Emily Harvale lives in]
although she would pre
Alps ... or Canada ...
several months of snow. Emily loves snow
almost as much as she loves Christmas.
Having worked in the City (London) for several
years, Emily returned to her home town of
Hastings where she spends her days writing ...
and wondering if it will ever snow.
You can contact her via her website, Twitter,
Facebook or Instagram.
There is also a Facebook group where fans can
chat with Emily about her books, her writing
day and life in general. Details can be found on
Emily's website.

Author contacts:
www.emilyharvale.com
www.twitter.com/emilyharvale
www.facebook.com/emilyharvalewriter
www.instagram.com/emilyharvale

***

Scan the code above to see all Emily's books on Amazon

Also by this author

The Golf Widows' Club
Sailing Solo
Carole Singer's Christmas
Christmas Wishes
A Slippery Slope
The Perfect Christmas Plan
Be Mine
It Takes Two
Bells and Bows on Mistletoe Row

Lizzie Marshall series:
Highland Fling – book 1
Lizzie Marshall's Wedding – book 2

The Goldebury Bay series:
Ninety Days of Summer – book 1
Ninety Steps to Summerhill – book 2
Ninety Days to Christmas – book 3

The Hideaway Down series:
A Christmas Hideaway – book 1
Catch A Falling Star – book 2
Walking on Sunshine – book 3
Dancing in the Rain – book 4

Hall's Cross series
Deck the Halls – book 1
The Starlight Ball – book 2

Michaelmas Bay series
Christmas Secrets in Snowflake Cove – book 1
Blame it on the Moonlight – book 2

ISBN 978-1-909917-63-7

Published by Crescent Gate Publishing

Print edition published worldwide 2020
E-edition published worldwide 2020

Editor Christina Harkness

Cover design by JR and Emily Harvale

Emily Harvale

Summer
at my
Sister's

CRESCENT GATE PUBLISHING

To all the wonderful volunteers and charitable organisations who help to keep our beaches clean and who work so hard to save the creatures who live in our seas, especially those who do such sterling work to try to save seahorses. The gentle seahorses need all the help they can get.

Map of Seahorse Harbour

There's an interactive map, with more details,
on my website: www.emilyharvale.com

One

'This had better be good,' I said, answering the landline phone in my bijou apartment after the fourth ring. 'I was about to slide into a lavender infused bath.'

'Josephine?'

I'd assumed it was one of my friends calling to see if I was going out even though I'd already told them all I wasn't, so I hadn't checked the caller ID. When I heard Mum's high-pitched tones, I cursed under my breath.

'Hi Mum. Is everything okay?'

'Oh. So you are there. I was about to hang up. I'm surprised you're in on a Friday evening. I thought you'd be out gallivanting with your friends.'

I held my tongue. Only an Olympic sprinter could have got to the phone faster than I had; and if she didn't expect me to be in, why had she called me on my landline and not my mobile? I took a couple of calming breaths, as my yoga instructor had taught me, reached for the glass of wine I'd already poured, and flopped onto the sofa.

'It's been a bit of a busy week. I wanted a long bath and an early night.'

'Early night? That's something I'd never associate with you. Anyway. Apart from the fact that I'm in agony, and your father is no help whatsoever, I suppose we're okay, but have you spoken to your sister recently? I'd be surprised if you have. You never seem able to find the time to call your father and me, even though I've just had a serious operation, but I thought perhaps you might make more of an effort for dear Diana.'

I took another deep breath and bit back my initial response. My friends had said something similar, to be fair – about me and the early night, which is why I'd thought it was one of them calling to persuade me. But my friends had teased me about it in an affectionate way, whereas Mum had reminded me that I'm a lackadaisical daughter and also, that Diana's her favourite. I don't mind that. Diana would be my favourite too, if I were Mum, but I do slightly object to being thought of as the useless twin.

'A hip replacement op isn't that serious, Mum,' I said, 'and it was weeks ago. I'm sorry you're still in pain. Perhaps you should speak to your doctor about it. As for Diana. I spoke to her last Saturday and we've texted a few times since. Why?'

'All operations are serious, Josephine. Especially at my age and with my poor health. Not that you care a fig about that. But this isn't about me. This is about Diana. How did she seem?'

Other than a dodgy hip, there was nothing wrong with Mum's health before the op and there'd been nothing wrong with it since. She was just down in the dumps because she couldn't go out and salsa every other night as she usually did. Which was probably one of the reasons she needed a new hip in the first place. And things were always about her, but this time she did seem more concerned about Diana.

'Um. She seemed fine. Why? Has something happened?' I sat upright, an uneasy feeling running through me like I'd just eaten a bunch of nettles.

'She won't tell me. Or your father. Not that he really questioned her. You never should've bought him that telescope for his birthday. He spends all day and night in his study, staring through the thing. Says he's looking at nature and the Universe but last night it was thick cloud so he couldn't have seen anything. Staring at our neighbours, I don't doubt. Probably that trollop who's just moved into number 25. Skirts up to her bottom and skin-tight tops down to tips of her fake breasts. Any day now I expect the police to knock on our door and arrest your father for being a Peeping

Tom. I hope you're pleased when we have to visit him in prison.'

There were so many things I could have said to that, but all I said was, 'I'm glad he likes it.'

I won't bore you with the tirade I got for the next thirty seconds but eventually she got back to the real reason for her call.

'I think you should go and visit her.'

'Who? The so-called trollop at number 25?'

A loud tut was followed by a sigh. I chuckled. Mum didn't.

'Don't be facetious, Josephine. You know full well that's not who I meant.'

'Diana? You want me to go and visit Diana. Why?'

Diana lived in Blackheath in South East London and I lived in New York, so it wasn't as if I could just pop round. Don't get me wrong. I was always pleased to see my sister, even if it was mostly via video call due to the fact we lived several thousand miles and time zones, apart, but I wasn't sure she always felt that way about me. Which proved yet again, that Diana was the sensible, Parnell twin. Although having married Alex Dunn almost sixteen years ago her surname was no longer Parnell.

'Apart from the fact that she's your sister, and not just your sister, but your twin and you should want to see her, like any decent, loving sister would–'

'I do see her, Mum. We video call one another at least once a week.'

Another tut. 'That's not the same and you know it.'

'I saw her at the end of May when we both came to Gib to visit you. And before that we met up in London when I popped over in March. Oh, and she came here to stay for a long weekend in January to hit the sales.'

'In that shoebox you like to call home.'

'My apartment is my home, Mum.'

'If you found yourself a wonderful man like Alex and settled down, you could have a beautiful home like Diana's. I don't know how many times I have to say this, but perhaps if you went to stay with them in Blackheath, or spent the summer with them in their house in Seahorse Harbour, Alex might introduce you to one of his friends. Maybe a gorgeous doctor, just like him. He knows all the right people. But you won't, will you? Why is that again? Remind me.'

I needed to take several calming breaths before I answered that. I had a good reason for not wanting to go and stay with them, particularly in Seahorse Harbour. The last time I was there was when I was seventeen and I hadn't been back since. Not that I would dream of telling Mum the reason. Or Diana, come to that. But I did tell one person, once. A long time ago. Aunt Elsie.

Secrets have a tendency to eat their way to the surface, no matter how hard we try to keep them shut inside, feeding them with guilt. I should know. I've been keeping secrets for most of my adult life. One day they might come tumbling out, especially if I returned to Seahorse Harbour.

'I prefer being on my own. I'm not the type to settle down. And I don't like staying in other people's houses.'

'So you keep saying. It's ridiculous, Josephine and you know it. You'll be thirty-five this summer. Isn't it time you did something with your life?'

'I am doing something with my life. It may not be something you like, but I'm having fun and that's all that matters.'

'Oh yes. It's all about fun with you, isn't it? Where's your sense of responsibility? Where's your ambition? You should have a wonderful home and a loving family by now. Like Diana. You should have a doting husband like Alex. You–'

'Thanks, Mum. I know the list of things you think I should have. It's not going to happen, so let's not discuss that further. Let's get back to the reason you called. Why do you think I need to go and visit Diana?'

'I give up, Josephine. But mark my words, one day you'll look around and realise you have nothing.'

'I have everything I need. I repeat. Why do you think I should go and see Diana?'

'Because there's something wrong and she won't tell me what it is. I'd go myself, but I'm still not allowed to fly. We've invited her here, but I knew what she would say to that. She's spending the summer in Seahorse Harbour, as always.'

'What makes you think something's wrong?'

'Mother's intuition. I can feel there's something wrong. Not having children of your own, you wouldn't understand, but Diana would know exactly what I mean. She'll have the same experiences with her two little darlings.'

'So she hasn't actually said anything to make you feel this way? As you say, she's got two adorable kids, a rich and successful doctor for a husband, a house in Blackheath and an idyllic second home by the sea. Oh, and let's not forget the ski chalet in Courchevel. She's got a cleaner, a gardener and an au pair. What could possibly be wrong in Diana's world?'

Unless Alex was having an affair?

'If I knew, I wouldn't be calling you and begging you to go and find out, would I?'

'Begging me? You're begging me? Okay. I'll give her a call tomorrow and ask her what's up.'

'Ask her what's up. Is that it? You need to go and see her, Josephine.'

'Look, Mum. This really isn't a good time. I can't fly to the UK right now. I told you the last time we spoke that my contract ends next week and I need to find another job. She sounded absolutely fine last Saturday and we've texted several times since. I'm sure if something was wrong, she would've said, but I'll definitely give her a call tomorrow.'

That much was true. Even if we didn't see one another that often, we talked every week and often texted in between. Despite our differences, Diana and I have always been close. When I say differences, I mean we're the chalk and cheese of the twin world. We don't even look alike. Diana's graceful, elegant and petite with hair the colour of dark honey kissed by bees and sprinkled with gold dust. My hair's mud-brown, according to Mum, although it's dyed a fiery red at the moment, which Mum hates, especially when I told her the colour was called 'vixen'. I'm the opposite of graceful and elegant. You can't really call me petite, either. I'm small in stature, but as for my hips and bust ... they aren't. Diana jokes that I got her hips and boobs as well as mine. Mum agrees. She says I was always greedy as a child.

We're different in our personalities too. Diana's the quiet one, Mum says. She's also practical, clever and sensible. Unlike me.

One story Mum likes to tell anyone and everyone who will stand still long enough to listen, is that one Halloween, when we were about five, our aunt Elsie bought witches' broomsticks for Diana and me. They were wrapped in sparkly paper embellished with luminous ghosts. Diana unwrapped hers carefully and in silence, whilst I tore at mine, shrieking with excitement. Once unwrapped, Diana immediately used her broom to sweep up the shreds of paper strewn over the kitchen floor by me. I threw my leg over mine and raced around the room before climbing onto the kitchen chair and up onto the table. I jumped off, trying to fly and landed awkwardly on the tiled floor, breaking my ankle ... in addition to Mum's favourite porcelain bowl which I accidentally kicked off the table when I jumped. Something else she manages to squeeze into many conversations. Especially around Christmas or her birthday. "Oh. For a moment I thought you'd bought me a gorgeous porcelain bowl. Like the one you broke when you were five. I did so love that bowl." Believe me, if I ever find a bowl like it, I'll buy at least ten of the damn things. But as Mum likes to remind me, it was irreplaceable. Mum didn't just shout at me on that fateful Halloween of the broomstick incident. Aunt Elsie got an earful too.

And I was getting an earful now.

'I realise you breeze through life as if you haven't got a care in the world, Josephine, and you think Diana's life is easy, but being a wife and mother is a full-time occupation. Yet Diana also runs a successful business, maintains two beautiful homes. Three if you count the ski chalet, although I accept that's looked after by the live-in help. Diana's dinner parties are the talk of Blackheath. She also hosts a popular book club, and yet she still has time to take care of her appearance. But does she ever complain? No. Whereas you ... but this isn't about your shortcomings. This is about dear Diana. I'm telling you, Josephine, something is not right. I've felt it for a while and the more I speak to her the more certain I am. I need to know what it is.'

I didn't bother to thank her for putting me firmly in my place. It wasn't the first time she'd done it and it wouldn't be the last. But yes. I did think Diana had a perfect, and pretty easy life. Don't get me wrong, I love my sister to bits and I was glad she's happy and fulfilled. But sometimes, in the small hours of the night when I woke up alone, I wondered what my life would've been like if things hadn't gone the way they had during that fateful, final summer in Seahorse Harbour.

Would my life have been like Diana's?

There was no point in dwelling on that. We can't turn the clock back, no matter how much we wish we could. And I did wish I could ... sometimes.

'I'll video call her, okay? If I pick up any sign of anything being wrong, I promise you I'll find out what it is. Deal?'

Mum tutted, sighed and tutted again.

'I suppose it'll have to do. Call me back as soon as you've spoken to her.'

'I'll ...' I didn't get to finish my sentence. Mum had rung off.

To be honest, I had misgivings the moment I heard Mum's voice. It was the third week of July but all it had done for most of the month was rain. I loved New York, but New York in the summer isn't that great when it's hot, wet and humid and you don't have air conditioning in your tiny rented apartment. I wasn't in the best of moods.

I was certainly surprised to receive Mum's call. For one thing, Mum only ever phoned me if there was a national disaster, a family emergency, or she had exciting news to share; I was the one who had to call her – once a week, unless I wanted an ear-bashing. Not that we had very much to say to one another. Mum and I have always had what she likes to call, different outlooks on life. Translated, that means that she dislikes everything I do and is constantly unhappy with my choices. She has no qualms about telling me so. Repeatedly. And that call had been no exception.

The second reason I was surprised by her call was due to the time difference. I lived in

New York; Mum lived in Gibraltar. It was 7 p.m. my time, which meant it was 1 a.m. in Gib. Mum likes to party, much to Dad's exasperation, but as she was still recovering from her hip replacement procedure and had texted me several times during the previous few weeks to say she constantly felt like death warmed over, I thought she'd be tucked up in bed. And yet she'd stayed up half the night and had called to tell me to go and see Diana. That meant she was genuinely concerned.

My lavender bath wasn't quite so relaxing after that and I had to refill the tub with hot water but as I soaked in the heavenly scent, all I could think about was Diana ... and Seahorse Harbour ... and that summer when I was sixteen. The summer that changed my life in so many ways.

Two

Needless to say, I hardly slept a wink. I video-called Diana, via Zoom, the following morning and, due to the time difference, I gulped lashings of coffee and wolfed down two large salmon and cream cheese bagels while Diana picked at her lunch, pushing her salad around the plate as if she thought it might contain something unpleasant, like a slug.

I knew that Mum was right. There was definitely something wrong in Diana's world. I could tell from the moment I saw her face.

'Hi, Di. How're you doing?' I tried to pretend I hadn't noticed. Perhaps she'd volunteer the information.

Diana shrugged and smiled but it wasn't her usual cheerful smile and it didn't reach her eyes.

'Hey you. I'm doing fine. How about you?'

'All good here. Just thought I'd give you a quick call and see if you've settled in.'

'Settled in? Oh. You mean the summer house? Er ... We're leaving on Monday

13

morning.'

'Monday morning? That's unlike you, isn't it? Doesn't Alex usually drive you all down on Friday night. I was expecting to see the sea in the background this morning. Not your kitchen in Blackheath. It's a stunningly beautiful kitchen and I do love looking at it, but I was hoping to see the sea. I wanted to pretend I'm basking on a sun lounger, listening to the waves and the gulls instead of New York traffic.' I laughed but she didn't join in.

'Sorry. We ... er ... we had a change of plan. Alex is ... so busy at the moment, what with the new wing of the hospital having just opened and the fact that they're short-staffed, he's juggling shifts and ... er ... he's not going to be coming with us. Not yet, anyway. He ... er ... he's hoping to join us in a few weeks, but...'

Her voice trailed off and I thought she looked as if she was about to cry. She dodged out of the way of the webcam and asked me to hold on for a moment. I held on for several.

'Di? Diana? Are you still there? Is everything okay? Di! I'm getting worried. Have you fallen over and killed yourself? Let me see your face. Right now, Di, or I swear I'm jumping on a plane and coming over there.'

A second or two later, she reappeared but her eyes looked a bit red and misty and her head was hung low in a futile attempt to hide her face from me.

'I'm fine. Just one of those days, y'know?'

'Oh I know those, but I think there's more to it than that, isn't there? Are you going to tell me or am I going to have to ask Alex what's going on?'

'No!' Her head shot up and she looked like a woman about to be tortured. 'No. Er ... It's nothing really. I just haven't been feeling well lately, that's all and what with Alex being so busy ... sometimes it's hard. But I'm fine, honestly. And the kids and I will soon be on the beach, so that'll cheer us all up. Please don't say anything to Alex, Josie. I ... I don't want him to worry.'

I wasn't sure I believed her explanation although I knew Alex would be busy. Alex was always busy. That's who he is. A one-man locomotive heading for the stars. Forgive the mixed metaphor. He's actually a surgeon who had just had a new hospital wing named after him, partly because he's a brilliant surgeon who deserved all the praise he was getting, and partly because he and his mum made a substantial contribution towards the building of it.

Alex and his mum, Bernice, weren't always rich. We met Alex when we were ten and he was twelve and he and Bernice were staying in a caravan in Seahorse Harbour Holiday Park. The first day we met him, he told us that when he grew up, he'd be a rich and famous surgeon.

Alex was determined nothing – and no one, would get in his way of that. And so was Bernice.

Bernice never spoke about Alex's dad, and nor did Alex. They still don't. Even Diana knows nothing about the man. If anyone asked Bernice she'd smile wanly and say, "He's no longer with us and it's still painful to say his name." When anyone asked Alex he simply scowled and said, "It's just me and Mum," almost daring them to pry any further.

But now Bernice was loaded, thanks to a lottery win she had about three years after Alex and Diana were married. Don't ask me how much. I have no idea. That's something else Bernice likes to keep to herself, although I'm sure Alex knows. Diana definitely doesn't. She would've told me if she did.

Alex doesn't seem to have changed much since the win. He's always loved praise and glitz and glamour. As one of the most highly respected and youngest heart surgeons in London, if not the country, he gets a lot of that, even without the lottery dosh.

But I've often thought Alex and his mum are joined at the hip. She tells him to jump and he asks her how high. Even now. Which is actually a little weird, bearing in mind he's a successful and talented, thirty-six-year-old man.

'Are you okay, Di?' I asked, peering at her

face. 'I mean, are you ill? You said you haven't been feeling well lately. Is it something to worry about?'

'No, no.' She shook her head. Almost violently. 'It's nothing like that. Honestly. I'd tell you if it was. I think I'm just ... a little out of sorts. A bit run down maybe. Nothing a sea breeze won't cure.'

'Cocktails always make me feel better so I'm with you on that.'

Now she did laugh. 'I meant the sea air, not the drink. You know I don't drink ... anymore.'

'And I don't drink any less.' I sniggered. I love those old one-liners. 'So it's just you and the kids then?'

She looked anxious. 'Me and the kids?'

'Going to Seahorse Harbour.' This conversation was definitely weird.

'Oh yes. For now. And Henry of course.'

'Ah yes. Henry. Who could forget that lovable hound?'

'You could. Obviously.'

'Yeah well. Dogs aren't my thing. You know I don't do well with living beings. With living anything, really. Which reminds me. I'm really sorry but that gorgeous plant you bought me a few weeks ago seems to have ... er ... decided it didn't like living in the City.'

'Josie, no!' She shook her head and laughed, although it wasn't a particularly happy sound. 'Please don't tell me you've killed it already.'

'Okay. I won't tell you that.'

'But you have?'

'I think it took its own life. I didn't do anything, honestly.'

'But you watered it, didn't you?'

'Er. I think I did. Once or twice. Possibly not. I meant to.'

She sighed and shook her head again. 'Oh, Josie. What am I going to do with you?'

Don't ask me why I said it. I had no intention of doing so. None whatsoever. But I did.

'You could ask me to come and stay with you for the summer. Or at least until Alex is free to come and join you.'

She blinked a few times and stared at the screen, her perfectly arched and shaped brows raised skywards.

'In Seahorse Harbour?'

'No. Mars. Of course in Seahorse Harbour. That's where you're spending the summer, isn't it?'

'It's where we spend every summer,' she said, somewhat wistfully I thought.

I gave a little cough and she smiled wanly.

'Do I have to ask twice?'

'What? Are you serious? Are ... are you actually asking if you can come and stay? You never come and stay with us.'

'Well, I'd rather stay with that sexy hunk

who now owns The Seahorse Inn but as I don't know him, I'll have to stay with you until he asks me. What did you say his name was again?'

'Mikkel. Mikkel Meloy.' She lowered her gaze ... and her voice.

'I still think that sounds more Irish than it does Norwegian. But he does look like a Viking and he could ravage me anytime he likes.'

'You've only seen him once, Josie and that was via my webcam at Easter.'

'Okay. Don't get snippy. You sounded just like mum.' I laughed. 'You only have to see a man like that once for him to make an impression. Is he still single?'

She looked away into the distance. 'As far as I know he is.'

'Hi, Josie!' My niece Becca appeared in the background, waving frantically. 'You two talking about Mikkel? He's sooooo gorgeous. Everyone's in love with him you know. Even though he's old.

'Hey you! He's only a couple of years older than me and your mum, you cheeky minx.'

Becca giggled. 'Yeah. Old. But not as old as Orla's dad. He used to be the heartthrob in Seahorse Harbour until Mikkel moved there. He's still hot, although Orla hates it when I say her dad is sexy – but he is. Not quite as hot as Mikkel though. Orla's crushing on him too. We've been reading Georgette Heyer books.

One of the women in Mum's book club loves them. Most of the heroines marry guys much older, so we're sort of getting into the whole, old men thing, even though it still seems a bit gross. They're sexy to look at sometimes but to have actual sex with them.' She shivered dramatically and scrunched up her face. 'Makes me want to heave just a bit.'

'You're not having sex with anyone, young lady. You're only fifteen.' I tried to sound stern but I think I failed because I was laughing.

I also tried to picture Liam's face. That's Orla's dad. He'd love to know that the thought of having sex with him made someone want to heave. Personally, when I was younger, I quite liked the thought of having sex with Liam Fulbright. Mainly because he was such a nerd, especially with his huge glasses, and I wondered if, like a super hero, he had a far, far sexier alter ego. I definitely got the impression there was something bubbling just beneath his lightly tanned skin and that long, lean body. But I hadn't seen Liam for years. The last time I saw him was when he was nineteen. And he was getting married to Una Cole – the most beautiful girl in the world.

'You can have sex with Mikkel and Liam and tell us all about it,' Becca said.

'Both at the same time?' I queried, laughing. 'I'm not really into that.'

There are no taboo subjects in our family.

We believe it's far better to talk about things like sex, openly and honestly and make teenagers aware of the potential risks, rather than make it something off-limits and therefore extremely exciting. And Becca's sensible, like her mum. I was certain she wouldn't do anything with anyone until she was sure she felt ready.

'Nor me,' she said, shrugging. 'Did I hear you say you're coming to stay for the summer? That'll be so cool. You never spend any holidays with us.'

'Yeah well. You know how it is, kiddo. Things to do. People to annoy. Got to earn a living. Stuff like that. But I'm going to spend this summer with you and Toby and your mum. If she actually says yes, that is. Planet Earth to Diana Dunn. Come in Mrs Dunn. People need to hear from you.'

'What? Sorry. I was miles away.' Diana glanced from me to Becca and back again as if she hadn't even realised her daughter had joined in our conversation. 'Er. You're really serious? You honestly want to spend the summer with us in Seahorse Harbour? You haven't been there since ... well ... for years. Do you really want to come?'

I didn't. Not in the least. But I had to find out what was going on with Diana and she clearly wasn't going to tell me via a video call. I knew my sister well enough to know that whatever it was, was serious. And serious stuff had to be talked about face-to-face in the flesh.

'Absolutely. My contract ends next week, so it's the perfect time. I'm owed some holiday so I may even be able to leave sooner. I'll have a word on Monday and see what they say. I was going to try to find a new job right away, but what the hell, I haven't had a break for years. Not a real break anyway. And I've still got most of the money Grammie left us. It'll do me good. Besides, I'd love to spend the summer with my sister.'

'And us,' Becca said.

I screwed up my face and shrugged before blowing her a kiss and winking.

'I'll see you soon, kiddo. And Di, I'll call you as soon as I can on Monday. Bye for now. Love you.'

'Love you too,' Diana and Becca said in unison.

It was only after I closed my laptop that I realised Diana hadn't actually said yes to me spending the summer at her home in Seahorse Harbour. She'd just asked if I were serious.

Three

Seahorse Harbour is one of those sleepy seaside villages that over the years has stretched out its arms and broadened its horizons with new homes and shops popping up along the coast either side. The local authority made the decision long ago – an imminently sensible one in my opinion – not to allow large developers in and only small, locally-based firms were permitted to build. This meant it still maintained the village atmosphere I fell in love with the first time Mum and Dad took us to Seahorse Harbour for two weeks in the summer when we were three or four. Grammie Yates, my mum's mum, and Mum's sister, Elsie came with us.

Every year after that, until I was seventeen, we all summered in Seahorse Harbour together, in the same rented house at the top of Church Hill, on the West Cliffs of Seahorse Cliffs, overlooking the village, the wide sweep of sand, the rocks and the tranquil waters of the bay.

Over the years we began to spend longer than two weeks every summer. We went at other times too. Sometimes just for long weekends. Once or twice for Christmas. And, oddly enough, after that year we met Alex and Bernice, they also spent every summer at The Seahorse Harbour Holiday Park, and, like us, began spending other holidays there too. The holiday park is open year-round, apart from two weeks at the end of January and the first few days of February. It's always open again in time for Valentine's Day.

Everyone, apart from me, continued to spend their summers at that rented house, and four years ago, when Grammie died and coincidentally, the rental house came up for sale, Diana and Alex bought it.

Alex also bought a ski chalet in Courchevel in the French Alps but I've never been there even though they invite me every Christmas.

'You been to Seahorse Harbour before?' the mini cab driver asked me as we trundled along the narrow lanes.

'Yes,' I replied, already feeling anxious. 'Years ago.'

I'd managed to leave my job a few days early, having told a little white lie to my now former boss and said there was a family emergency. He'd said in that case I should go right away. I got the first flight I could, just after 8 on Monday evening and thanks to the time difference, had landed at Heathrow around 8.20 on Tuesday morning. I was feeling a bit spaced out by the time I'd collected my cases, got the tube from Heathrow into London and drunk copious amounts of coffee during the forty-minute wait for the train from there down to Easterhill. That's the nearest station to Seahorse Harbour and it's four miles away as the crow flies but seems like twice that distance via the narrow country lanes once you leave the town.

'So you know how Seahorse Harbour got its name?'

I did, but I could see his smiling face via his rear-view mirror and it was obvious he wanted to tell me. I learnt a long time ago that it's often better to let people say what they want to say rather than impinge on their happiness by cutting them short.

'I can't remember,' I said, preparing myself for what I knew was to come.

He shifted position so that he was sitting more comfortably, no doubt. With one arm resting on the steering wheel and the other slung across the back of the passenger seat so that he could see me better as I sat, now somewhat nervously on the back seat, he proceeded to tell me what I already knew. I sat upright just a little and he probably thought I was engrossed. The truth was, I was concentrating on the road ahead. I thought at least one of us should.

He beamed at me. 'It's because there're actually real seahorses living here.'

As opposed to fake ones? I was tempted to ask but I didn't.

'They're in an area of water called The Shallows, at the foot of Seahorse Cliffs. I'll point it out to you as we get near. You can't see it from the road but you'll get an idea of where it is.'

I knew where it was. The Shallows is an inlet at the foot of Seahorse Cliffs, as the man said, where the seagrass in which these magical creatures live, is abundant. That's mainly due to the fact that the only way to access The Shallows is from the sea and thanks to the mouth of the inlet being notorious for rip currents, most people stay away, leaving the grasses and the seahorses, together with all the other creatures living there, in peace.

'Seahorses are in decline,' he said, 'so we're lucky to have them here. They live in stuff called seagrass and folks don't want to swim in waters containing that so it's pulled up in some places. In others, it's torn up by dredging or by fishing trawlers. In some, it's killed off by chemicals in waste. Do you know that seahorses are used in the Chinese medicine trade?'

'No.' I did, but I sounded convincingly surprised, although I was more surprised that we hadn't veered off the road yet.

'Yep. I think it's bloody disgusting. It's reckoned they take something around 150 million seahorses a year. Can you believe that?' He whistled and shook his head.

I hadn't realised it was such an enormous number but I agreed it was disgusting.

'And this is just as bad. About a million are taken to die in the sun and then sold as souvenirs. Makes my blood boil. And theirs, no doubt. Bloody cruel. Then there's the pet trade. Don't get me started on the morons who want to keep exotic creatures as pets but haven't a clue how to look after them. Another million or so of the gentle creatures end up there and most don't last long with their new owners.'

'That's truly awful.' I meant it.

'Not in Seahorse Harbour though. Folks decided early on that its namesake needed protecting, so the seagrass is tended and the seahorses are watched over by a small but dedicated team of volunteers. They're called The Seahorse Riders and they organise fund-raising events throughout the year. Mostly in the summer when tourists like you are plentiful.'

And willing to part with our holiday money for a glimpse of the beautiful creatures and a T-shirt or other souvenir – but never an actual seahorse – to take home as a reminder. Usually along with an annual subscription to the newsletter, and a cuddly, seahorse-shaped stuffed toy to go with it, if I remember correctly.

'You can sign up to save a seahorse,' he confirmed without me saying anything, 'and take home a T-shirt or two. Or an ornamental seahorse from Fulbright Ceramics. They're fantastic. Got my wife one for our anniversary. Lots of different sizes and each one unique.'

'Fulbright Ceramics?' I felt an odd sensation at the mention of Liam's name.

Diana had told me that Liam had bought The Olde Forge and converted it into a pottery called Fulbright Ceramics, where he now made and sold the most beautiful items. She'd even shown me a couple of photos of it. That was a big surprise. For years, Liam worked in the City and commuted every day, but death makes people re-evaluate their lives and when Una died, that's exactly what Liam did and decided it was time to make a change, apparently. Diana said it was because he needed to stay at home and look after Orla who was only just turned thirteen at the time. But a potter was the last thing I'd ever envisage Liam becoming. I hadn't realised he was good with his hands. I knew he was good with his brain.

'Yeah. It's near the church. You can't miss it. There're two signs outside. One says 'The Olde Forge' because that's what it once was. The other says 'Fulbright Ceramics' because that's what it now is. Tell Liam, Jonno sent you.' He beamed at me again. 'That's me. Liam's a mate of mine and he'll give you a good price.'

'Thanks. I'll do that.'

'Good on yer. Now look to your left and you'll see Seahorse Cliffs. That's the other reason Seahorse Harbour got its name. The shoreline's shaped like a seahorse. One lying on its side on the sand.'

I knew that too, but I looked in the direction he was pointing. You couldn't really see it from the road but the land mass swept out in the shape of a seahorse's head, together with the long, pointed snout, aptly named Seahorse Point. At the very tip of the point there's a vertical drop of about thirty feet. As kids we used to tombstone off there. That's jumping off into the sea below in case you haven't heard of tombstoning. It's not really a very sensible thing to do – which is why we did it. The swell can easily push you against the rocks or pull you into the rip current of the inlet, so you have to swim as fast as you can around the 'outside' of the seahorse's head, and it's a fairly long way back to shore. Which is also what Jonno was telling me, I realised, or something very similar.

'Tombstoning's banned in Seahorse Harbour now because several people have died, but it doesn't stop kids – and often adults, from doing it. Only last year, two twenty-eight-year-old guys, one of whom was getting married the following day, lost their lives by leaping off Seahorse Point after a few drinks too many and getting smashed onto the rocks and dragged under water by the rip current.'

I'd heard about that too. Toby, my thirteen-year-old nephew told me all about it and the expression on his face was one of admiration.

'Don't you think of going tombstoning, Toby,' I told him, via video call, naturally.

'You did it,' was his reply.

'Yes. And I was an idiot. Just like those guys were. There's nothing clever about throwing yourself off a cliff into treacherous waters, which is why your mum never did it. She was far more sensible than me and I hope you are too.'

He shrugged in reply and I had an uneasy feeling that it wouldn't be long before Toby gave it a try, if he hadn't already. I mentioned as much to Diana and she said she'd have another word with him about it.

Diana never did it because Mum and Dad told us in no uncertain terms not to, and Diana always did what she was told. I hoped Toby took after her. Me, on the other hand, well, I rarely did what I was told. Which is one of the reasons I was always changing jobs.

When we were young, about eight or nine,

I think, I told Diana that a witch must've put a spell on her to make her so obedient. She said that I was the one under a spell. A naughty spell, she called it, and she promised that one day she would find a way to undo it. I didn't hold out much hope for her chances.

'So no tombstoning, okay?' Jonno continued.

'No tombstoning. Got it.' I gave him a thumbs up and a smile.

'From Seahorse Point the bay curves in and out to form the neck and body of the seahorse. That's where The Shallows are.' He pointed in the general direction of the inlet as we drove past. 'There's also a cave near the mouth of the inlet, called Weeping Eye Cave. When the tide comes in, especially when the sea is rough, water pours into the cave and, due to the angles, rock formations and pressure build-up inside, is forced upwards. A jet of water spurts out from a small hole on the top of the cliffs, which is called The Weeping Eye. It's a popular, tourist attraction. But don't stand too close or you may fall in. And don't peer into the eye on a stormy day. The water spout might rip your head off. It's pretty powerful.'

I knew all of this, of course. I'd been soaked by water from The Weeping Eye, more times than I could remember. And almost fallen in it, once or twice. When the tide is out, you can actually climb down into the cave, but it's pretty dangerous and only an idiot would do it. So yes, I've done it. Alex and I climbed down there once when we were about fifteen, during another summer in Seahorse Harbour. Diana wouldn't join us. You can also swim into the cave via the inlet – if the Rip Current doesn't get you. Only those who know the waters and the tides really well, do that. And yes. I did that once too. With Liam, as it happens. He knows everything there is to know about the sea and the tides around Seahorse Harbour. Or at least, he did.

From the air, in a hot air balloon or one of the small, twin-prop sightseeing planes you can take from the nearby air club in Easterhill, the seahorse shape of the bay is even more noticeable and The Weeping Eye really does look like an eye. You can see the edges and sides of the cliff, like an iris, leading down towards a shimmering blue pool below. That pool is a magical place to swim – when the tide is out. When the tide comes in, it's like a swirling vortex.

I know what Seahorse Harbour looks like from the air because Dad treated Diana and me to a hot air balloon ride for our sixteenth birthday. I loved every second of that flight. He often jokes that that's when I got the travel bug.

I think he's probably right.

'And now we're heading down the hill into the village of Seahorse Harbour,' Jonno continued. 'Is it like you remember?'

It was almost exactly as I remembered. As the cliffs petered down towards the village and the sand, nothing much had changed. A couple of new lanes led away from the cliff edge and the road, into the fields and cliff behind, where a few new houses had sprung up, and some of the shops along the road leading into the village were new, but the village itself looked the same as it did the last time I was there.

'Those black rocks there are ridged, just like a seahorse is,' Jonno said, pointing to the rocks to our left, 'and they form a sort of circle and curl out into the water and round again, just like a seahorse's curled tail. Kids hunt for crabs and such in the rock pools there, and right in the centre, there's one pool that's deep enough to swim in. Not that many people do.'

I had. But I didn't think there wasn't much point in saying so.

The village of Seahorse Harbour is nestled in a valley but most of it is set on some rather steep hills leading up from the promenade called Sea Walk. There are some shops and businesses dotted along Sea Walk which itself sits raised slightly above sea level and most of which is sheltered from the sea by the seahorse's rocky tail. In particularly stormy weather, the waves have been known to breach the rocks and crash onto the promenade, but none of the shops or businesses has ever been flooded, at least not in living memory.

The General Store, or TGS as we often referred to it, is on Sea Walk. It sells everything from food to newspapers to bucket and spades, and houses a sub post office. Close by, there's a bakery called Beach Bakers and a café called Seahorse Bites. These places may have changed hands since I was last in Seahorse Harbour, but I know they're still there because Diana has mentioned them.

In the centre of the village there's a quaint little church with the rather grand name of St Mary Star of the Sea. There's an ancient oak tree to one side with a bench where you can sit and look straight down either Lower Church Hill or Sand Lane, to the sea. Between these roads is Memorial Gardens. A splendid hotel sat there once, but it was bombed in the Second World War and now there are steps leading down to lawned areas and bushes and plants.

Other than that, there are a few souvenir shops, an ice cream kiosk with pretensions to be an ice cream parlour, and a small sea life centre called Seahorse Tales where kids from nearby schools go to learn about the seahorses and other marine life and where The Seahorse Riders offices are based. It's also where injured or sick seahorses are looked after. Seahorse conservation is taken very seriously in Seahorse Harbour. And rightly so. It's predicted that seahorses will become extinct within thirty years or less, if nothing is done to save them.

'There's a vet,' Jonno said, 'but no doctor, so if you need medical assistance you have to head to Easterhill.' He chuckled. 'Asher's pretty good at fixing most things though, so we give him a try first. He's the vet. Asher Bryant. He's also a mate of mine.'

'Will he give me a discount too?' I teased.

'He'll probably ask you out for a drink,' Jonno said, winking at me, 'but I expect you're already taken.'

'Taken? Oh no. Nope. Not me. I'm single. And planning to stay that way, thanks.'

Asher was clearly new. Or at least he wasn't the vet last time I was in Seahorse Harbour. Old Barney Short was. But he was in his seventies back then so he'd no doubt long-since retired. Or possibly passed away.

'Pretty girl like you? Good luck with that.'

'I don't do relationships,' I said. 'Young, free and single, that's how I like it and that's how it'll stay, believe me. Even when I'm old.'

I didn't bother to mention that I was about as good at keeping relationships alive as I was at keeping house plants.

'Not here to meet the love of your life then?' He seemed oddly disappointed.

'Definitely not. Just to have some sun, sea and fun. And to visit my sister and her family. She has a house here.'

'Really? Then why did you ask me to drop you at the pub?'

I gave him a slow smile. 'Because I need a glass of wine before I face them.'

'As bad as that?'

'Not bad at all. But I'm jetlagged. I need one glass to prepare myself for teenagers and a rather mad dog.'

'Doesn't your sister have wine?'

'She doesn't drink.'

'At all?'

'Nothing alcoholic.'

'Better nip to TGS then and pick yourself up a few bottles.' He sniggered. 'Oh that's The General Store. People round here call it TGS.'

'D'you live here, Jonno? You seem to know an awful lot about the place and you said Liam and Asher are your friends.'

He nodded, grinning at me. 'Yep. I met the wife here. She was here on holiday. We live in one of the new houses in The Heights. That's one of the roads we passed coming down the hill. We moved here from Easterhill about four years ago, just after they were built. Cost an arm and a leg but it's worth every penny for the view.'

'I won't argue with you on that.'

Easterhill is the nearest town and it's four miles inland to the north of Seahorse Harbour. It's where the air club, Easterhill Air and small air strip are, which were once part of the

Easterhill Estate. Lord Easterhill had a bit of a penchant for light aircraft and gliders but when he and his wife died, leaving no heirs, they left the airstrip, aircraft hangers and the planes to the town of Easterhill and it was turned into an air club. The stately home of Easterhill was sold and is now a luxury hotel, spa and golf course. The grounds of the estate were divided between that and Easterhill Air.

Jonno pulled up outside the pub at the top of Sand Lane and turned to face me.

'Here we are then. The Seahorse Inn. Are you sure you don't want me to drop you at your sister's place first? Where does she live? Will you have to lug your bags up one of the hills?'

I laughed. 'Don't worry, I'll be fine. One of my many jobs was once a flight attendant and I've also been a holiday rep and worked in various positions in hotels. I'm used to lugging bags around.'

'Well-travelled then?'

'Definitely.'

'No place like home though, is there?'

I wasn't sure how to answer that.

'How much do I owe you?'

'Seven-fifty, please.'

I handed him a ten-pound note. 'Keep the change.'

'That's very generous. Thanks.'

'That's for the guided tour.' I grinned at him.

He grinned back. 'Let me get your bags.'

He leapt from the car and opened the boot, depositing my bag and cases right by the door to the pub, just as a tall, blond, broad shouldered man opened it. I noticed the muscular tanned legs first and I recognised him immediately. It was the man I'd seen via Diana's webcam – Mikkel Meloy. And he was definitely far better looking in the flesh. Taller and broader with a smile that would melt knicker elastic if it was any hotter.

'Hi Jonno.' He shook hands with Jonno as they sort of leaned into one another and slapped each other on the back.

'Hi Mik. Got a customer for you. And a rather pretty one too. But before you get any ideas, she's not looking for a man, just a glass of wine to prepare her for a visit to her family.' He laughed and so did Mikkel.

I realised I might have told Jonno a bit too much, but I couldn't help but return Mikkel's smile. It wasn't just hot; it was also infectious.

Four

'Hi. I'm Mikkel. Mikkel Meloy. My friends call me Mik.'

He held out his hand to me and I eyed it nervously, unsure whether or not to take it.

'You're not going to pull me into a hug and slap me on the back, are you?'

His dark blond brows shot up and then he gave a roar of laughter as he shook his mane of golden blond hair.

'I promise not to slap you on the back.' His voice was strong and gravelly with just a slight trace of a Nordic accent. 'And if you'd rather I didn't hug you, I understand. But we're very friendly people.'

'Norwegians?'

The gorgeous smile lit up the deepest blue eyes I've ever seen.

'I meant in Seahorse Harbour, but yes, I'm originally from Norway and we're very friendly there also.'

'I'm from London, and lately, New York. We carry pepper spray in our handbags.'

He must've seen I was joking because he laughed and raised both hands in the air.

'I'll wait until you're ready to hug me then. Do you want a drink?'

'No. I'd like a pound of sausages.'

A crease formed between his brows but he soon laughed again.

'Ah. Pretty and funny. I like that in a woman.'

'I'm off then,' Jonno said, grinning. 'If you decide you want a lift to your sister's give me a call.' He handed me a card. 'It's almost lunchtime so I'm popping home for a sarnie. I'll be out and about again by the time you've had your wine.'

'Thanks, Jonno, but I'll be fine. I will give you a call if I need a cab while I'm here though.'

He waved goodbye to me, gave Mikkel a friendly slap on the arm and was gone in a matter of seconds. Mikkel slung one of my bags on his shoulder and grabbed my cases, wheeling them into the pub.

'They're not mine,' I said.

He stopped for a second, tutted and shook his head.

'You like to play games,' he said. 'I like to play games too.'

From the look he was giving me I had a pretty good idea of the sort of games Mikkel Meloy liked to play. And most of them would involve getting naked, I suspected.

I coughed to clear the images popping into my head and followed him inside. The change from bright sunlight to the dark interior soothed my eyes and meant I had to remove my sunglasses.

Mikkel deposited my cases right in front of the bar and was behind it in three strides. Long, well-defined, tanned legs, gorgeous-looking bottom hidden beneath khaki shorts, manly waist and a black T-shirt stretched tight across those broad shoulders, kissed at his neck by the curled tips of that golden blond hair, made me drop onto the nearest stool, feeling a little overcome.

'Wow!' I said out loud, not realising I had done so.

'Like it?' he asked, beaming at me.

For a moment I wondered how to respond and then I realised he thought I was commenting on the interior of the pub as he glanced around and held out his hands as if offering me the entire room.

I quickly took in the white-washed walls, the ropes and nets and other fishing paraphernalia hanging from the black beams and the low, white-washed ceiling. The walls bore photographs of Seahorse Harbour through the ages, some sepia, some in colour, together with paintings of the sea, seahorses, or ships. There were several ceramic seahorses on the large window sills. I'm not sure what effect he was going for but it somehow worked.

'Very nice,' I said, nodding my approval.

The only things that hadn't changed since I was last in The Seahorse Inn were the name, the black beams and the large fireplace in the far wall. I sat in front of that during a very cold October, many years ago with the man I loved and he told me his decision. A decision that would change my life.

'I bought it last year,' Mikkel was saying. 'I also own the restaurant on Sea Walk, called Hippocampus, so if you are looking for good food and wine during your stay, that's the place to go. The name is from the genus of the seahorse, not the part of the brain, if you are wondering.'

I wasn't, but I smiled and nodded.

'You bought the old boatyard and boat shed and turned it into a rather snazzy restaurant. The last time I was here, I ran in and out between the damaged and discarded boats, the sails and ropes and nets and the flotsam and jetsam the former owner, Harry Boatman had acquired during a lifetime of one hundred years spent residing in a tiny boathouse on the beach. And when I say boathouse, I mean that in the literal sense. Is that still here? Or did you demolish it?'

He gave me a hurt look.

'Only a monster would destroy the boathouse. I'm many things but a monster, I am not. You know the place then? You knew Harry?'

'Yep. Long time ago. I was seventeen the last time I was here.'

Harry's 'house' was an old sailing lugger turned upside down, with the bow cut off and boarded up, part of which formed a door. Inside was a chair and table, a pot-bellied stove with its chimney pushed through the hull of the boat, a few shelves and a bed made from the remaining wood of the bow. He lived in that house as man and boy. That's why they called him Harry Boatman. I'm not sure if anyone knew his real surname. Or perhaps it was Boatman and just a happy coincidence.

'He died last year. I bought it on condition that he remain until the end. He knew it would be soon. The doctor told him when the cancer was diagnosed that he had just months to live. But he was, as you say, one hundred. He went peacefully in his sleep.'

'Did he have relatives?'

'No one who could be traced. He left the money to The Seahorse Riders.'

'Wow. I bet they were pleased.'

He smiled. 'It was a lot of money. I think they were. I have built a nightclub on part of the boatyard. It's called Neptune's and it's next to the restaurant.'

'Dinner and dancing then? Things *have* changed in Seahorse Harbour.'

'You disapprove?'

I shook my head. 'Nope. The place needed a good restaurant, and a nightclub's a great idea, especially for the tourists in the summer. What are you going to do with Harry's place?'

He leant on the bar. 'I'm considering refurbishing it and renting it out as a holiday home.'

'Hmm. I'm not sure I'd want to spend my holiday in a boathouse right next door to a potentially noisy nightclub, although the close proximity to the restaurant and the sea might prove an attraction. But I'm sure you know what you're doing. So, what does a girl have to do to get a drink around here?'

He looked genuinely startled. 'I am so very sorry. I apologise. I was enjoying our conversation so much that I forgot about your wine. It's on me. White or red?'

I laughed. 'A pub owner forgetting to serve his customers. Whatever next. White please. Chilled, if possible.'

He threw me an odd look and a smile, took a bottle from the wine chiller and poured me a very large glass.

'Stop! That's enough. You don't owe me that big an apology.' I laughed merrily.

'I do,' he said, continuing to fill the glass and then sliding it towards me and leaning on the bar looking directly into my eyes.

'Trying to get me drunk?'

'Trying to make you stay longer.'

I met his gaze for a second or two before I had to look away and take several gulps of the cold wine in an attempt to cool off. It was a very warm day but the heat I was feeling had nothing to do with the weather, or the jeans and sleeveless blouse I was wearing.

Luckily for me – or unluckily, depending on your viewpoint, a few more customers came in and Mikkel dragged himself away to serve them, but every so often he glanced in my direction and I could almost read his mind. I knew I'd better get out of there pretty damn quick or I might just end up spending the afternoon … and possibly longer with the magnificent Mikkel Meloy.

Don't get me wrong, usually I would've jumped at the chance of being in the arms, and possibly the bed, of a man like Mikkel. Call me a tart if you like but I'm a firm believer in the adage that life is for living. And I live it the way I want. I also believe in sexual equality. If men can sleep around then so can women. Not that I've slept with that many men. Not really. Not compared to some of my friends. And don't think I sleep with any man who asks me, because I don't. But when a man as hot as Mikkel looks at me the way Mikkel did, well, I thank the Universe for bestowing such a wonderful gift on me and enjoy it while it lasts.

The problem is, it never lasts long. Not the

sex, I don't mean. That can sometimes last for hours ... if you're doing it right and you're with a man who knows his onions, so to speak. I'm talking about relationships.

Sometimes a hook-up is simply that. A hook-up. It's not meant to last for longer than either party intended. But sometimes, you meet a man you want more than just a few hours of passion with. You go out on a date. And then another and another and suddenly, you're in a relationship. That never happens with me.

I go out on dates, but either I seem to screw things up, or I realise pretty quickly that he's not the man of my dreams. And as far as I'm concerned there's no point in starting a relationship unless you want it to go somewhere. Some of them call me a few times after I've made a complete mess of it, but they eventually give up. Some I tell not to even bother. It's clear there was nothing but lust involved.

I did have one serious relationship once. When I was sixteen. Not that that one lasted very long either. Just one year. But it broke my heart and I decided then and there not to fall in love again.

Mum says I never stick to anything, but I've stuck to that. Love is off the table, as far as I'm concerned. Sex, however, that's firmly on the table ... or wherever else may come in handy.

I would definitely be visiting The Seahorse Inn again, but today, my sister and her family were waiting and even I couldn't be such an awful sister as to send her a text saying, 'See you later. Met a hot guy and having sex.' Especially as I'd then have to tell her that I stopped off at the pub and Mikkel was the hot guy.

Diana would understand, but she wouldn't be terribly happy that I'd gone to bed with someone literally minutes after arriving in Seahorse Harbour.

I emptied my glass, gave Mikkel a wave and headed for the door.

Before I knew it, he was right beside me.

'I will see you again, won't I?'

He was certainly keen. I liked that in a man.

'Absolutely. You can count on it.'

'Where are you staying?'

'With my sister.'

'And that is...?'

I nodded towards the other side of the village. 'Over there.'

He let out a long sigh. 'You like keeping secrets?'

'It's called being mysterious.'

He grinned. 'It's called being infuriating. I don't even know your name.'

'You're right. You don't. Thanks for the

wine. And the conversation.'

I walked away but he was in front of me in a moment.

'Seriously?' His brows were raised almost to his gorgeously floppy fringe. 'You're not going to tell me anything about yourself?'

'The only thing you need to know right now is that I like white wine. Chilled. And that I'm spending the summer – or part of it at least, with my sister in Seahorse Harbour. It's hardly a big place, is it? And you own the only pub, restaurant and nightclub within four miles. I think we can both safely assume we'll bump into one another before too long.'

He shook his head and gave a small laugh. 'I forgot. You like to play games.' He stepped a little closer. 'Then this is goodbye for now. I will be counting the hours until we "bump" into one another again. And then, my pretty, mystery woman, we'll play a few more games. Just you, me and a bottle of chilled white wine. Or better still, chilled champagne.'

I looked up into his eyes. 'You had me at chilled white wine. For chilled champagne, you can have me wherever you want.'

God. I can be such a flirt at times. But I love it and I can't help myself.

He made a sort of choking sound and ran a hand through his thick blond hair.

I raised my brows and gave him a look to tell him to let me pass and he stepped aside, grinning and giving me a sweeping bow, indicating the path ahead.

'I'll put several bottles on ice,' he said, looking up at me with those incredibly deep blue eyes.

Five

Men are a bit like puppies, I've always thought. You tell them they're a good boy and you give them a treat and tell them if they're very good they can have more. And for a time, they'll be all wide-eyed and waggy-tailed and their tongues will be virtually hanging out. But just like a puppy, most of them have a short attention span. At least in my experience.

One minute, they're telling you they love you; the next, they're telling you it just won't work and that they're marrying someone else.

But we won't go there. I still couldn't bear to think about that final summer in Seahorse Harbour. Or that devastating October.

I made my way across the road and glanced towards the church. I stopped for a moment and looked at it. It was such a beautiful building. Small, but perfectly formed. A bit like me. Yeah right. I wish.

St Mary Star of the Sea was built by the Normans three years after they invaded England, via Sussex, and it's been standing there since 1069. When I see such an ancient building, I often wonder what stories it could tell. Imagine how many hundreds, probably even thousands of weddings, christenings and funerals a place like must've had inside those thick, stone walls.

I was wishing I hadn't drunk all that wine. The day seemed to be getting hotter and the wine had gone straight to my head. The only food I'd eaten since yesterday was the food on the plane and that's never enough to feed a mouse. I decided to sit for a while on the bright yellow bench beneath the ancient Oak in the centre of the village, beside the church. From here there was a view directly out to sea and I watched a yacht bob along in the distance and seagulls soar and swoop low over the glass-like, turquoise water. I breathed deeply, pushed my sunglasses onto the top of my head, shoving back the tumbles of wavy red hair and closed my eyes, suddenly remembering long-ago summers. I heard someone walking past but I kept my eyes closed. Until I heard my name.

'Josie? Is that you?'

My eyes shot open at the sound of a man's voice. It sounded a lot like Liam Fulbright's had all those years ago, only deeper, stronger and more commanding somehow. But the man standing in front of me looked nothing like the Liam I remembered. Liam had been tall and gangly and never quite as tanned as everyone else. His hair was always short, as if the scissors had taken fright and cut off far too much. Bits of it stuck out everywhere, a bit like a porcupine. His eyes were dark blue, but nothing to write home about, especially as they appeared more bulbous thanks to the thick glasses he wore. But I had always thought there was something simmering just beneath the surface and that one day, whatever it was, would burst forth and Liam would be transformed.

It seemed I was right. Unless this wasn't Liam Fulbright.

'It's Liam. Liam Fulbright. I don't suppose you remember me? We spent several summers together, a lifetime ago. Becca told my daughter, Orla you were coming. You haven't changed a bit. Except, perhaps your hair. I think it was chestnut brown in those days.' His smile was warm and friendly.

I shaded my eyes from the sun.

'Liam Fulbright? Really? Wow.'

I put on my sunglasses so that I could see him better and got to my feet. He towered over me. But then so did everyone. Diana and I stopped growing when we reached five foot three.

'Don't tell me you've walked from the station?'

'What? Oh. Er. No. I got a cab but stopped for a quick drink at The Seahorse Inn.'

'And ended up on the bench here? Just the one drink? Or did you have several?'

I didn't answer immediately. I was still trying to take in how much he had changed.

'Er. No. Just one. But I think the jet lag and heat is getting to me.'

'So you stopped to admire the view.'

He half-turned to look at the sea and then his eyes focussed on me again.

'Well, it is a rather gorgeous view,' I said, scanning him from the tips of his black, Converse trainers to the roots of his lustrous chocolate-brown hair.

Gone was the spiky haircut and in its place, soft, natural waves sat around a deeply tanned and exceedingly handsome face. The firm jaw held a hint of stubble, the dark blue eyes, sparkling in the bright sunlight were free of glasses and when he smiled, his sensuous-looking lips parted to reveal perfect, naturally white teeth. He was at least six foot or more and his legs were long in his jeans. His pale blue cotton shirt, although not tight, showed that his chest and shoulders were broad and his forearms, where the sleeves had been rolled back, were certainly toned. Not in a body-builder way, but in a way that made it clear Liam Fulbright was no slouch.

'I agree with you on that,' he said. 'I couldn't imagine living anywhere but here and seeing that view every day.'

'No. I could easily get used to a view like this. I mean, like that. The sea. The sea view is gorgeous. Er ... I was so sorry to hear about Una. I should've sent a card or something. Sorry. I'm a terrible person, I know.'

He reached out and touched my shoulder and I swear to you, my skin seared beneath his hand. Or perhaps my shoulders had got sunburnt. I was wearing a sleeveless blouse and I'm not sure how long I was sitting on that bench in the full midday sun.

'No you're not, Josie.' His voice changed tone. I could detect a hint of anger. 'To be honest, I wouldn't have known if you had or not. I was in a bit of a state and didn't really take in anything at the time. Everything was a bit of a blur.'

'I can imagine. Er. How are you doing now? Becca and Orla have become close friends, so I do hear your name from time to time. I was so surprised when Diana told me about your pottery. I had no idea you were interested in that sort of thing.'

He gave me a questioning look. 'That sort of thing?'

'Creative stuff, I meant. I thought you'd be wearing a suit and tie and working in that bank until the day you died. Oh God, I'm sorry. Poor choice of words.'

He laughed. 'No need to apologise. I thought so too. And if Una hadn't got cancer ...

well, who knows what might have happened? Even if she hadn't died, I suppose there's a chance I might still have chucked it all in and become a potter. Or ceramicist, I should say. I make items from other materials, not just clay.'

'But why pottery? Sorry, ceramics. Did you do any before?'

'Before Una died? Not really. I did some at school, and I really enjoyed it. I knew I couldn't continue commuting to London after Una's passing and leave Orla on her own. She was only thirteen and although several people in the village offered to look after her – and did for a month or so in the beginning, it broke my heart to leave her every morning, knowing she'd be in bed when I got home each night. We only had the weekends together and she was becoming a bit withdrawn. So I made a decision and handed in my notice. I had no idea what I was going to do. The bank let me go right away even though I had to give three months' notice, but they paid me for the time. It's all about confidentiality and once you decide to leave they don't want you sticking around and stealing their clients to take elsewhere. Although they knew I wasn't doing that. It was great for me and it gave me time to think about my future. Our future. I did a couple of classes with a ceramicist in Easterhill and found I had a knack for it. I bought The Olde Forge with savings and part of Una's life insurance. The rest is for Orla. For uni or for whatever she wants to do with it. Sorry. I don't know why I'm telling you all this. You're probably bored to tears.'

He laughed and ran a hand through that gorgeous hair and I had an urge to do the same. I didn't though.

'Not at all. It's interesting.'

'You always were a good listener, I seem to recall. Let me help you up the hill with your cases. Or do you want to admire the view some more?'

I was tempted to say I wanted to stay for the next three hours, but the view I wanted to admire, was him, not the sea.

'Walk in front of me and I can.'

I hadn't meant to say that out loud. I really was a tart. Two gorgeous men in one day. The summer wasn't going to be anywhere near as bad as I expected.

'Sorry. What?'

His lips twitched as if he wasn't sure if he'd heard me correctly and didn't know whether to smile or not.

'Er. I meant the sooner I get to Diana's the quicker I'll get to admire the view some more. And I'll have plenty of time this summer to admire the views around here. It would be great to have a hand up this hill. I'd forgotten how steep it was.'

That was true. The view from Diana's

house was incredible. And I had forgotten how steep the hill to the house was.

'So you're really staying for the summer?' He seemed surprised. 'You haven't been here since ... well, for at least seventeen years. I think the last time I saw you was at my wedding.'

'Yep. It was. I've been really busy.'

'You must've been. I'm glad you're here now. It'll be nice to catch up. I hear you've been all over the world and you're now living in New York.'

'Yeah. But I'm not sure for how much longer.'

He shook his head and smiled. 'Getting itchy feet?'

'No. Need to find a new job. I'm not sure where that'll be. I love my apartment in New York but the last contract I had working for a travel company was pretty boring. Sitting behind a desk, planning other people's holidays isn't my idea of fun.'

'And you were always keen to have fun. I remember that.'

I sighed but smiled. 'Don't you start. I get enough of that from Mum. "Will you ever settle down, Josephine? Why can't you be more like Diana? Why don't you find yourself a nice man and get married and have babies so that I can tell you how useless you are at being a mother along with everything else."' I looked at him and grimaced. 'Sorry. Not sure where that came from.'

'Does your mum still treat you as if you're second best?' His voice was tinged with anger.

'Yeah. But she doesn't mean any harm. No, seriously. Don't look at me like that. She honestly doesn't. She just wishes I could be a clone of Diana. And so do I sometimes.'

'Don't ever say that, Josie. You're great and don't let anyone tell you otherwise.'

I harrumphed at him and laughed. 'Come on, Liam. You don't know what I'm like. The last time you saw me was just before my seventeenth birthday. I'm a walking disaster, believe me. But I'm happy with my life. Most of the time. And that's what matters.'

'Perhaps I don't know you as well as I would've liked, but you were kind and friendly and caring. You were also the life and soul of the party. Any party. And if there wasn't a party, you'd start one. I remember that. I always thought, if you ever fell in love, it would be with a very special man.'

I met his look and it made me feel a little uncomfortable.

'I'm not sure I'll ever settle down,' I said. 'I don't think I'd be any good at it. Not like Diana. And talking of Diana, I'd better get going or she'll be sending out a search party.'

He laughed. 'Or you could text her and let her know you're here.'

Summer at my Sister's

'You see! I didn't even think of that.'

Six

I wasn't sure who was the most pleased to see me: Diana, Becca, or Henry the crazy, mixed up dog. I say 'mixed up' because Henry isn't just a cross-breed. I think there must be at least four different breeds in his make-up. He's brown and white and tan and there's a big autumn-red shape over one of his eyes. He's got the face and wiry brows of an Irish Wolfhound, the long fur coat of a Briard, the legs of a Great Dane and the tail of a Golden Retriever. That tail can clear a coffee table in seconds. Judging by the size of him I think there may also be a little bit of horse. He comes up to my waist when he's got all four paws on the ground. When he's got two of them on my shoulders, almost knocking me over, he's about seven feet tall. You'd have thought I would have known that this is how he would greet me. He's done it every time I've seen him, although thankfully, Diana doesn't always bring him with her when we meet up.

Diana and Becca attempted to pull him off as he started to eat me. They said he was just being friendly and trying to lick my face but I wasn't completely convinced. I tried to push him off me with both hands and he wasn't budging an inch.

I shot a look at Liam, who seemed to find it rather amusing.

'A little help ... would ... be nice,' I said between mouthfuls of fur and trying to avoid dog drool.

'Henry. Down boy.' My nephew Toby wandered into the hallway and with three little words, did what Diana, Becca and I couldn't, using all our strength.

Henry launched himself off me and trotted over to his master without a backward glance while the force of his retreating paws shoved me backwards, sending me tumbling ungainly towards the floor. Luckily, Liam caught me in his arms before I landed on my arse.

'Thanks,' I said, scowling up at him. 'You were no help at all.'

He was laughing but as he stood me upright, one hand cupped my right breast. I'm not sure who was more surprised but he quickly rectified the situation almost dropping me flat on my back in the process. Somehow he managed to save me – again, and this time was extra careful as he helped me straighten up.

The strange thing was, the feel of his hand on my breast sent all sorts of odd sensations darting through me and I was a bit embarrassed. But whenever I feel like that I overcompensate.

'Blimey, Liam,' I said, shaking my head and tutting. 'I've only been back in Seahorse Harbour for an hour or two and you're already trying it on.'

I swear I could see red beneath that tan. Was the man actually blushing?

'I ... er ... sorry. It was an accident. I wouldn't dream of ... er.'

'I was teasing you, Liam.'

I grinned at him and after giving me another very odd look, he grinned back.

'Can't take you anywhere, can we?' Becca said to me, laughing, as she grabbed me and gave me a hug.

Diana was also giving me a peculiar look and she shot a look at Liam before smiling and pulling me into her arms once Becca had let me go.

'It's so great that you're here,' Diana said. 'I can't believe it.'

'Join the club,' I said, wiping what I'm sure was dog saliva from my hair as we eased apart. 'Hey, Toby.' I waved at my nephew who was engrossed with his phone while Henry the mad hound sat patiently at his feet staring up at him. 'Thanks for saving me.'

'Anytime. Glad you're here.'

'Aren't you going to give your auntie a big hug?'

Toby grimaced as I inched my way towards him, cackling and he began to back away. Henry's head whipped round and he gave a soft snarl, raising one side of his upper lip which sort of flapped about a bit as if he had a nervous twitch. I hesitated and raised my brows questioningly. He'd never growled at me before. My nephew had, but never the dog.

'He's harmless,' Toby said. 'But I'm training him to attack on command, so don't even think about trying to hug me.'

Diana laughed. 'And by attack, he means that Henry will slobber all over you.'

'Yeah,' I said. 'He already has.'

'Liam?' Diana looked past me. 'Would you like to come in for a cup of tea? Or a beer? Or maybe a glass of wine.'

'You've got wine?' I shrieked, as Liam opened his mouth and closed it again.

'For guests,' Diana said, with a smile.

'I'm a guest. Lead me to it.' Becca took my hand and led me forwards. 'My bags,' I said, glancing over my shoulder.

Liam looked perplexed, as if he wasn't sure whether to come in or not, but he suddenly made a decision. 'I'll bring them. Thanks, Diana. I'd kill for a cold beer.'

Henry slobbered all over my hand as Becca and I walked from the spacious hallway towards the two long, solid wood stairs which led down to the massive, open plan kitchen directly ahead. Toby continued to stare at his phone as he fell in step beside us. How he could see where he was going was beyond me. His sandy-brown hair flopped over his face from both sides. He swept the whole lot back with one hand while the thumb of his other hand flew across the keys.

The kitchen in Sea View Cottage was at least five times the size of my apartment. It led into a cavernous dining area to the left, which led into a rather grandiose sitting room, although one section of the kitchen also had a spacious but somehow cosy, sitting area overlooking the garden. The kitchen had two sets of folding doors, one straight ahead, the other to my right, opening onto a spacious decked area which surrounded two sides of the house, and that, in turn, led onto an immaculate lawn edged by gorgeous, healthy plants, shrubs and trees.

Sea View Cottage isn't really a cottage, it's a large, impressive and ultra-modern house, with lots of glass instead of walls. At least it is now. It might've been a cottage once, centuries ago, and it did still retain some 'original features', but whether they were original to the cottage or brought in from somewhere else, I couldn't tell you.

One feature that is original is an outside toilet, which each successive owner had left, no doubt as it was handy if you were in the garden.

Although as the house had at least four other loos and a couple of en suites, there were plenty to choose from. But Diana thought The Privy as it was called, was quaint. It even had a sign on the door. Inside, it looked nothing like it had and it had been connected to the mains drainage at some exorbitant cost when Diana and Alex bought the house. It had even featured in one of those upmarket, home-style magazines, along with the rest of the house, of course.

Thanks to the position of Sea View Cottage there were views of the sea to be had from three sides; the front, the back and one side, and as it was such a gorgeous day, Diana suggested we sat in the garden. Liam deposited my bags in the hall and helped Diana get the drinks while Becca, Toby, Henry and I nabbed the best chairs. I took one of the sun loungers right beside the pool. Yep. Sea View Cottage has a pool. That was another thing added by Alex and Diana. It sits to one side of the decking where it gets the sun for most of the day.

'It's mainly for the children,' Diana told me when the hole was being dug. 'Sometimes the rip currents extend further out than just the inlet. At least with a pool we know the kids will be safe.'

'Seahorse Harbour Holiday Park has a pool,' I casually pointed out.

Diana had screwed up her nose. This was

during another one of our video calls.

'The holiday park is great and I know Alex loved his holidays there but I'm not sure The Lido is quite as well tended as it once was. As Dad said just the other day, "Why swim in a pool of everyone else's pee when you can swim in a pool with just your own?" Mum gave him an earful.'

'Of pee?'

Diana laughed. 'You know what I meant. Bernice was staying with us at the time and she overheard and—'

'Hovering in the background as she does,' I interrupted.

Diana's eyelashes flickered. 'Yes, well, she likes to be included.'

'She's a nosey, bitchy, jumped up old cow. But she's your mother-in-law and I know you'd never dream of saying that.'

Diana cleared her throat. 'She's not as bad as that. But anyway, Mum hates it when Dad embarrasses her in front of Bernice, so when he said about the pee, Mum was livid. She shoved him out of the way and made a big thing about how he likes to have his little jokes and how he knows that none of us would ever pee in a pool.' She shook her head and laughed.

'Poor Mum. She just makes things worse, doesn't she? I bet she's proud that you're having your own pool though.'

Diana confirmed she was. Mum was even

more proud when Diana's house, pool and The Privy were featured in that magazine, especially as the caption below one of the photos said it was 'The premier home in Seahorse Harbour'. Mum loves stuff like that.

Diana and Liam joined us in the garden, both carrying trays. Liam's had the drinks, Diana's had bowls and plates of nibbles.

'Toby. Please ask Henry to get off that chair,' Diana said.

'Why? There're plenty.' He frowned at her beneath his hair.

'They're for people, not for dogs. Must we do this every time?'

She sounded slightly fraught. That wasn't like Diana. Henry flopped his legs over the arm and rested his head on his paws, so he wasn't going anywhere and Toby had returned his attention to his phone.

'Are we having a party?' I asked, changing the subject.

'What?' She glared at Toby for a second before smiling at me. 'Oh. I thought you might be hungry.'

'I'm always hungry,' Becca said.

She reached for a devilled egg, which happened to be my favourite, as Diana knew.

'Me too,' I said. 'But not always for food.'

I gave Liam a meaningful glance, but either he didn't hear me or he chose to ignore it.

His hand on my boob earlier was clearly

still having an effect. All I could think about as I watched him put his tray on the long glass table, slide a finger up the outside of his beer bottle to catch a large drip of foaming beer and then suck the foam off his finger, was that I wouldn't mind being that bottle.

Seven

I was hoping to broach the real reason for my visit with Diana later that afternoon but Liam stayed for almost an hour and then Becca wanted to show me her room. I'd seen it loads of times via video call but she was adamant I needed to see it 'in real life'. I had to admit it looked even more gorgeous in reality than it did on a screen.

She proceeded to ask me why I'd never come to stay before and although I gave her the usual excuses: work commitments; living in different countries; having jobs with unsociable hours and few holidays, she didn't seem to buy it.

'I've visited you in Blackheath loads of times,' I said.

'But never to stay. Just for the day. Yet you go and stay with Gran.'

'Yeah. But that's on pain of death, not because I want to. Your gran would kill me if I didn't go to Gib to stay for at least a few days every year.'

'So does that mean you don't stay with us because you don't want to? If Mum threatened you like Gran does, would you come?'

'Er. No. I mean that's not why I don't stay with you. It's not because I don't want to, it's honestly because I ... er ... well, life is complicated, kiddo. You'll understand when you grow up.'

'I'm grown up now.'

She certainly was. She'd never questioned me like this before. It was as if she'd just started seeing my excuses for what they were. I had to do something to distract her. I didn't discuss my reasons for staying away from the family with anyone. I had no intention of trying to explain myself to my fifteen-year-old niece. I asked her to tell me what she and Orla had planned for the summer and luckily she was excited to do so. It got us off the subject of me, but it took more time than I'd imagined. It was going to be one heck of a busy summer by the sounds of it.

I went to find Diana and found Toby and Henry instead. Toby was taking Henry for a walk and when I asked him where his mum was he shrugged and said, 'Search me.'

'Okay,' I replied. 'Spread your legs and put your arms in the air.' I sniggered but he looked at me as if he thought I was a little bit bonkers, so instead I asked if I could join him on his walk.

Again he shrugged. 'S'pose.'

Toby had turned into a teenager of few words.

I asked Becca if she wanted to join us but she was meeting Orla, so I headed off with Toby and walked in virtual silence while he constantly tapped or scrolled his phone screen.

'Any chance you could put that on hold and chat for a minute or two?'

'Huh? 'Bout what?'

'About anything. How's school?'

''Kay.'

'Who's Kay?'

'Huh?'

This was pretty hopeless. It seemed Toby suddenly liked to drop the first letter of some of his words, but he didn't get my joke. I don't recall our conversations being quite so stultified via video call.

'Never mind.'

We strolled down the hill I'd puffed my way up earlier with Liam, which brought us out just behind the church. Fulbright Ceramics was a little over to the right, from here and I was tempted to abandon Toby and pop inside The Olde Forge and see if there was anything tempting on offer. But Liam was no doubt working and I decided I'd probably flirted with him enough for one day.

Nevertheless, as we passed by I did take a sneak peek via the open double doors and I nearly had an orgasm on the spot. Liam was sitting at his potter's wheel, his legs astride a wooden frame, one foot on a wooden pedal-type-thing that jutted out and seemed to be attached to the wheel by a chain, but from where I stood it was hard to tell. The Olde Forge was as deep as it was broad and Liam and his wheel were at the rear of the old stone building.

Sunlight danced on his hair and his forearms, and made the conical lump of what looked like wet mud between his hands gleam as he ran his fingers up and down, inserting his thumbs inside and teasing the clay into shape.

If you've ever seen the film, *Ghost*, you'll understand that I could see myself sitting at that wheel right then, in place of Demi Moore.

'You coming?' Toby asked, stopping a few feet ahead.

'I think I am. Er. Sorry. Yes. Right with you.'

I dragged my eyes away, coughed to clear my throat and considered nipping into The Seahorse Inn for a chilled white wine to slake my thirst, but the thirst I was feeling at that moment, not even chilled white wine could satisfy. And besides, I'd also flirted enough there too and my hormones couldn't cope with watching another sexy man in action. Plus, abandoning my nephew to 'scratch that itch' as Rhoda, my best friend, in New York called it, wouldn't be a good idea on my first day in Seahorse Harbour.

We walked past some cottages opposite Memorial Gardens and made our way onto Sea Walk, between Nice Ice, the ice cream kiosk-cum-parlour and Beach Bakers, where the pastries and cakes in the window were definitely calling me and momentarily erased all thoughts of sexy men from my mind. Sadly, I'd eaten three devilled eggs, two ham and asparagus wraps, and something else delicious but I had no clue what it was, so a cake oozing with cream or a pastry drowning in icing, probably was a bit much, even for me. Maybe on the way back. I'd need some sustenance to get me up that hill.

Without warning, Toby yelled in an animated fashion, waving frantically and dashing off along the promenade. Henry bounded after him, nearly knocking me flying in the process.

'Where's the fire?' I called after them.

They both stopped in front of a tall, solidly built man with hair the colour of treacle and skin just a few shades lighter. He either spent a lot of time in the sun, or several hours in a tanning salon. Henry gave him the same greeting he had given me but the man stood his ground and after a moment or two, eased the dog away as easily and as gently as if Henry were a tiny puppy. Then he ruffled Toby's hair.

I couldn't believe my eyes. No one ruffles Toby's hair and gets away with it, but apart from a huge grin, Toby didn't even flinch. Who was this man with special powers?

I hurried towards them and he glanced in my direction. I smiled as I closed the distance, and he gave me a questioning look.

'Hello,' he said, his voice as solid as the rest of him. 'I haven't seen you around here before.'

'She's my aunt,' Toby said. 'She never comes here.'

'No,' I said, taking in the fact that this was the third gorgeous man I'd seen since I arrived. Why didn't Diana tell me the place was full of sexy, god-like males? I'd have tossed aside all my fears and heartbreak and been in Seahorse Harbour faster than the speed of light. 'I'm merely a hologram. I'm not really here.'

'Ah. That explains it. I'm Asher. Asher Bryant. It's lovely to meet you, hologram of Toby's aunt.'

Henry wasn't the only one drooling. I'm pretty sure I was when Asher smiled at me.

'The vet! Jonno mentioned you.'

'You know Jonno?' He seemed surprised.

I laughed. 'He drove me here from Easterhill Station today and he told me about you.'

'Oh? Because you have a pet.'

'Er. No. Because he was regaling me with the delights of Seahorse Harbour.'

His brows shot up. 'And he mentioned me?' He laughed and rubbed his clean-shaven jaw. 'It's good to know he's talking me up. I quite like the idea of being one of Seahorse Harbour's delights.' He gave me a wink as if he didn't really believe it. 'I'll have to buy him a pint.'

'And I'll have to get a pet.'

Our eyes met and we smiled at one another.

'You kill every plant Mum buys you,' Toby said.

Now the boy could manage an entire sentence? Typical. I'd forgotten he was there. I'm such a terrible aunt.

'That's true. And yet she keeps buying them.' I gave Asher a sheepish grin. 'I don't suppose there's something I can have that doesn't need any looking after whatsoever, is there? Something that can feed itself and doesn't need much space? Like a pygmy goat, perhaps?'

'Even goats need care and attention,' Asher said. 'You could have one of those virtual pets. As you're a hologram that might work quite well.'

'Perfect.'

'We're going swimming,' Toby said, clearly bored with our silliness. 'Want to join us?'

Oh God! Y-es pl-ease. Thankfully I didn't say that out loud. Although as I hadn't got my bikini, and thought we were just going for a walk and possibly a paddle, I didn't relish the prospect of watching this hunk and Toby having fun in the sea without me.

Asher shook his head. 'I'd love to but sadly I've got patients. Another time though?' He looked at me and gave me another of those mind-numbing smiles.

'I'm here for the summer so anytime you want to ride the waves, or anything else, is fine with me.'

'You surf?' Asher's enthusiasm was evident.

'Surf? Er. No. I have enough trouble staying upright on solid ground. I was joking.'

'Mum said you did,' Toby said, frowning. 'Years ago. Before I was born.'

'Yes, well that was a very long time ago.'

'It's like riding a bike,' Asher said.

'And I've fallen off one of those too. I'll happily sit on the beach and watch.'

Asher grinned. 'We'll get your aunt riding before the summer's out, won't we, Toby? Or at least staying upright on a paddle board.'

Toby nodded and grinned. 'I've got an old board she can borrow. No wet suit though. She wouldn't fit into any of mine.'

Asher looked me up and down, sending tingles all over my body. When he gave me another rather sexy smile, I was sure steam must be shooting out of my ears.

'I think I've got a suit that might fit. My sister's about the same size as you. She leaves it here for when she comes to stay.'

'Coo-ey, Asher!' A chubby woman waddled towards us, beaming at Asher and cuddling a chihuahua. They both wore bright pink bows on their heads and had the same sort of screwed up eyes, as if trying to keep out the sun. 'I thought that was you. I was on my way to the surgery when I spotted you. I don't have an appointment but my poor Peaches really needs your help.' She leant forward even though she was at least two feet away. 'She won't stop licking her bottom.' She glanced around. 'And that's not a very ladylike thing to do in public.'

'Really?' I said. 'I do it all the time.'

The woman gave me a stern look, but Toby and Asher grinned. Peaches bared her teeth and Henry whined and hid behind Toby's legs. I'm not sure if it was Peaches, the woman, or the idea of me licking my bottom that frightened Henry.

'Let's walk to the surgery together, Mrs Street and I'll see if something's causing a problem. Enjoy the beach you two.'

'Good luck, Peaches,' I said, glancing over my shoulder once – or maybe twice, as Asher, Peaches and Mrs Street walked towards Church Hill.

Well. Asher Bryant was gorgeous. But he

hadn't asked me my name and he didn't glance back at me once. Not that I saw anyway. But I suppose his mind was probably on Peaches' bottom.

Toby, Henry and I jumped from the promenade onto the sand. Toby stripped off his T-shirt and jeans and ran into the water wearing the swim shorts he had on underneath. Henry ran in after him and sent an arc of water in my direction. Luckily I managed to jump out of the way of most of it but my hair, my sleeveless blouse and my rolled up jeans were wet and we didn't have a towel. The water was as warm as a bath and I wished I'd brought my swimsuit down with me. If I remained on the beach for long, I knew I'd throw caution to the wind and go in the sea with my clothes on. After fifteen minutes or so I called to Toby and indicated I was off and I left him, Henry and a couple of other boys around Toby's age, diving in and out of the gentle waves and made my way towards my aunt Elsie's.

Eight

'Holy mopeds, it *is* you!' Elsie pulled me into a bear hug on the doorstep of her cottage. 'I didn't believe Diana when she popped in to see me on Monday and told me you were coming to stay. I never thought I'd see the day when you came back here, but I always hoped you would.'

Aunt Elsie is Mum's elder sister and, like Diana and Alex, she bought a property in Seahorse Harbour with the money Grammie Yates left her. Grammie was Elsie and my mum's mum. But the cottage Elsie bought is actually a cottage, and about half the size of Diana's house. I'd seen it via video call, but I'd never visited in the flesh. I knew it consisted of a sitting room, a kitchen diner and a pantry on the ground floor with two bedrooms and a bathroom on the next. There's also an attic which Elsie had converted into a master bedroom with an en suite. The front garden is small and filled with an abundance of plants and flowers of all colours, shapes and sizes. It's as if someone tossed seeds and bulbs in the air and let them grow where they landed. There's neither rhyme nor reason to Elsie's garden, front or back. The back garden is larger and as she welcomed me into her home and led me outside, the scent of honeysuckle, lilac and lavender filled my nostrils.

'Sit yourself at the table and I'll get us a G&T.'

Elsie isn't your typical aunt. She offers alcohol, not cups of tea. Perhaps that's one of the reasons I love her so.

She also rides a moped painted in psychedelic art, and wears clothes in equally vibrant colours and patterns.

Her name is Elspeth, and like Mum, whose name is Tabitha, no one ever calls them by their given names. They're known as Elsie and Tibby and that's how they introduce themselves to anyone who hasn't met them. Like me and Diana, Mum and Elsie led opposite lives but always kept in touch and were extremely close.

That was until a few years ago when something happened between them and caused a bit of a rift. Neither one will talk about it and I'm not sure Dad even knows the reason, but now, although they still attend family gatherings, they barely speak to one another.

I haven't seen Elsie since last Christmas and that was only for the day. Unusually, Diana and her family weren't going to Courchevel for Christmas, so everyone was invited to spend it at Diana's home in Blackheath. Mum and Dad were staying for a few days but Elsie arrived on Christmas morning, as did I, and she left in a cab with me at 6 p.m. shortly after Christmas tea.

I asked her then, for the umpteenth time what had gone on between her and Mum, but all she said was, "Sisters sometimes don't agree on certain things. It'll all come out in the wash. Best leave it alone till then." I hadn't asked her since and I wouldn't dream of asking Mum. Diana did, but Mum wouldn't tell her anything either so we were all in the dark about the rift.

Elsie's home, Seaside Cottage is just a short stroll up from Sea Walk and the sands and rocks beyond forming the curly tail of the seahorse-shaped bay. It has a direct view of Seahorse Point and the entire bay from the front, and at the back, stands a tall hedge of holly, quince and forsythia. Behind that there's a wood called Little Wood, which leads all the way up the hill behind several houses, including Diana's, so the gardens are secluded. Just like Elsie's front garden, there's an abundance of colourful and exotic flowers all happily swaying together in the gentle breeze.

I sat at the white, metal table on a Lloyd loom chair piled with colourful cushions, beneath a grape-covered arbour where several bees and wasps were buzzing, busily going about their daily chores.

'This place is Heaven,' I said, when she brought our very large G&Ts.

'I love it here,' she replied, with a beaming smile.

She hoisted up the voluminous sheer sleeves of her full-length, floral kimono which hung open over sunshine yellow and red Capri pants and a bright red, low cut blouse, and sat on the chair opposite. The belt of her kimono, tied in a huge dangling bow at one side, seemed to be wrapped around her pink, blue and purple curls that tumbled to her shoulders. As I said, Elsie isn't your average aunt.

She wasn't like this when she and Mum were younger, according to Dad. Mum was the tearaway, which I find incredibly hard to believe and Elsie was more like Diana. But after Elsie's husband died very young, more than thirty-three years ago, Elsie's entire outlook on life changed. Dad told Diana and me once that he thought Mum and Elsie had switched bodies, like in the movies, and even Mum and Elsie admit that it was as if their behaviour was reversed. But for as long as I've known Elsie she's always been like this. Full of life and happiness. Whereas Mum is more reserved and has an innate ability to sour my mood with just one sentence.

Elsie's older than Mum by five years. I'm younger than Diana by five minutes. Not that that means anything. Mum often said that if I wasn't careful, I'd end up like Elsie. She saw that as a negative. I saw that as something to aspire to. If I could be as spritely and fun-loving as Elsie when I reached her age of sixty-five, I'd be a happy bunny. She even went out on more dates than me.

She leant back in her chair and raised her bare feet up onto a large pouffe covered in a pink flamingo-patterned material.

'Cheers,' I said, leaning forward and clinking our glasses of G&T.

'Cheers, honeybee.'

She took a few sips, eyeing me over the rim the entire time.

'What?' I laughed. 'Have I got spinach in my teeth or something?'

She cocked her head to one side and the large bow flopped across her face. She moved it out of her line of vision and threw me a sort of screwed up smile.

'How's it been so far, being back here after all these years?'

'Fine. Better than fine, actually. I stopped for a drink before I went to Di's and met the divine Mikkel.'

'Ooooh yes. He could ravage me anytime he likes.'

'Me too.' I laughed again. That's exactly what I had said to Diana. 'And afterwards, on the way up the hill, I bumped into Liam Fulbright. I can't believe how much he's changed. He's like a super hero. Although he wasn't very heroic when Henry leapt all over me and tried to eat my face.'

'Has Liam changed?' She furrowed her brows before nodding. 'Yes, I suppose he has since you last saw him. And even more so after Una died. But that's to be expected. Such a shock that was. Liam was devastated. And for very good reason.' She gave a cough. 'You always liked him, didn't you?'

I blushed and took a gulp of my drink. 'Uh-huh.'

'At one time I thought you and he might ... well, that wasn't to be was it? Because you... But we won't talk about that. Unless you want to.'

I darted a look at her and shook my head. 'Nope. Nah-huh. Definitely not.'

'That'll be a no then. So how's New York?'

'Fantastic as always.'

'And the men?'

I shrugged. 'Not quite as fantastic. At least not the ones I date. But I haven't finished telling you. I also met Asher Bryant today. God. He's pretty hot, isn't he?'

'And built like a brick s—'

'Elsie!' I guffawed.

'I wasn't going to say what you think, honeybee. I was going to say like a brick, sausage factory.'

I chuckled. 'A brick sausage factory? You

mean he's tough and...'

Elsie tutted. 'I mean he's solid, tasty and meaty, like a man should be.'

'He's got a gorgeous smile. But so has Mikkel. And as for Liam. Oh God, Elsie. I walked past The Olde Forge and Liam was throwing a pot. That's what it's called when they're making one, isn't it?' I waved a hand in the air. 'It doesn't matter. Anyway. My hormones were blowing trumpets.'

Elsie giggled like a girl. 'I often walk past The Olde Forge. Sometimes several times a day. I frequently go in and wander around the tables and the shelves where he displays his wares. I've got so many pots, vases, ornaments, bowls and well, everything, that either I've got to buy a shed to house them or I've got to stop going in to look at Liam.'

I giggled too. I could just see Elsie ogling Liam.

'Has he ... dated anyone since Una died? Diana mentions him sometimes but not that often actually. And I can't believe she hasn't shown me a recent picture of him, especially now he looks the way he does.'

Elsie swished her glass and the ice cubes clinked against the sides.

'I think he went on a date with Lucy Willis. She's a school teacher in Easterhill and Orla's in her class. She's renting a cottage in the village. Only moved here last September.

They're friends, but I'm not sure if they're just friends or if they're friends with benefits.'

'Oh I see.'

'There's Orla to think about. Liam dotes on her.'

'And Una's a pretty tough act to follow. I remember the day they got married. I watched her walk down the aisle and I couldn't believe that a woman as beautiful as that existed. Or that she was happy to live in Seahorse Harbour. Didn't she come from London, originally?'

Elsie nodded. 'I think Liam was intoxicated by her. Everyone was the moment they saw her. As you say, she was a beauty. But sometimes beauty is only skin deep and ugliness lurks not far beneath.'

'Are you saying there was a bad side to Una? I thought she was all sweetness and light.'

'She was. At first. But people change. Or perhaps they don't. Perhaps some other people just bring out the worst in them.'

I sat forward in my chair. 'Ooooh, Elsie. Are you saying Una did something bad? Like what? I'm dying to hear.'

She shook her head. 'No, honeybee. Not right now. Another time, perhaps.' She took a sip of her drink. 'I know you said you don't want to talk about it but you've finally come back to Seahorse Harbour after all these years. That calls for a celebration. Perhaps you're ready at last to put the past behind you? I've got some bubbly in the fridge.' She knocked back her G&T and got to her feet. 'Let's open that, put some music on and dance around the garden.'

'That's not why I'm here, Elsie. I'm here because of Diana.'

'Diana?' She stopped in her tracks and stared at me.

'Yeah. Mum called me last Friday and said she thought there was something wrong with Diana and that I needed to come over here and find out what it was. I hadn't noticed anything, but I video called Di the next day, and Mum's right. There's definitely something wrong. So I got on a plane and here I am.'

'And Alex?'

'Here's still in London. Di says he's rushed off his feet and won't be coming here until later in the summer.'

'I see. Well. That's a coat of a different colour.'

'Have you noticed anything? Has Di said anything to you?'

'She only arrived yesterday and didn't stay long when she popped in to see me. She did look tired and I mentioned it but she shrugged it off and said she's been busy. That's no doubt true. She runs that baby clothing business, that book club, all those dinners and parties for Alex and his cronies, not to mention running back and forth to Bernice's every time the woman clicks her fingers. And then there're the kids. It's no wonder she's tired. Tibby's worried, is she? Hmm. That's interesting. Perhaps it's time I had a word.'

'With Diana?'

'With my sister.'

'Really? It'd be great if you two could heal the rift between you, but I'm not sure how that helps Diana right now.'

'It might help. We'll have to see. Has Diana said anything at all to you?'

I shook my head. 'Nothing. I'm completely in the dark. All I know is that when I phoned her, I'm pretty sure she started crying but she moved out of sight and then said she'd been feeling unwell. I haven't had a chance to talk to her yet. I don't want to say anything in front of the kids.'

'No, no. Quite right.' She hesitated for a second. 'I think I'll still get that champagne though and we should definitely have a dance. Dancing always makes everything seem so much better.'

That's one thing Elsie, Mum and I agreed on.

Nine

'What's up then, Di?'

I finally got a chance to talk to Diana about 10 p.m. that night. After returning from Elsie's, I'd gone to my room for a nap and had slept until 7 p.m. when Diana called me down to dinner. Afterwards, we all sat in the garden. We played croquet for a while, and hit a shuttlecock back and forth over a make-shift net before collapsing on the chairs and sun beds. The hot day had drifted into a hot and humid night and when Becca and Toby went to their rooms around 9, saying they were both shattered, I helped Diana clear up. We then had coffee, sitting side by side while dipping our feet and ankles in the pool. Well, Diana had coffee. I had wine.

'What do you mean? Nothing's up. I told you on Saturday that everything's fine.'

'Pull the other one. I didn't believe it then and I don't believe it now. There's definitely something wrong. I could see it the minute you answered on Saturday, and I'm sure you had a little cry. Please tell me, Di. I might be able to help.'

'I'm just a bit run down, that's all.'

'Don't buy it. Sorry. I wasn't going to say this, but Mum's worried about you too. She called me on Friday night and told me I should come and see you.'

Diana glared at me and then tutted and shook her head.

'I should've known. She kept badgering me. She even got Dad to have a word. But I told them what I'm telling you. Nothing is wrong. I just need to recharge my batteries, that's all. It's been a pretty hectic year. What with my business, the book club, the kids, the hospital wing and all the parties and publicity for that, and Alex working all hours of the day and night...' She looked tearful and shook her head. 'I'm tired. We're all tired. That's it. If that's why you've come all the way here, I'm afraid you've had a wasted journey.'

'Seeing my sister is never a waste of a journey.' I nudged her arm. 'I'm not sure I believe you, Di, but I won't push you to tell me what's up. Just know that whatever it is, we can deal with it. Okay? I'll be here when you're ready to talk.'

She blinked several times in rapid succession as if fighting back tears. I reached out and linked my arm through hers, leaning into her shoulder.

'Thanks,' she said, her voice little more than a whisper.

'That's what sisters are for.'

She rested her head against mine and we sat in silence for a time, the only sounds being the lapping of the water against the sides of the pool and what I think was an owl hooting in the distance. The sky was the colour of ink; the stars, silver dots and a sliver of a pinky-white moon was barely visible.

I could've sat there for hours, especially as Diana had had the common sense to have thrown down plump cushions for us to sit on. Something I would never have thought of until after my bum was as numb as could be. The serenity was broken by my mobile phone.

I pulled it from the pocket of the dress I'd hastily thrown on when Diana had told me dinner was ready, and screwed up my nose at the screen. My friend Rhoda had put an app on my phone that displayed any image you wanted from a wide selection to identify a specific caller. For her caller ID, she'd selected an image of a curvaceous, big-boobed, big-haired blonde sitting astride an aeroplane in flight. That was amusing because her hair's jet black, she's stick-thin and she hates flying, but as she always says, "A girl's gotta have dreams." The image on my screen at that moment was of a cartoon-like Medusa running around maniacally waving her arms in the air whilst all the snakes on her head bit her on the arse.

'Oh bugger. It's Mum.' I glanced at Diana and she sighed.

'Don't answer it.' There was an almost pleading look in her eyes.

'She'll only call again if I don't. And she'll keep calling until I do. And she'll contact the police, the ambulance and the fire brigade to come and check on us.'

Diana sighed again and nodded. 'Okay. But could you tell her I've gone to bed with a headache?'

'And make her worry that you're dying from a brain haemorrhage. I don't think so. We'll just tell her we've had a busy day and we're both very tired so we'll only chat for a few minutes.'

Which is exactly what I said, and almost thirty minutes later, after I pretended my battery was dying, I said a final, 'Good night, Mum' and switched off my phone.

'I wish I hadn't given up drink,' Diana said, rubbing her forehead with her fingers. 'Now I really do have a headache. Can't she ever take a hint?'

'Not unless it's given with a hammer on her head, no.' I glanced at Diana. 'Are you okay? Shall I get you some painkillers?'

'No thanks. I'll be fine. But I'll love you and leave you for the night, if that's okay?' She swung her legs out of the pool and stood upright. 'Help yourself to more wine, or anything else you fancy from the fridge or cupboards.'

'Thanks. You don't happen to have Mikkel, Liam and Asher stashed in your cupboards do you because I quite fancy all of them?'

It took her longer than usual to smile and she didn't seem to find it funny, so her head must've been killing her.

'No. And you can't have sex with all three of them, Josie. That just wouldn't be right.'

'Er. Okay. Sorry. It was just a joke.' I stood up too.

'Was it? I never know with you.'

'Hey!' I gave her arm a gentle squeeze. 'You'd better go to bed and get some sleep. You're getting a bit ratty. I'll wash up this stuff.'

'Sorry.' She closed her eyes and shook her head. 'Ignore me. I didn't mean that.'

'Not a problem-mo. Pleasant dreams. I'll be up in a minute. And you have a lie-in tomorrow. I'll get up and make breakfast.'

She laughed at that. 'You'll be jet lagged and you know it. I'll be fine. Pleasant dreams, Josie.' She leant forward and gave me a kiss on the cheek, taking one of my hands in hers as she did so. 'I'm glad you came. Truly I am.'

'Me too. This is going to be a summer to remember. One we'll still talk about when we're old and grey and smacking our toothless gums together.'

She gave me the oddest look and a strange sort of smile before turning and walking indoors, leaving me to clear up her cup and my glass. That may not seem like a big thing, as I'd offered to do it, but Diana never let her guests tidy up, not even me. In fact, especially not me. She didn't trust me not to break something.

Yep. There was definitely something wrong with my sister, and I really needed to find out what that was as soon as possible.

Ten

Needless to say, Diana was right. I had a serious case of jet lag on Wednesday morning. Although I suppose that large glass of wine at The Seahorse Inn, followed by wine at Diana's and then the battleship-sized G&T at Elsie's, not to mention the bottle of champagne, rounded off with more wine at dinner and then a little more throughout the evening, might not have helped the situation.

Whatever.

The last thing I needed was to have my face licked by a drooling hound.

'Get off me, you bloody camel.'

I gave Henry an almighty shove ... followed by another ... and then another. The fourth attempt finally worked. The only problem was the stupid mutt had got himself tangled in the bedding, including somehow, the fitted sheet, so when he tumbled to the floor along with the duvet, sheet and two pillows, he took me with him.

I landed, somewhat inelegantly with one

leg still caught and as Toby called his hound from somewhere in the house, and the damn dog shot off like a bullet from a gun, he dragged the bedding and me behind him.

It was only for a couple of feet, but far enough for me to bang my leg against a chair and my shoulder against the writing desk. No one but Diana would put a writing desk in a bedroom. Except, perhaps, Bernice. Anyway, by the time I'd eventually got to my feet and showered, I had two large bruises forming. The straps of my floral cotton top, and the cut of my Royal blue shorts, showed them off rather nicely.

'Good morning,' Diana chirped, as she glanced over her shoulder from the cooker, all bright and breezy in a canary-yellow, summer dress, her hair expertly coiffed and her make-up perfect … at 7 a.m. in the morning. I ask you, who does that if they're on holiday? And who gets up at 7 a.m. unless they have to go to work? 'Did you sleep well?' She turned around, holding a frying pan containing sizzling bacon. And then she saw my face. 'Oh! What happened to you?'

'Henry happened to me.' I limped towards the table, overacting just a tad.

'Did he come in and wake you up?' Becca asked, grinning broadly.

'If trying to murder me in my bed is classed as waking me up, then yes. He did.'

Toby glanced up from his phone. 'Should've closed your door.'

'I did.'

'Couldn't've.'

'Couldn't've? Is that even a word? I did close the door, I assure you.'

Toby shrugged.

'Did it click?' Becca asked.

'Did it what?'

'Click?' Diana repeated. 'The door has to click to be properly closed. It's the way they're designed.'

'Thanks for telling me. It's a pity no one mentioned that last night.'

'Is that a bruise?' Diana pointed at a blackening circle at the top of my arm and my shoulder.

'Yep. Courtesy of Henry and your writing desk. I've got one on my leg that almost matches. The chair did that.'

'Goodness.' Diana shook her head. 'Are you okay?'

'I'll live. Not sure I can say the same for Henry.'

Toby glared at me. 'You didn't shut the door. That's not his fault.'

Diana chortled. 'Josie was joking, sweetheart.'

'Josie wasn't,' I mumbled, winking at Becca.

'Would you like a full English breakfast?'

Diana asked, dishing up the bacon onto four plates. 'Becca has a busy day planned for us.'

'Is Henry joining us?'

''Course,' Toby replied, scowling at me.

'Oh joy. I'd better pack a first aid kit and several swathes of bandages. So what's on the itinerary then, Becca?'

'I told you yesterday.'

That's true. She had. It involved something to do with cleaning and the beach but I couldn't remember what and I had no idea I was included. I thought she was telling me what she was going to be doing with her friend Orla.

'It's The Seahorse Summer Sand Shine-Up,' Diana said. 'We do it every year during the first week of the school holidays and again during the last. The entire village joins in. We collect litter from the beach and any that's stuck amongst the rocks. The Seahorse Riders ensure the inlet's cleared. It's surprising how much gets trapped by the currents. You'd think it would all be swept out to sea, but it's not. Of course, The Seahorse Riders and some of the locals help to keep the beach clean throughout the year but this is really to encourage people to remember our beaches aren't rubbish dumps.'

'Wonderful. A day picking up rubbish. That does sound like fun.'

'It is,' Diana said.

'Mikkel will be there.' Becca grinned at me.

'So will Orla's dad.'

'And Asher,' Toby said, although I don't think he quite realised the significance of mentioning gorgeous men, or that they might be an enticement because he added, 'and Aunt Elsie.'

'Well, if Elsie's going you can definitely count me in,' I said, beaming as Diana put a delicious-looking breakfast in front of me without a word.

'You'll get to meet Orla,' Becca said. 'I've told her all about you.'

'All?' I squealed, with a large piece of bacon half in, half out of my mouth.

That was a bit disconcerting. Liam was Orla's dad. I hope Orla didn't repeat it all to him.

Becca nodded, tucking into her mushrooms. 'I told her you've been absolutely everywhere in the world.'

'I haven't been everywhere, exactly.'

'That you've got a gorgeous apartment in the middle of New York.'

'Er. That might be a bit misleading.'

'And that you only date gorgeous, rich and very sexy men.'

'I wish. Are you sure you told her about me and not someone else?'

Becca tutted. 'I said that you go to all the trendiest clubs.'

'That's true! Yay.'

'And that you're never, ever getting married.'

'Oh.'

'Because you can have all the sex you want without any commitment.'

'Becca!' Diana gave her an admonishing stare. 'That's not the sort of comment you should be making in front of your brother.'

'Why?' Toby's head shot up but he was sniggering. 'We talk about sex. Both you and Dad said it's okay.'

'It is, darling. But sex should be between two people who are in love and who are committed to a loving relationship. Sex without a commitment is not something we condone.'

'Quite right,' I said.

Toby mumbled something inaudible and returned to his phone and his breakfast, eating with a fork in one hand and texting with the other.

'Not at the table, darling,' Diana said.

Toby ignored her and carried on, throwing a rasher of bacon in the air for Henry, who had been sitting silently by his side between me and Toby. The dog jumped up and caught it in his mouth with a slap of his jaws and a splattering of saliva which, needless to say, headed in my direction and landed on my neck.

'Henry!' I yelped. I swear that dog sniggered.

'Toby! That's enough. Josie will think you

have no manners.'

Diana glared at him and he glared right back.

'So,' I said, wiping my neck with the pristine napkin Diana had provided, 'What time does this sparkly beach thing start?'

'At 9 or just after,' Becca replied.

'Are you wearing that dress, Di? Don't you think it might get messy if we're collecting rubbish?'

Diana looked at me. 'Oh no. We use special poles with grippers on the end. And you and I and Elsie will remain on the sand. The youngsters clamber over the rocks.'

'I see. Well, that sounds very civilised. Can we go to the pub for lunch?'

'We take a picnic.'

'Oh. We'd better remember to bring all our leftovers and wrappers home then, hadn't we? Or that sort of defeats the object.'

'We always do.' Diana held the coffee pot aloft. 'More coffee?'

Diana didn't sound quite so cheery after me mentioning the pub. Perhaps this whole 'not drinking' lark was getting to her.

'Lots, please.' I smiled at her. 'Does this thing go on all day?'

'It ends around 4, or whenever all the rubbish is cleared. People often go for a swim afterwards.'

'So I'd better take my swimming stuff?'

'That would be a good idea.'

I so wanted to retort, 'Yeah. And it would be a good idea if you lot told me these things. Like shutting the bedroom door until it clicks.' But I didn't. Instead, I just said, 'Fine. I'll go upstairs and get it.'

My mobile was ringing as I walked into my room. I forgot I'd left it on charge. I peered at Medusa and the snakes biting her arse and sighed deeply.

'Morning, Mum. How are you on this lovely, sunny morning?'

'I'd be a lot better if you would do what you're supposed to be doing and tell me what's going on with dear Diana.'

'I can tell you this much. Diana is getting mood swings and Toby is playing up. Does that help?'

'Wh-what do you mean by mood swings? And how is Toby playing up? He's always been such a good little boy.'

'Yeah well, things have changed. He's thirteen now and you know what teenagers can be like. I think he's trying to push his luck to see how far he can go, and as his dad's not here he–'

'What do you mean, his dad's not there?'

'Er. Precisely that. His dad's not here. Didn't Diana tell you? Alex stayed in London. He's busy at the hospital and can't get away.'

'Stayed in London? You mean he's not in

Seahorse Harbour?'

I sniggered. 'Er. Yes. That's what I just said.'

'This isn't funny, Josephine. This is serious. Alex and Diana always spend summer in Seahorse Harbour.'

'Oh, Mum. Come on. Don't make this into one of your dramas. He'll be coming down later. He's just got a lot on his plate at the moment, that's all.'

'Is it? Are you sure? Has Diana said anything to you? Are they ... are they having ... marital problems?'

Mum made that sound as if they'd got the bubonic plague. But that was one of the first things that had occurred to me. I'd wondered if Alex was having an affair, although I wouldn't say that to Mum.

'I have no idea, Mum. Diana won't talk to me about what's wrong just yet. But I'm sure she will. Given time.'

'Given time? If there's something wrong with their marriage, Josephine, time may be a luxury we don't have.'

'We? Er. I hate to point this out, Mum, but there is no 'we'. If Diana and Alex are having problems, they'll sort it out between themselves. All we can do is be here if Di needs us or wants to talk about it. And so far, she clearly doesn't.'

'You really are hopeless sometimes,

Josephine. I knew I should've come over there myself.'

'I'm not hopeless. And you can't fly yet, remember? Look, Mum. Just leave it with me, will you? I said I'd find out what's going on and I will. And I'll do that a lot better if you don't phone me every night and morning, okay? Now I'm hanging up because we're going to make the beach all clean and shiny. Give Dad my love. Bye.'

I didn't wait for a reply and I put my phone on vibrate. At least then I wouldn't hear it ring.

Eleven

The beach was packed. I didn't realise so many people lived in Seahorse Harbour.

'They're not all from here,' Elsie said, as if reading my mind as she came and stood beside me.

She was wearing a pair of white shorts, much shorter than mine and her deeply tanned legs made mine look somewhat anaemic. For a sixty-five-year-old, she had exceptionally good legs. Her floaty, patterned top contained every colour known to man, and probably a few, man wasn't sure of yet, and her bright orange sun hat was large enough to shade half the bay. It matched her espadrilles perfectly and the ribbon ties of those were the same as the multi-coloured ribbon tied around the brim of her hat, which also had more ribbon down the sides and tied beneath her chin. Presumably, so that the wind wouldn't whip it off.

Except there was no wind. Not even a breeze. It was going to be another very hot day.

'You look lovely,' I said.

Oddly enough, despite the colours assaulting my eyes, she did.

'So do you, honeybee. Any news on the Diana front?'

Diana had gone off to chat to someone on the 'clean-up committee' and to get us our litter grabber sticks. Becca had gone to find Orla, and Toby and Henry had ... gone somewhere. I didn't notice where.

'Nope. Nothing yet. Mum called me last night and again this morning and I'm afraid I snapped at her.' I looked Elsie in the eye. 'Did you call her? You said you might.'

Elsie shook her head and her hat slapped my face – twice. I stepped back out of its reach. I'd already been assaulted by a mad dog and now a hostile hat was attacking me. Summers at the seaside were supposed to be about sun, sea and fun, not trying to avoid dismemberment and death.

Okay. That was possibly a slight exaggeration.

'No. I did think about it,' Elsie said. 'But I feel it's best to wait a while and see what develops.'

'Mum didn't know Alex wasn't here either. She was as surprised as you were. She now thinks they may be having marital problems.'

'That's a distinct possibility.'

'Is it? I ... I did wonder if Alex might be having an affair.'

Elsie met my look and held it. I got the feeling she wanted to say something but she just looked me in the eye until someone called her name. She turned and waved and I avoided the hat as she looked at me again.

'Let me know if you have any news, won't you?'

'Absolutely. And the same goes for you. If Di talks to you about what's troubling her before she talks to me, you'll tell me, won't you?'

Elsie smiled and reached out her hand, brushing a lock of wayward red waves away from my face.

'Of course I will, honeybee. But you know as well as I that she won't talk to me about anything like that. You're the only one who has ever trusted me enough to do so.'

I watched Elsie walk towards her friend. A man dressed in a pair of pale grey, linen trousers, a white V-necked T-shirt, a grey and white striped linen jacket and topped off with a straw boater hat with a grey and white striped hat band. He wasn't as colourful as Elsie but he looked dashing and charming as he tipped his hat and held out his crooked arm for her. His hair was white, as was his trim beard and he was probably around Elsie's age or perhaps a few years older.

'Hello,' a male voice said, behind me.

I recognised the Nordic accent and turned

with a broad smile on my face.

'Do I know you?' I asked, lowering my sunglasses to the end of my nose and staring at Mikkel over the frame.

He laughed as he took my hand and kissed it.

'I was hoping I would be unforgettable. As you were.'

'Nice. I like your style.'

I scanned him from head to toe. He wore tan leather deck shoes, no socks – thank heavens – dark brown cotton shorts cut to two inches or so above his knees, and a loose-fitting, tan T-shirt.

'Should I give you a twirl?'

I laughed. 'That's not very gallant. You're supposed to behave as if you hadn't noticed I was checking you out.'

'My mistake. I should like you to give me a twirl. Or is that not gallant either?'

I grinned, spinning around slowly on the spot and raising my arms above my head before running my hands down my sides.

'I definitely like your style,' he said, giving me a low, wolf-whistle. 'I have several bottles of champagne on ice. Perhaps, when we finish here, we might … What has happened to you?'

'What?' His expression had changed completely. From flirtatious to concerned. 'Oh. My bruises.' I glanced at my shoulder and my leg. The bruises were now black and large. I laughed and shook my head. 'Nothing serious. Just a murderous dog and some argumentative furniture.'

He furrowed his brow as if he didn't really understand. 'A murderous dog?'

'I was joking. It's okay. The bruises look worse than they are. So what were you saying about this champagne?'

I stepped a little closer and looked up into his eyes and then I heard a strange gasp behind me and Mikkel looked over my head as I turned around.

'Diana!' Mikkel said, his tone rather more elevated than before.

'Mikkel,' Diana replied, looking at me, not at him, her face flushed as if she'd been running. Which I was pretty sure she hadn't. Diana rarely ran.

'I ... I hadn't realised you were here,' he said.

'We arrived on Monday afternoon.' She looked out towards the horizon.

'Is Alex here?' He glanced from side to side.

'No. But he is joining us later.' She smiled wanly at me and met his eyes. 'I see you've met my sister.'

'Your ... sister!'

He stared from her to me and back again and oddly, the expression on his face was the sort of thing you see in horror movies. You know? When someone has just realised all hope is lost and they're about to die an exceedingly painful and gory death.

I gave a little cough and beamed at him. 'I'm Josie Parnell. Diana's twin sister.'

'I ... I had no idea,' he said, looking at both of us again in turn.

'My sister has come to stay with us for the summer.'

'Or until Alex gets here,' I said, wondering why they both looked so awkward.

Were they attracted to one another? Was that it? It couldn't be anything other than that. Diana wasn't the sort to have an affair. It just wasn't in her make-up. She adored Alex. She always had. From the very first time she saw him, she told me, long ago. And she still loved him. I was certain of that.

'It's lovely to see you again, Mikkel,' Diana said. 'Josie? Are you coming with me ... or would you prefer to...?' Her words trailed off.

'I'm coming with you, of course,' I said. 'See you later perhaps, Mikkel?'

'What? Oh yes. It was good to see you again, Diana. Please don't be a stranger.'

He watched as she turned away and then he reached out and touched my arm as I turned to follow her. 'I wish I'd known who you were.'

I turned back to look at him.

'Why? Would it have made a difference? Is there something you want to tell me?'

He looked into the distance for a split second and then he smiled at me. It wasn't quite as sexy and flirtatious as before but it was definitely getting there.

'No,' he said, shaking his head. 'It makes no difference. I was ... just surprised. Diana – and Alex, were very helpful to me when I arrived and made me feel most welcome. We ... became friends. I hadn't realised she had returned. That's all.'

I didn't buy that for one minute.

'So the champagne is still on offer? Shall I ask Diana to join us?'

He shrugged. 'The champagne is definitely on offer. As for Diana. Of course, she is welcome. But I think it might be better if she didn't.'

I smiled, turned and walked briskly after Diana but I spotted Asher and he waved. He was wearing flip flops, a pair of blue and cream swim shorts with dolphins on, and a plain, cream linen shirt, open over a blue T-shirt.

'Hey hologram of Toby's aunt.'

'Hey, Asher. How's the bottom? Was anything stuck up there?'

He raised a questioning brow and then laughed. 'Oh, Peaches. I'm afraid I can't answer that. Vet and patient privilege, you know. But I will say that she's far more comfortable now and the problem is solved.'

'Intriguing.'

'What's happened to your arm? And your leg?'

'A rabid dog attacked me. He pulled me from my bed and tied me up in the sheets then threw me against the furniture.'

'Henry did that?'

'Why are you sniggering? I'm seriously injured and all you do is laugh?'

He shook his head and coughed. 'From the look of those bruises, you're not in any pain. They look worse than they are, I'm fairly sure of that. But I'm happy to give you a once over, just to be on the safe side.'

I grinned. 'Thanks. But I'm fine. This beach clean-up thing is busy. Doesn't anyone around here work on a Wednesday?'

'Most people know one another so if anyone needs a vet, or a loaf of bread, or a pot, or whatever, they know where to find the appropriate person.'

'I hardly know anyone.'

'Ah, but you know a man who does. And Diana knows everyone, so you're fine.'

'True. Are you and Diana friends?'

'Excuse me?'

'It's a simple question.'

He tipped his head to one side. 'But you asked it in a way that made it sound as if it meant something more.'

'Did I? I didn't mean to.'

'Well then, yes. I'd say we're friends. I've

been to dinner with her and Alex, and they invite me to parties, and for drinks. But I've never been to their house in Blackheath or anything so I'd say we're casual friends, not close friends. Why?'

'And Mikkel?'

'Am I friends with Mikkel? Yes. Good friends. He hasn't lived here long but we became friends very quickly.'

'And Mikkel and Diana?'

He stiffened slightly.

'I think that's a question for Mikkel and for Diana. But as far as I know, Mikkel is, like me, a casual friend. What's this about?'

'Nothing really. I'm just wondering who is and who isn't friends with Diana. And with Alex of course. Did you know it's her thirty-fifth birthday this summer? And mine too, obviously. We're twins, after all.'

'No. I didn't know that. I knew she had a twin sister but until yesterday, I had no idea what you looked like. You're very different. Both in looks and in temperament, I suspect.'

'We are. Completely. I was thinking about the possibility of us having a birthday party, which is why I was wondering who her friends here are.'

I lied, but I think I was fairly convincing. And actually, a birthday party wasn't a bad idea. I'd have to have a word with Diana and see if we could sort that out. I'd planned a weekend binge of drinking, eating and clubbing with my friends in New York, but clearly that wasn't going to happen now, and I had to do something to mark such an auspicious event. Thirty-five was going to be a big thing for me. It was going to be the start of me behaving like a responsible adult. At least that's what I'd told my friends, although they all fell about laughing, so I'm not sure they believed me.

'Oh I see,' he said, smiling. 'Well, unless you're planning a surprise party – and I think, given the circumstances, that's not really possible – why don't you simply ask her?'

'Yes. I'll do that. I'd better go and find her or she'll think I've got lost. See you later, perhaps.'

'We'll all be in the pub when we've finished here, so if you fancy a drink, I'll see you there.'

'Great. Maybe.'

I waved as I walked and then I saw Diana talking to Liam over to one side, near Nice Ice, the ice cream kiosk with delusions of grandeur. They were half hidden by the plants and flowers in the large lead troughs dotted along the sections where the roads met the promenade of Sea Walk. I got the impression they were having a serious conversation. I stood still and watched, not really certain why. Possibly because Liam was only half dressed and looked incredibly sexy. He had a wet suit pulled up to his hips and the rest of it flopping down, covering his bottom, which was a shame. I'd like to have seen that in tight-fitting rubber. His torso was naked but I could only see him sideways on. It took me a while to look at Diana.

She stepped from one foot to the other, half-turned away and then turned back again. At one point, she reached out her hand as if she were going to grab his arm, but she dropped it to her side and looked as if she were tutting, or sighing. She didn't look happy, in any event. I was so intent on them, I didn't notice Becca and Orla had come and stood near me and were looking in the same direction I was.

'Mum?' Becca shouted, waving to Diana. Diana and Liam looked round and darted a look at one another, before looking at me and Becca and Orla. 'Orla and I are going over to the rocks. We'll see you later.' Then Becca turned to me. 'This is my friend Orla, Josie. Orla, this is Josie.'

I dragged my eyes from Diana and Liam and smiled at the stunningly beautiful girl, who was the spitting image of her mother, Una.

'Hi Orla. It's lovely to meet you. You're as beautiful as your mum.'

'You knew my mum?' She seemed surprised and threw a look at Becca who shrugged.

'I didn't really know her,' I said. 'We came

here every summer and one year, your mum was here too. She and your dad fell in love almost at first sight, so although we all hung out together, they only really had eyes for one another. One year later, they were married. I haven't been back here since because I got a job crewing a yacht for a friend of my aunt Elsie. And after that, I worked all over the world doing different things.'

I had no idea why I was trying to excuse my absence from Seahorse Harbour. Orla wouldn't care.

'Oh, I see. But you remember her?'

'No one who met your mum would ever forget her. She was the most beautiful girl I think I've ever seen. Until now.'

I smiled at her and she smiled back, lifting her chest with pride, but it only lasted a moment and then she gave me a serious look.

'And she and my dad were really, truly in love?'

'Yes. Head over heels.'

That was a strange question. It almost seemed as if she had reason to doubt it. Perhaps, when the cancer was diagnosed, things became ... tense. Difficult, maybe. People probably change when they or those they love are facing mortality.

Orla glanced towards Nice Ice and I followed her gaze, but Diana and Liam were no longer there.

'Come on, Orla,' Becca said. 'We're being called over to the rocks. See you later, Josie.'

'Yes. See you. Have fun. It was lovely to meet you, Orla. See you again soon.'

'Yes. I hope so. You're exactly as Becca said.'

She and Becca ran off towards the rocks and the bunch of people gathering there. I watched them for a moment, wondering what Orla had meant by her question about her mum and Liam being in love. It was really rather odd.

Or perhaps it was just a young girl who didn't know whether or not to believe in love at first sight.

I knew how that felt.

Although everyone seemed to be acting strangely today. Perhaps it was the heat. It was already stifling and the temperature was set to rise.

I turned around and came face-to-face with Liam and I nearly jumped out of my skin.

'Oh hi. You scared me half to death.' I thumped my hand against my heart and took a few over the top deep breaths, just for added effect.

'I'm sorry. I didn't mean to.' He looked a bit sheepish. 'I was just talking to Diana.'

'Yes. I saw you.'

'You did? Yes of course you did.' He nodded. 'And you've just met Orla?'

'Yes. She looks almost exactly like Una.

Not much like you, I'm afraid.'

He stiffened visibly. 'I think that's probably a good thing. Una was beautiful to look at.'

'You're not so bad yourself, Liam.'

'What?' That seemed to fluster him and he ran a hand through his hair and gave a sort of strangled laugh. 'I was a dork then, and I'm not sure I've changed that much. Except I no longer wear glasses.'

'You were a lovely dork. But you've changed a lot. I hardly recognised you yesterday. Contact lenses?'

'No. Laser surgery. It was ... a present from Una.'

'Wow. That's some present.'

'Yeah. It certainly was.' He didn't seem thrilled.

'Well, I think you looked good before, but now you look even better.'

He shrugged. 'Not everything's about looks.'

'I didn't say it was. Take the compliment, Liam. And tell me why you're wearing – or should I say, half-wearing – that wetsuit.'

I was struggling to stop myself from looking down to where I could see a fine line of hair trailing up from his barely visible swim shorts. Instead, for some reason, I tried to count the hairs on his hard chest. There weren't masses of them. Just a smattering towards the centre above a fairly impressive six-pack, and then that line of hair leading down–

'Because I'm about to get into the water,' he said, interrupting my thoughts. 'We've got a couple of inflatables and I'm just waiting for the others.'

'Inflatables? What? Like blow-up dolls, you mean?'

I know it was a ridiculous thing to say, and I don't know why I said it.

He frowned and then he shook his head. 'Is everything about sex with you, Josie? You haven't changed at all. It's all about having fun, isn't it?'

'It was a joke, Liam. A silly one, I'll admit. But it was just a joke. And no. Not everything is about sex with me. Or fun. I can be serious too. If I need to.'

'Really? Orla told me last night that she's going to be just like you. That she's never getting married and is going to travel the world and have sex with anyone she wants without any commitment. That's not something a dad wants to hear from his sixteen-year-old daughter.'

'What? And you think I told her that? I only met her for the first time ten seconds or so ago, as you're well aware. I suspect she got that idea from Becca. I'm perfectly willing to tell her that's not quite how it is if that'll make you happy.'

He studied my face for a moment. 'It would. But as I saw you talking to Asher just now, and earlier looking very cosy with Mikkel, I'm not sure it'd do much good. Actions speak louder than words.'

'Who are you? My mum? Why shouldn't I be talking to Asher and to Mikkel? We're all single. At least I think we are. I know I am. And we were just talking. It doesn't mean I was about to leap into bed with either of them. And you can talk. What about you and Diana? That conversation looked pretty intense to me. Almost like a lover's tiff. Diana's married, Liam. In case you may've forgotten.'

'I haven't forgotten. Believe me.'

He glowered at me and I glowered back and then someone called his name and without looking in their direction he said, 'Excuse me. I've got things to do.' And he marched off without another word.

Twelve

Needless to say, collecting litter from the beach wasn't as much fun as Diana had made it out to be. Or perhaps it was because my heated discussion with Liam had soured my mood. How dare he lecture me!

I didn't see him at all after that but I did bump into Asher and Mikkel once or twice. And bloody Liam had even spoilt that. For some reason, I couldn't seem to summon up the enthusiasm to flirt with either of them.

When we stopped for lunch, I went for a walk by myself and because I was in such a bad mood, I slipped and fell on the rocks and grazed my leg. It was turning into a bitch of a day and I was glad when it was over. But at least the beach, the rocks and the sea, were rubbish free, so that was something.

I didn't even go to the pub for a drink. I told Diana and Elsie I had a headache and was going back to Sea View Cottage to lie down. Diana came with me. Elsie and her friend, who she introduced to me as Gray – short for

Graham, I assumed – went to The Seahorse Inn.

'Are you okay?' Diana asked as we trudged up the hill.

I was aching all over from hunching over my litter grabber stick all day, my fall and from Henry's wake-up call. I'd grazed my hands on the rocks as well but I hadn't noticed until we were halfway home.

'Fine. Just tired. You know? A bit like you keep telling me you're feeling. But we both know that's a lie, don't we?'

Diana stopped and looked at me. I stopped too and met her look. It was a few seconds before she spoke.

'Okay. So I haven't been completely honest. But it's nothing for you to worry about. Or Mum. Call it ... an early mid-life crisis or something. I ... I've just been looking at my life and thinking I need to make some changes, that's all. It's nothing earth shattering.'

'Really? That's it? That's why you were crying when I called on Saturday? That's why you're not your usual happy self? Is it also because Toby's being a typical teenager and rebelling against you?'

'I'd hardly call it rebelling. He's simply finding his feet.'

'Probably not the best time for you to decide to give up alcohol though. Why did you give up drink at Easter? Was it really just to lose a bit of weight, because if so, I hate to say this, but I'm not convinced it's working.'

Okay. That was a bit bitchy. It was the truth. But bitchy nonetheless. Diana had put on a few pounds but most people would still kill for her figure – including me.

She glowered at me. 'I ... It wasn't just about the weight. It was for general health reasons too. Drinking alcohol to excess does no one any favours. That's something you might want to think about.'

'Ooooh.' I laughed, suddenly. I think the last time Diana and I had had a bit of a set-to was in our teens. Or maybe once or twice since then. I can't recall. 'Well. I think that's probably made us both feel a little better. I apologise for my dig about the weight. You look as stunning as ever and have no need to lose even half a pound.'

Diana sighed and smiled wanly. 'And I apologise for the drink comment. To be honest, I'd love a glass of wine right now.'

'Really? Want to go to the pub?'

'No! I mean ... I'd rather go home, have a shower and relax by the pool. I think my deodorant has given up the ghost in this heat and my dress is clinging to me. And not in a good way.'

'Okay. That sounds good to me.' I linked my arm through hers. 'I need you to help me up this hill. I'm wounded. Why didn't you buy a house at the foot of the cliffs instead of right near the top?'

'Better views. And besides, I love that house. It has such happy memories for me.'

'Yeah. I get that. Di? Does it bother you that Toby's playing up? He's normally such a good kid. It's just a stage, isn't it? I know nothing about kids really so I don't know if it's something you need to nip in the bud or let it go and see what happens. But you're such a great mum and I must admit I was a bit surprised by Toby's reactions.'

She sighed again. This time as if the weight of the world were on her shoulders.

'I think it's just a stage but it's so unlike him. Alex ... hasn't been around much over the last few months ... because he's so busy. Perhaps Toby's missing spending time with him. I've tried to talk to Toby about it but he just ignores me, or tells me not to nag and...' She shot a look at me. 'Well. The other day, before we came down here, we had a bit of a scene and Toby said the reason his dad spends so much time at work is because I'm such an old nag bag.'

'Toby said that? You're kidding?'

That really was a surprise. But maybe all teenagers said stuff like that. I think I recall saying something like that to Mum. On more than one occasion. But Toby wasn't like me. He was more like Diana. For him to be rude and intentionally hurtful to his mum was quite something.

'I was so upset when he said it. It even made me wonder if it was true. Was that why Alex has ... been working such long hours?'

'You're not an old nag bag, Di, and don't let anyone persuade you that you are. Alex works long hours because he's an exceptional surgeon and because he adores his job. That doesn't mean he doesn't also adore you. But you knew how much he wanted to be a doctor when we met him. Even as a twelve-year-old, that's all he could talk about. I can still remember how excited he was when we told him our dad was a doctor. He wanted to meet him right away.'

'Yes. I remember. That's one of the main reasons he married me. So that Dad would help him get his foot on the ladder. Which of course, Dad did.'

I shot a look at her but her gaze was fixed straight ahead.

'Wh-what makes you think that? Has he ... has Alex said that?'

Now she did look at me and there was a really odd look in her eyes. Her smile was strange too. As if she knew that I knew something but that she knew even more than me. If that makes any sense at all.

'You and I both know it's true, Josie. It doesn't bother me. I was well aware of that when he asked me to marry him. But I loved him beyond all reason and I wanted to marry him, no matter what.'

'Wow. I never knew you ... I mean I had no idea you thought that.'

'I don't regret it. I still love him beyond all reason.'

'So ... Alex isn't one of the things in your life you want to change? Don't look at me like that. You said you were going through an early, mid-life crisis and you wanted to make some changes in your life.'

Her eyelashes fluttered as if she were fighting back tears but as we walked on in silence for a while, I could see she was thinking.

'I can't imagine my life without Alex in it,' she said, eventually, looking up at the house which was just a few feet away from us now. 'And I hope I never have to find out what that's like.'

I didn't ask Diana about the conversation I'd witnessed between her and Liam. I was still hoping she'd tell me about it, but she didn't. Neither did I mention the odd way she and Mikkel had behaved. Perhaps it was all my imagination and I was seeing things that weren't there.

After showering, we'd swum in the pool and chatted about the day with the kids when they returned. They told us how much rubbish had been cleared. The amount was truly staggering. Thirty large black sacks were filled with plastic bags and bottles, broken glass, food wrappers and crisp bags, cigarette butts, used condoms and dirty nappies. That was particularly gross.

No wonder our oceans are polluted and the marine life and sea birds are dying. Why can't people simply take their rubbish home with them? Do they leave rubbish in their own gardens when they have a barbecue? I expect some probably do.

After that, Diana and I made Spaghetti Bolognese for supper, and Diana had one glass of wine. Just one. But she didn't seem to enjoy it.

I wanted to stay up and talk but I'd caught the sun and I was completely worn out, so after a quick game of monopoly with the kids, I went to bed. My room, with the en suite, was about the size of my New York apartment and it had two windows and a set of French windows, which opened onto a small balcony, just large enough for a bistro table and two chairs. I could see the sea and Seahorse Point but I couldn't see the sand in the bay due to the line of the church and houses and buildings in the village.

The white based, floral curtains let in masses of light, unlike my black-out curtains at home, and for the second night running, I didn't get much sleep. All night I kept dreaming of Liam and Diana and even though I knew it was probably nothing, I couldn't help wondering whether something was going on between them.

At least I didn't get a wet, slobbery wake-up call. I'd made sure the door had clicked before I'd gone to bed.

Thirteen

During breakfast, the next morning, Diana told us that she had some work to do in respect of her baby clothing business. I offered to help but she declined my assistance, saying it would be quicker if she did it herself, if I didn't mind, and suggesting I might like to have a day to myself.

I'd spent the morning lounging by the pool but Becca and Toby had other ideas. They wanted to go and lounge around a different pool, so I was roped into accompanying them to the Lido at the holiday park. Mind you, Diana had to look after Henry, so I think she got the worst end of the deal.

It was years since I'd been to Seahorse Harbour Holiday Park, and the Lido there, which was once little more than a paddling pool, was now something to rival the Olympic-sized pool at Easterhill Spa.

Sun loungers surrounded the azure waters of the pool, on a pristine, white-tiled area, with tables and chairs placed on a raised concrete section behind. At one end of the pool was a row of outdoor showers and at the other end, a row of water jets where toddlers, and some teenagers and even some adults, screamed with joy and excitement as they ran back and forth whilst the jets shot up around them.

There was an ice cream parlour called Ice Dreams, a pizzeria called Pool Pizzas, with a definite Italian vibe and bistro-style tables and chairs outside, a hotdog kiosk with hotdogs similar to the ones I often got on my way to work in New York and, best of all, a bar.

Becca, Orla and Toby bagged some sun loungers whilst I got us drinks. Non-alcoholic cocktails for them, an alcohol-filled one for me. It was gone 1 p.m. after all.

The school holidays had started during the middle of the previous week, but the place was half-empty and there were plenty of sun loungers to be had. Each sun lounger had a handy little side table bolted to it, with a shelf beneath and a little cupboard you could lock with a key. The key was attached to a rubber wrist band that you could wear while you swam, or ate, or whatever else you wanted to do.

'What a brilliant idea,' I said, repeatedly snapping the rubber band Becca had on her wrist. Until she thumped me on the arm.

'Sorry I'm late.'

I turned to face Liam and I nearly dropped my cocktail.

'Liam? We've only just arrived ourselves. Are you joining us?'

He creased his brows. 'Yes. Orla and Becca said you'd invited me. Didn't you?'

I hadn't. I glanced at Orla and Becca who were sniggering beneath their sunhats.

'Er. Not exactly.' His face fell. 'I mean, I mentioned it. But I didn't think you'd be able to make it. What with your business and everything.'

I could've added, and the fact you got into a strop and marched off yesterday, but I didn't.

He brightened. 'I allow myself the odd hour or so off.'

'Very wise. Um. Would you like a drink?'

'I'll get it. Would you like another? I might as well get it while I'm there. Looks like there's a bit of a queue forming.'

'That would be nice. Thanks. I'll have sex on the beach, please.'

He blinked twice whilst Becca and Orla sniggered louder and Toby tutted. I half expected another lecture, but instead a mischievous grin slowly spread across his mouth and it even reached his eyes. They sparkled in the sunlight.

'I'll see what I can do,' he said,

I cleared my throat as he turned away, images of Liam and me on the beach, popping into my head one after another. I glanced at Becca and Orla.

'I'm going in the pool,' Toby said, tossing his towel onto his sun lounger and diving in the water head first.

Luckily, we were sitting at the deep end.

'So are we,' Becca added. 'We'll give you and Liam time to chat.'

'Is there something going on here I should know about?'

Becca lifted her shoulders, arms and hands in an exaggerated shrug.

'Nope. We just thought you might like someone your own age to talk to.'

They ran off giggling, arm in arm and I spread my towel over the lounger. I removed the purple sarong and thin cotton, lavender shirt I was wearing and adjusted my purple bikini straps before placing my phone and my bag in the little locker provided. I stretched out on the lounger, sitting in what I hoped was a seductively graceful pose, cocktail in my hand, sunglasses pushing back my red wavy hair which I spent a few minutes getting just right, and waited for Liam to return.

'Wow,' he said, standing in my sun. 'You're a sight for sore eyes.'

'Thanks. You're not so bad yourself.'

I shaded my eyes and admired his bare torso beneath his now open, white linen shirt.

'I'm hot.'

'Yes, you are. But you're also in my sun, so if you wouldn't mind sitting, that'd be great.'

He gave an awkward laugh. 'I meant it's a very hot day.' He put my cocktail on my table and sat on the edge of the lounger beside mine, his hands clasped around his beer. 'I'm sorry about yesterday. I was totally out of order.'

'I'm sorry too,' I said. 'Let's forget it.'

'Great.'

He put his beer down whilst he removed his shirt and shorts, revealing plain navy-blue swim shorts beneath. He swung his long, muscular legs up and leant back on the lounger. I watched him surreptitiously and when I was sure he had relaxed, I leant towards him and looked him in the eye.

'Will you do me, Liam?'

He choked on the gulp of beer he'd taken but I saw his gaze trail over my body.

'W-what?' he mumbled.

I'm such a tease, but I couldn't help myself. I held up the bottle of sun cream and waggled it in my hand.

'I said, will you do me, please? I've done my front but I can't reach my back and I don't want to suffer from sunburn.' I gave him my sweetest smile.

He narrowed his eyes but he eventually smiled.

'You couldn't ask Becca or Orla?'

'I could. But they'd already gone. I'll do you, if you'll do me.'

'Okay, Josie. But shall we do without the sexual teasing?'

'Sexual what?' I fluttered my eyelashes. 'I don't know what you mean. Can't a girl ask a guy to slather cream on her naked back and offer to do the same for him without being accused of being a tease? What is the world coming to?'

'Turn over,' he said, taking the bottle from me.

I adjusted the lounger so that it fell flat and slowly turned, holding his gaze for as long as I could and when I lay on my front, I lifted my arms towards the top of my head.

'Can you undo my top? Or do you need a hand with that?'

'I think I can manage.'

His fingers brushed my skin as he undid the clasp with one flick and my back tensed as my top fell away.

'Ticklish,' I said.

'Then we may have a problem.'

'No. I'll just bite my lip until it's over. Mind the bruises though.'

He poured cream directly onto my skin, trailing it down my spine and then he ran one finger from my neck to just above the top of my bikini bottoms, then back and forth along the line of elastic.

Now who was doing the sexual teasing?

Well, two could play at that game.

'Oh, Liam,' I moaned softly. 'That feels so good.'

He ran his palms over me, up and down and eased his fingers around my sides, almost touching my breasts with his fingertips at one point.

'Oh, Liam! Yes.' I moaned a bit louder.

'Shush,' he commanded, laughing and continued as before. 'Done.'

'And my legs?'

'Your legs?'

'Uh-huh. I don't want them to burn. I might find it difficult to sit if they do.'

I heard him cough and then the cool cream made me tingle. He smoothed it over me starting from my ankles and working his way up my calves and over the backs of my thighs. I opened my legs slightly and, after a moment's hesitation when his hands stayed where they were, he slid them in between. I sucked in a breath as his fingers glided towards the high cut of my bikini.

'Oh God, Liam. You're so good at this. Oh yes. Right there,' I teased.

He stopped just short of making my day.

'That's you done.'

I lifted my head and grinned at him.

'Aww. I was kind of hoping you wouldn't stop.'

To my surprise, he slapped my bottom. Only a gentle tap.

And then he leant forward, his firm chest pressed against my back as he whispered in my ear, 'I was kind of close to not wanting to. And you damn well know it, Josie.'

Tingles ran up and down my spine as he slowly moved away and it took a few seconds for me to compose myself. Once I had, I offered to do him, but he grinned and said he'd stay on his back for now. We lay in silence for a while and then Becca and Orla returned, leaving Toby playing with some other boys in the pool. I reached back to do up my top but Liam stretched over and did it for me.

'Er. Thanks,' I said, slightly surprised at how fast he'd done it.

'Anytime,' he replied, with a grin.

'There're a couple of incredibly hot guys here,' Orla said.

Liam grinned at her across me and Becca.

'That's not really something your dad wants to hear, sweetheart.'

'Oh, Dad!' She laughed. 'Don't be such a prude. I'm sixteen. It's legal for me to have sex.'

'It may be legal but that doesn't make it compulsory. If I had my way you'd wait until you're at least twenty-five.'

'Yeah right. Good luck with that, Dad. Hey, Becca. Look at him. The one in the shorts with the parrots on. He's cool.'

Liam looked at me, still grinning but with a trace of concern in his eyes.

'Is cool better than hot, or not as hot? I forget,' he whispered.

'About the same, I think,' I whispered back. 'Or maybe a little lower on a scale of one to ten.'

'What would you give him, Josie?' Becca asked. 'On a scale of one to ten.'

She had obviously heard me and was pointing at a man who looked to be in his late thirties. He was as white as fresh snow, apart from his face and arms, which were almost the same colour as his burnt-ginger hair, and his face was as round as an orange beneath a large sombrero-type sunhat. His beer belly hung over the top of his bright yellow speedos, which seemed a bit too small for him.

'Four.'

'Four?' Orla said. 'He's gross. Minus four maybe.'

'Nah-uh.' I shook my head. 'He has potential. Remove those awful trunks and put him in a pair of light-coloured swim shorts and throw away that hat and give him some snazzy shades. Get him to do a bit of exercise to rid him of that belly and define his jaw and cheekbones, add a bit of a tan and he's definitely a four. I don't think he could be much higher though.'

'Hmm. Possibly,' Orla agreed after a moment or two.

'I don't like ginger hair,' Becca said, 'so that would have to go, but yeah. I can see he could look better.'

'Yep,' I said. 'It's important to look beyond what you see at first glance. Sometimes there's a hidden gem.'

'What about him?'

Becca pointed at a teenager with dark hair, dark eyes, dark shorts and a very dark smile. He was standing on the other side of the pool and had the look of an Italian, the body of an athlete and the confidence of a politician.

'Twelve,' Orla said, in a swoon-like tone.

'Definitely double figures,' Becca agreed.

'Trouble,' I said. 'You don't want to put a number on that.'

'What?' Liam looked at the teenager and at Orla. 'I agree with Josie, sweetheart. Stay away from boys like that.'

Orla tutted.

'What happened to looking beyond what you see at first glance?' Becca asked, grinning at me.

'Sometimes all you need is one glance,' I said.

'To fall in love?' Becca sighed. 'I'm definitely in love.'

'Me too,' Orla said, with an even longer sigh.

'I think we've got our work cut out with these two,' Liam said, not all together thrilled, by the sounds of it.

'Nothing to do with me.' I threw him a smile. 'I'm only the aunt. Not my responsibility.'

'You're also my godmother.' Becca laughed, her eyes still focussed on the dark-looking teenager.

'Am I? I don't remember signing up for that.'

'I've got photos of you at my Christening, and you definitely did.'

'Damn. In that case I'm locking you in a room until your eighteenth birthday.'

I'd never forget Becca's Christening. When I held her in my arms that day and promised to do my duty as her godmother, I felt a protectiveness I'd never felt before. It wasn't the first time I'd held her, although I hadn't seen her much, I'll admit. But making those promises, even though I didn't believe in God, brought out something in me I didn't know was there. Some sort of maternal instinct, I suppose. It also reminded me of what I might've had. If things had worked out differently.

The teenager ran and leapt in the air, tucking his knees up to his chest and bombing into the pool which sent a wave of water over everyone within range. Fortunately, not us.

'Definitely trouble,' I said.

We handed out scores to a few more men and teenagers and when one stunning woman sashayed past, I nudged Liam.

'Score please,' I said.

'Seriously?' He watched her for a moment after I nodded, removing his sunglasses to get a better look.

'In your own time, Liam.'

He grinned at me, put his sunglasses back on and leant back against the lounger.

'Seven.'

I did a double take and shrieked, 'Seven? You have got to be kidding. She was at least a nine. Look at her.'

'I did,' he said. 'Definitely a seven.'

'God. I'd hate to know where I am on your scale then.'

He grinned. 'You might be surprised.'

'Oh? Pleasantly or otherwise?'

'My lips are sealed.'

'Oh come on, Dad.' Orla laughed. 'You can't leave it like that.'

'I can and I shall.'

'Coward,' I said. 'I won't be angry or upset. I won't sulk. I know I'm not in her league.'

He pulled his sunglasses down his nose with one finger and looked at me over the frame. 'Beauty is in the eye of the beholder. Didn't anyone tell you that? I'm not saying. So you may as well give up.' He pushed his glasses back in place.

'Fine. I bet it's a three.'

He laughed. 'You're definitely not a three. One day, I might tell you.'

'You're no fun.'

Orla, Becca and I continued for a while and then got bored until a man walked past and I spotted something I really liked the look of.

'Oh my God!' I said. 'Did you see the size of the nuts on that?'

'Bloody hell,' Becca said, whistling.

Liam shot bolt upright.

'I don't think I could get one of those balls in my mouth,' I added.

'Josie!' Liam snapped. 'May I have a word?'

I looked at him in surprise. 'A word?' And then I realised what he'd thought, and I tried hard not to burst out laughing. 'Um. Discombobulated.'

He'd got to his feet and he stared at me, confusion in his dark blue eyes.

'What?'

'Discombobulated. You said you wanted a word. That's a word I rather like. Dis-com-bob-u-lated. It has a nice ring.'

He sucked in a breath as Orla and Becca repeated the breakdown of the word, giggling as they did so.

'I meant, may I speak to you in private?'

'Oh.' I stretched out my hands to him. 'Okay. But you'll have to pull me up.'

He tutted but he grabbed my hands and yanked me so hard that I fell against his chest.

'Get a room,' Orla teased, giggling loudly.

'I think they might be,' Becca said, as Liam led me away, still gripping one of my hands in his.

'We're not,' he snapped.

I looked back at them over my shoulder and gave them a wink and a smile.

Liam saw me and he tugged my arm. 'Stop it, Josie. Stop it right now.' He twisted round to face me when he found a relatively quiet spot near the ice cream parlour. 'Enough's enough. Okay?'

'Er. I'm not sure why you're suddenly so mad,' I said, playfully walking two fingers up his chest.

He brushed my hand away.

'Stop it. Look. I'm all for having fun and, although it fills me with fear, I don't mind Orla eyeing up young guys. I know it's perfectly natural and I'm glad she feels comfortable enough to do that in front of me. But I do object to you commenting on the size of a man's ... private parts. It's totally inappropriate to say things like that in front of my sixteen-year-old daughter.'

I snorted with laughter.

'It's not funny, Josie.' He looked really cross. 'I realise you're sex mad and I know everything is fun to you and I don't suppose anything's off-limits, but please try to understand where I'm coming from.'

'Oh I do, Liam. From your arse. I wasn't talking about a man's anything. Well, unless you count the massive–'

'Josie!'

'–Chocolate sundae he was carrying, which was covered in huge hazelnuts, ginormous marshmallow balls and dripping with chocolate fudge sauce.'

I nodded to the photo of one over at the ice cream parlour.

He blinked several times as he looked from me to that and back again.

'Ch-chocolate sundae?'

'Have you swallowed a mouse? Yes. A chocolate sundae. I think you're the one who's sex mad, Liam. All I wanted was a delicious-looking ice cream. Now do you have anything else to say? Like an apology perhaps? Or can I go back to my sun lounger and work on getting a tan?'

'Shit! I'm so sorry, Josie. I thought...' He ran a hand through his hair. 'Yes. Yes of course. I ... I have nothing else to say. I'm really sorry.'

I smiled as I turned away.

'If you're *really* sorry, you can buy me one of those sundaes. And make sure it's covered in those nuts. I'm rather partial to nuts. Of all shapes and sizes. And to balls. Marshmallow balls, that is.'

I returned to my sun lounger and neither Becca nor Orla asked where Liam was but they kept whispering and sniggering until a few minutes later, Liam reappeared with chocolate sundaes for us all. And another cocktail for me.

He didn't stay long after that. Just long enough to eat his sundae and give me several sheepish and apologetic smiles.

'I'd better get back to work,' he said, quickly donning his shirt and shorts. 'Try not to have too much fun without me.'

'I can't promise that,' I said, and Orla and Becca grinned at one another.

Toby was already back in the pool with his new friends, including, unfortunately, the dark teenager. Orla and Becca went to join him. I waited until they were out of earshot and Liam had gathered his things.

'See you later,' he said, moving away as I picked up my cocktail and took a sip.

'You can count on that. And Liam?'

'Yes?'

He turned back to look at me with a slightly wary expression in his eyes.

'In case you're interested, you're an eight-point-five. I would've scored you higher but you have a tendency to lecture me.'

I sucked the cherry off the cocktail stick and rolled it around with my tongue.

His mouth fell open and then a slow and extremely sexy smile curved across his lips.

'And you're a nine. I would've scored you higher but you have a tendency to do what the hell you like. And that bothers me. It bothers me a lot.'

I wasn't quite sure what he meant by that, but I have to say I was thrilled and elated that Liam had scored me a nine. As he walked away, I bounced my feet up and down on the lounger and waved my hands in the air, stopping abruptly when he glanced around once, shook his head and grinned at me.

A nine!

I mean, dear God. That was just one point away from perfect.

Fourteen

'But we always have a party at the end of our first week here,' Becca said, crossing her arms and pouting as I joined them in the kitchen for breakfast on Friday morning.

'We do,' Toby agreed.

Henry barked twice, so I assumed he was agreeing too.

'What's going on?' I asked, pouring myself a mug of coffee from the snazzy, black coffee machine on the black marble counter.

Diana sighed and shook her head, putting slices of bread in the matching black toaster and then turning and leaning against the counter.

'We usually have a cocktail party on either the Friday or Saturday evening of our first week. But as ... Alex isn't here, I wasn't planning to have it.'

'Why not?' I queried. 'It sounds like fun.'

She held my gaze for a moment. 'It would seem a bit ... strange without Alex. People might ... well. We should wait until he joins us in a few weeks.'

'Why? You could say you're having it because I've come to stay. Who do you usually invite?'

'Everyone,' Becca said, leaning her arms on the back of a chair.

'Everyone? What everyone in the whole wide world?' I grinned at her.

'Duh.' Becca pulled a face. 'Don't be daft. Everyone in Seahorse Harbour.'

'Oh. That makes sense. I'll help with everything, Di. Come on. It'll be great.'

'And you promised we'd still do all the stuff we always do when you told us Dad wasn't coming.' Toby frowned at her.

Oddly enough, so did Henry. At least he looked like he was frowning. His wiry brows hung low over his blue-grey eyes and his mouth flopped downwards at both sides.

'Oh all right,' Diana said, as the toast popped up. 'But both you and your sister will have to help Josie and me. Okay?'

'Deal.' Toby returned to his phone.

'So when's it going to be, Mum?' Becca asked. 'Tonight or tomorrow?'

'Tomorrow. We'll need to give people a little bit of notice and we'll need to do a shop. That means going into Easterhill.'

'We couldn't, by any chance go to Easterhill via Easterhill Spa, could we?' I gave Diana a pleading look. 'I could do with a massage and a mani-pedi. And I'll treat you to one if you say yes.'

'You'll be lucky to get an appointment. But okay.'

'Can I come?' Becca asked. 'And Orla?'

'We'll never get appointments for four,' Diana said. 'And someone needs to stay with Toby and Henry.'

'I can look after myself,' Toby said.

'You're thirteen. I'm not leaving you here alone all day.'

'I won't be alone. Henry's here.'

'They could stay with Liam,' Becca said. 'He wouldn't mind. They've stayed with him before.'

'Well. I suppose I could ask. I'd better see if we can get appointments first.'

'And what about Elsie?' I said. 'She'd probably like to come too.'

'Five really is asking too much, I'm sure, but I'll see what I can do.'

'Mention Dad,' Becca said. 'He's a celebrity in the golf club and the air club. Rich and handsome heart surgeon, and the best golfer and pilot in the county. They love him.'

'That won't work for the spa, sweetheart, although they do usually manage to fit me in if I call up at short notice.'

'Fingers crossed,' I said, as she called the number from her contacts list.

'Hello. This is Diana Dunn. … Yes that's

right. ... It's lovely to speak to you again too. I know this is a long shot but do you by any chance have any appointments free today for some massages, manicures and pedicures. ... You do? How wonderful. ... For five people? ... Yes, that's right. Five. I'm sorry. ... Oh, that's fantastic. Thank you. ... Yes. We'll see you then.'

'No luck then?' I laughed.

'I can't quite believe it,' she said.

'The power of celebrity,' Becca said. 'I'll call Orla. What time are we leaving?'

'In half an hour.' Diana still looked stunned.

'I'd better call Elsie,' I said. 'And someone had better break the news to Liam that he's got Toby and Henry for the day. I bet he'll be pleased.'

As it happened, Orla asked her dad, and Liam said he'd be happy to do it. Elsie was thrilled to be having a girl's day out, and I couldn't wait for a pampering session.

I also needed to buy a new dress. I hadn't expected to be attending a cocktail party in Seahorse Harbour, although as I was spending the summer at my sister's, I suppose it should've occurred to me that I might.

Diana was renowned for her dinner parties at her house in Blackheath, as well as her successful book club which, from what both she and Mum had told me, sounded more like a cocktail party for women than it did a group to read and discuss the latest books.

Before we left, Diana texted those she could about the party and said we'd have to drop a few written invites in to those for whom she didn't have the number, like Lucy Willis, the school teacher who moved to the village last year.

'You mean to tell me that Lucy, who's lived in Seahorse Harbour since last September, isn't on your contacts list yet? I don't believe it.'

Diana always tried to make friends with everyone the moment she met them, even though she only came to Seahorse Harbour for the summer and a couple of other times during the year.

'Very amusing. I did invite her round for a drink when we spent the October half- term here, but we didn't seem to gel. I tried again at Easter. But she doesn't seem to like me.'

'Doesn't like you? Crikey! She must be the only person in the world who can resist your charms. I can't wait to meet her. Do you think she'll come?'

Becca answered before Diana could.

'She'll come if she knows Liam's here. She's got a thing for him. Orla told me Lucy's always popping round lately.'

'Really?' Diana and I said in unison.

I wasn't sure I liked the idea of Lucy popping round to Liam's. And from the expression on Diana's face, nor did she.

'Isn't she Orla's teacher?' I asked.

Becca nodded. 'Yep. But Orla thinks Lucy wants to be more than just her teacher. She wants to be Orla's new mum.'

'Blimey. Er. Does Liam want that to?' I glanced at Diana who looked a little flushed.

Becca shrugged. 'I think they went out once, at Christmas, so Orla says. But when Orla asked him about it, he said that they're just friends. She doesn't think they've been out together since. Not on a date, anyway. But Lucy often asks Orla how her dad is and if he's seeing anyone.'

'That must be very awkward for Orla,' I said, feeling a bit annoyed that a teacher would put their pupil in such a position.

Becca grinned. 'Not really. Orla thinks it's funny. She likes to wind Lucy up. She's dying to tell her about you.'

'Me? W-why would she tell Lucy about me?'

Becca tutted. 'Duh-uh. Because it's so obvious that Liam likes you.'

'Is it?' Diana said, her tone a little strangled.

'Well', I said, tossing a lock of hair over my shoulder. 'He did tell me at the Lido yesterday that I was a nine.' I laughed. 'But he was probably teasing me. We do that. Tease one another. We always did when we were younger.'

'A nine? Gosh. But is that all it is?' Diana asked, her voice low now. 'Teasing, I mean?'

I nodded. 'Yeah. I think so. You know how much I love to flirt. I'm not saying Liam's not hot – because he is. Very. But ... I don't know. When we were younger I ... but things happened.'

I looked away for a moment to catch my breath. I'd almost let something slip. I'd have to be more careful. I was forgetting where I was and who I was with.

'Did you have a crush on Liam?' Becca sounded genuinely surprised, but a huge grin swept across her face.

I coughed and shrugged. 'Not a crush, exactly. I really liked him though. And we got on extremely well. But things changed. I changed. Then Una arrived and Liam fell head over heels in love, so that was that. We'd better get going. We've got to pick up Orla and Elsie.'

I hurried to the door before anyone could say anything else in the hope that the topic was forgotten for now.

Which thankfully, it was.

Fifteen

Easterhill Spa was even more fabulous than I'd remembered. The last time I was there the spa area was only half the size. They'd since built a modern addition, connected to the main house by an atrium with an elaborate glass roof which extended up to the height of the second floor and housed the spa reception, an ornate marble fish pond with a cushioned-covered marble seat encircling it, and enough ginormous potted palms to give Kew Gardens a run for its money.

Soothing music played in the background and we were given the fluffiest towelling robes and towels I'd ever felt, together with a pair of flip flops which also had a towelling toe-post and straps.

We were shown into a changing area so white and bright it nearly blinded me. Okay, Maybe not blinded me but it certainly woke me up. The cubicles had padded bench seats and a row of hooks.

Once changed, we were each led into a

different treatment room which thankfully was far less glaring and more serene. My masseuse had the hands of an angel. Not that I have any idea what an angel's hands are like. She soothed away all traces of tension and tightness and even gave me a little bottle of an arnica and lavender oil mixture to help heal my bruises, although they had started to fade just a little now that I was getting a bit of a tan.

The pedicure was given whilst I sat in a reclining massage chair, which was a completely different experience to the massage I'd just had, but hey, why not get your money's worth? Even the chair I sat in for my manicure was like sinking into a cloud. No wonder these treatments cost an arm and a leg. But we all walked out of Easterhill Spa feeling fifty times better than we had when we staggered in – and now we all had sparkly, painted fingernails and toenails.

On reflection, we should've shopped before our trip to the spa because by the time we'd bought all the food and drink for the cocktail party and I'd spent an hour finding a new dress, we could've all done with another of those massages.

But a relaxing swim in the pool when we got back to Sea View Cottage certainly helped. And then it was all hands to the pump to prepare for the following evening, although thankfully, Diana had somehow managed to engage a local team of catering staff and servers for Saturday night. No wonder her parties were famous. She knew exactly who to contact at short notice and precisely what was needed to make the evening a success.

Saturday went by like a flash and whilst Becca and Toby helped a little, they were really more of a hindrance. Diana and I were both glad when they asked if they could go to the Lido for a couple of hours. Apart from the fact that meant we were left looking after Henry. But I'd discovered Henry wasn't very bright and if you pretended to throw a stick or a ball for him, he'd search for the thing for ages before he realised you hadn't thrown it.

The catering staff arrived at 6 and by 7 we were all dressed up and ready to welcome the guests.

'This is Lucy, Josie,' Diana said, greeting Lucy as if they were dear friends by linking her arm through hers. 'Do make yourself at home, Lucy. I believe you know everyone here but let me know if there's anyone you haven't met.'

'Pleased to meet you, Lucy,' I said.

'Yes. And you.' She didn't look pleased.

Lucy wasn't quite what I'd imagined. I'd envisioned a bit of a plain Jane, with glasses and hair tied up in a bun. Don't ask me why. Probably memories of my teachers. But Lucy had long, jet black hair, startlingly vivid green eyes and skin the colour of porcelain. She was tall, slim and wore what looked like a designer label, emerald green, halter neck and backless jumpsuit. She made me feel under-dressed and a bit of a plain Jane myself.

'That's Lucy?' I said as she sashayed away. She'd obviously been a model at one time or another. No ordinary person walked like that. She even did one of those cat walk turns and her eyes bore into me as she lifted her chin as if to say, 'That's right, baby. I'm the competition and you've already lost Liam to me.' Not that I ever really thought I had a chance with Liam.

'You've met Lucy, I see,' Elsie said, coming up behind me and handing me an orange-coloured cocktail with two slices of orange and three cocktail cherries on a colourful parrot cocktail stick.

'I have. What's this?'

'It's a Hurricane. Dark rum, white rum, passion fruit, an orange and a lemon, some sugar syrup and a few splashes of grenadine.'

'Sounds like it might give me a hurricane of a headache if I had too many. I'm not a lover of dark rum.'

'Get it down your neck and it'll bring a smile to your face that even little Lucy won't erase.'

'There's nothing little about Lucy. She's the most unlikely looking school teacher I've ever seen.'

Elsie laughed. 'I heard she comes from

money, but I don't know if that's true.'

'Let's hope she goes back there.'

'Ah.' Elsie beamed at a slightly overweight woman with short, spiky, white-blonde hair who was marching towards us. 'Have you met the Reverend?'

The woman stuck out her hand and grabbed mine in a handshake firmer than many men's.

'Hello there. You must be Josie. I've been hearing all about you. I saw you on the beach at the Seahorse Summer Sand Shine-Up and I meant to come and say hello but I lost track of time – and of you.' She laughed, still holding my hand in an iron-like grip. 'I'm the ear of the Lord around here. My name's Persephone. And yes, I'm aware of the irony. Persephone being the Greek goddess of the Underworld and all that. Married to Hades. Persephone, not me. People call me Perse, as in Percy the man's name but spelt with an 'se'. Are you having fun? Do you go to church? We're C of E, you know, despite the name. Thanks to that old bugger, King Henry and his desire to marry Anne and rid himself of the Pope. There was a big thing about changing the name but St Mary Star of the Sea has a certain ring to it, don't you think?' She beamed at me with a set of blinding-white tombstone-like teeth.

'Er.' I wasn't sure where to start so I smiled and said, 'Hello, Perse. It's lovely to meet you, but no, I'm afraid I'm not religious.'

'Never mind. Plenty of time for that. What're you drinking? It looks fairly lethal. Ah, there're Liam and Orla. Must go and say hello. Lovely to meet you, Josie. I'm sure I'll see you around.'

She finally let go of my hand and I shook it up and down to get the feeling back into my fingers.

'What in the name of God was that?' I asked Elsie, who was laughing. I took a swig of my cocktail. 'She's more of a hurricane than this drink. Is she really the Reverend?'

Elsie laughed. 'Yes. And you'll find yourself in church before you know it. Let's go and find Gray. He's lurking about here somewhere. Probably outside on the deck. Or would you also like to go and say hello to Liam and Orla?'

I tutted. 'Don't give me that look, Elsie. Let's go and find Gray. I can catch up with Liam later.'

But I couldn't help looking in his direction as I followed Elsie across the kitchen towards the open, folding doors, and although he was chatting to several people I hadn't yet met, he glanced up, met my look and his gaze held mine as I continued on my way, crashing into Toby because I wasn't looking where I was going.

'Hey!' Toby yelled, having been splattered with some of my Hurricane. 'Are you drunk already?'

'No I'm not,' I replied, dragging my gaze from Liam as a huge grin spread across his face. 'I'm sure that was your fault.'

'Yeah. Blame me. Where's Mum?'

'She's...' I glanced around the room. I couldn't see her. But more worryingly, I could no longer see Liam. Orla was chatting to Becca and they were giggling as usual. 'Oh, I don't know. I think I saw her talking to Mikkel a few minutes ago.'

'Can I have some of your drink?'

'You've already had some.' I smiled as I wiped splashes of my drink from his cheek.

'I thought you were fun.'

'That's just a vicious and unsubstantiated rumour and a slur on my good character.'

'You *are* drunk.'

'No. I'm just teasing.' I put my hand on his shoulder. 'Come with me, little man and I'll show you how much fun I can be. Oh yuk. That sounded gross even to me. I didn't mean that. I'll get you a cocktail. A non-alcoholic cocktail.'

'Thanks for nothing. I noticed you met the Reverend.' He grinned at me and nudged me in the ribs, spilling even more of my drink, only down me this time.

'I'm so glad this dress only cost me a hundred and fifty quid. Thanks, Toby.'

'Sorry.'

I shook my head. 'Don't worry. It's not your fault. It'll come out, I'm sure.'

'Allow me.' A hand held out a napkin towards me. A hand I recognised. I looked up into Liam's eyes, which were twinkling with mischief as he patted at the low neckline of my midnight-blue, body-hugging, crêpe dress.

'Er. Thanks.'

Toby tutted, shook his head and walked away saying, 'I'll get my own drink.'

Liam was fighting a grin. I could see it in the way his lips kept twitching at one corner. He looked into my eyes as he held the napkin just above the plunging V-shape of the dress – and my ample cleavage.

'Shall I?' he asked.

'Not if you want to live.' I grabbed the napkin from him and handed him my almost empty glass. 'I'd rather you didn't stick your hand down my dress at my sister's posh cocktail party.'

'Does that mean I could if we weren't at your sister's posh cocktail party?'

'In your dreams, Liam.'

I dabbed at my cleavage.

'I could lick it off if you'd prefer. I'm sure no one would notice.'

'You know. I'm almost positive that some old git nagged me about sexual teasing the other day.'

I tapped a finger against my dark red lips and assumed a thoughtful expression.

'Who's teasing?' he said.

I looked him in the eye and stepped a little closer, allowing my gaze to wander over his black trousers, crisp white cotton shirt, black jacket and navy-blue, red and white dotted bow tie.

'What would you do if I took you up on that offer?'

His grin faltered for a second but soon came back.

'I'd ensure I made a good job of it. I'd get every last drop, no matter how long it took.'

'I'll bear that in mind. I think this was yours.'

He gave a little gasp as I stuffed the napkin into the waistband of his trousers, threw him a sexy smile and walked off in search of Elsie. But I was surprised that my body was tingling in the most unexpected places, yet again.

'Toby was...' I began as I met Diana a few minutes later coming out of Alex's study. '...looking for you,' I continued as Mikkel followed her out.

Diana and Mikkel exchanged glances and Mikkel smiled.

'Diana was just showing me some photos of the new hospital wing that's been named after Alex. I hadn't seen it.'

'Ah,' I said, not believing a word. 'It's really something.'

He had the internet like everyone else. He could've seen it anytime he wanted. But perhaps that was just me seeing one and one and making sex. Or something along those lines. There was definitely something strange going on with him and Diana. But surely it couldn't be that? Diana adored Alex. She wouldn't have an affair. She simply wasn't the type. I was letting my imagination run away with me. I'd thought there was something going on between her and Liam the other day too. Perhaps Liam was right. Everything was all about sex with me.

'Well,' Diana said, flushing a deeper pink than the cerise dress she was wearing. 'I'd better find Toby and see what he wants and then get back to my other guests. Have a good time, Mikkel. And you, of course, Josie.'

'I'm having lots of fun, thanks.' I grinned at her and then at Mikkel as we both watched Diana walk away. 'The hospital wing, eh? And there was I thinking that chilled champagne was on ice just for me. I'm getting another drink. Want one?'

He met my look and smiled. 'Absolutely. And the champagne has been on ice since the day you walked into my bar. You never seem to want to pop the cork.'

'I've been busy,' I said. 'And it looks like you've been busy too.'

'It's not what you think,' he said. 'Diana loves her husband.'

'I know she does. So what's going on?'

He shook his head. 'Nothing. Nothing is going on.' And he sounded almost sad about it.

'Hey mate.' Jonno, the cab driver appeared in front of us and he and Mikkel did the hugging, slapping thing. 'Hello young lady. You look lovely tonight. Are you enjoying your stay so far? I had no idea you were Diana's sister. Why haven't we ever met before?'

'Hello, Jonno. More than I expected, yes. I haven't been to Seahorse Harbour for years, as I told you. I travel a lot and I currently live in New York.'

'I see. This here's my gorgeous wife, Sandra. Isn't she a picture?'

'She certainly is. Hello Sandra. It's lovely to meet you. I'm Josie. Your husband brought me here from the station on Tuesday and gave me a guided tour.'

Sandra, who looked at least ten years younger than Jonno and as if a slight breeze might blow her over, smiled at me. She was extremely pretty, with long curly, brown hair and the kind of face that didn't need any make-up to look good. When she spoke, she sounded like a church mouse.

'Jonno loves to tell everyone about the seahorses. That's how we met. He gave me a guided tour when I came here on holiday with my friends.'

Jonno wrapped an arm about her and I wondered if she might snap, but she was obviously much stronger than she looked.

'I took her and her friends all around the houses because I didn't want Sandra to get out. It took me twenty minutes to summon up the courage to ask if I could see her again?'

'And he didn't charge us a penny so I had to say yes, didn't I?'

'And we've been together ever since,' Jonno added with evident pride and adoration.

'Yes. I came here for two weeks and I stayed for ten years. So far. Although we lived in Easterhill because that's where Jonno had a house.'

'Wow. Love at first sight then?'

'It was for me,' Jonno said. 'Sandra here took a bit of persuading. But by the end of two weeks, when I asked her to stay, she did. Much to my eternal thanks and huge amazement.'

'Are you here with anyone?' Sandra asked, looking up at Mikkel.

'No. Not me. Young, free and single. That's me.'

'Until you find 'The One', that is.' Sandra had a lovely smile.

I shook my head. 'I think, 'The One' got away a long time ago. But that's fine. I'm happy. Well, I will be once I've got another Hurricane. Can I get either of you a drink?'

Jonno and Sandra raised their glasses.

'We're fine thanks,' Sandra said, with another lovely smile. 'And Jonno's driving so he's only having one.'

I liked Jonno and Sandra. If I lived in Seahorse Harbour, I'd have liked them to be my friends. Did that sound sad? I suddenly missed my friends in New York. Especially Rhoda. We'd texted one another a few times but due to the time difference we had yet to talk. I decided I'd give her a ring the following day.

'Aren't you coming to my club?' Mikkel asked them. 'Some of us are going there after this.' He glanced at me. 'Are you joining us?'

'At your club? At Neptune's? Is Diana going?'

Mikkel shook his head. 'She said she needs to stay here and look after Becca and Toby.'

'Oh. Then I'd better stay too. It wouldn't be fair to run off and leave her.'

'If you change your mind. You're more than welcome.' He smiled. 'I've got some chilled champagne.'

'I bet you have,' I said. 'I'm going to get myself another Hurricane. I'll see you all later.'

Mikkel had been coming with me but now he stayed with his friends, which was fine with me. I went to see what had happened to Elsie and Gray and saw them chatting to Asher. He also looked gorgeous in his tux. So many people had dressed up even though Diana had said it was a black and white cocktail party but come as you like, casual or formal or in fancy dress. That had made me laugh. I hadn't expected that from Diana. I thought she was a traditionalist. Toby told me later that it was his suggestion.

'If Dad were here, it would be a black tie event as usual.'

That sounded rather incongruous somehow, from a thirteen-year-old.

'Hi Asher. You're looking rather handsome,' I said. Well. It was the truth.

'You're looking pretty stunning yourself. I haven't seen you since the beach clean-up. You didn't come to the pub.'

'No. Diana and I were tired. I'm not used to hard work. I've been spending my days in an office for the last couple of years. You know, feet up on the desk, shooting paper planes across the room to try and kill my colleagues. Drinking coffee and eating doughnuts all day. Physical and manual work is tough. Although I'd rather do that than stick my hand up a cow's arse, like you do.'

He burst out laughing. 'Not often, I'm glad to say. Are you coming to Neptune's tonight?'

'No. Diana's got to look after the kids so I'll stay here with her and possibly help her clear up. Or maybe just watch, and make paper planes out of napkins.'

'Is everyone going to Neptune's?' Elsie asked.

Asher grinned. 'Several of us. Want to join us?'

'Don't think I wouldn't,' Elsie said. 'And I'd still be dancing while you youngsters were gasping for breath. But why don't I stay and watch the kids? Then you and Diana can go out and let your hair down.'

'I'm happy to stay if you'd like some company,' Gray offered.

'That's settled then.' Elsie grinned. 'Where's Diana? You should tell her now. She'll probably need an hour or so to see it as a good idea.'

But to everyone's surprise, Diana only needed a few minutes.

'It's been years since I've been to a nightclub,' she said when Elsie told her. 'Do you want to go, Josie?'

'To a nightclub? That's like asking the Pope if he wants to go to Heaven. And I do have a new dress and I do like to dance. But if you'd rather not, that's fine.'

She looked thoughtful for a moment and then nodded.

'Why not? It might be fun. And it's only down the road so if I decide not to stay, I won't have far to go.'

'If you decide not to stay, tell me, and I'll come home with you,' I said.

'Don't be silly. I'm a big girl, Josie. And nothing bad ever happens in Seahorse Harbour. This isn't New York, you know.'

'That's what everyone says about a place

until something bad does happen.'

The party continued for another hour or so before people slowly began to drift away. The invite had said from 7 until 9 so by 9.15 only those going to Neptune's remained.

'I mustn't be too late,' Diana said, as we waved goodbye to Elsie and Gray and headed down the hill, arm in arm. 'Toby asked if he can have some friends round tomorrow afternoon for a barbecue. That means more cooking in the morning.'

'Oh joy.'

Asher, Mikkel and Liam walked ahead of us and I couldn't help but notice that Lucy and the Reverend tagged behind them rather than walk with us. Sandra and Jonno went home, and Orla was staying the night with Becca. Mikkel had said that a few of the other people at the party might join us, but in the end, it was just the group of us.

Neptune's wasn't really what I'd imagined. On the outside, it was a deep bright blue and shiny with an image of the god himself etched into each large, glass door. Inside, the floor looked like the seabed; the walls had videos of marine life swimming in the sea, including seahorses, whales, sharks, dolphins and colourful fish. It was all a bit surreal and made me feel a little dizzy at first. The bar staff were dressed as mermaids and mermen and the bar was made to look like a coral reef. But the music was great and the dance floor was large, surrounded by fantastic chairs in the shapes of various shells and tables that looked like standing crabs about to scurry off with your drinks. It was fun and not at all pretentious.

Asher, Mikkel and Liam spent a lot of time seated, chatting away as if the rest of us weren't there, but every so often I saw them watching Diana, Lucy, Perse and me and I really hoped they'd get up and dance.

In the end, I had to go and insist they join us, and just as I did that, a slow dance played and Asher grabbed my hand. I have to admit, I was a bit disappointed, especially when Liam then went and danced with Perse. But better that than Lucy. Mikkel made a beeline for Diana but she dashed off to the loo so he danced with Lucy instead.

It was some time until I got to dance with Liam but when I did, he slid his arms around my waist and pulled me close. He'd removed his bow tie as soon as we left Diana's and undone two buttons of his shirt. He'd taken off his jacket as soon as we sat down in the nightclub. I rested my head against him but even in heels, I only came up to his chest. That was a pity. I'd like to have nuzzled against his neck.

'Did I tell you how beautiful you look tonight?' he said.

'No. But you can tell me now.'

'I think I just did.'

'Oh. Was that it? You scrub up well yourself.'

'Scrub up well?' He laughed. 'Thanks.'

'Lucy's not what I'd pictured.'

She was now dancing with Asher but I could see her glancing surreptitiously at us.

'Isn't she?'

'She's stunning.'

'Is she?'

'Do you like her?'

'Yes. She's nice.'

'I bet she's a ten.'

'A ten?' He eased a little away from me so that he could see my face, and then he smiled. 'Oh. The scoring, you mean. No. I wouldn't say she's a ten.'

'A nine?'

'Nope.'

'Oh come on, Liam. She's got to be a nine.'

He laughed again and this time I could feel his muscles through his shirt.

'If you're going to tell me how high I should score people, why do you bother to ask?'

'I'm being polite.'

'Oh. Is that what you're doing? I thought you were being bossy and controlling.'

'I'm not bossy and controlling. You take that back right now.'

He laughed. 'I think that proves my point.'

'Smart arse.'

I grabbed his bottom and squeezed it. I couldn't help myself. It was firm and perfect and I was tempted to do it again.

He slid his hand down and gave mine a gentle pinch. 'Nice arse,' he said.

I thumped him on the chest and he made a sound like, 'Ouff'.

'That was rude,' I said.

'Whereas you grabbing mine is fine.'

'Exactly. Have you and Lucy been on a date?'

'What?' he looked at me again, and there was something in his eyes I couldn't fathom. 'Why do you ask?'

'Just curious. I saw her watching you at the party and she's giving us a very odd look right now.'

'Is she?'

I thought he'd look round but he didn't.

'Yes. She is.'

'Perhaps she's saying the same about you to Asher. You are, after all, staring at her, aren't you?'

'No.'

I was, obviously, although I thought I was doing it sneakily.

'What's the sudden fascination with Lucy?' he asked.

'I'm not fascinated. Are you?'

'With Lucy? No.'

'Good. But you didn't answer my question.'

'What was that?'

'Did you go out on a date with her?'

'Oh that question. You're right. I didn't answer.'

I waited but he just pulled me a little closer and it felt so good that for a moment I forgot what I was going to say next. I closed my eyes and breathed in his scent. He smelt of soap and lavender and sandalwood.

'Um. Are you going to?'

'Answer? No.' And then the song came to an end. He smiled and eased away from me. 'Thanks for the dance. It was ... interesting.'

And that was it. The three men returned to their seats, their drinks and their conversation and we four women danced until Diana decided she wanted to go.

'You can stay,' she said.

'No. I'll come back with you.'

We said goodbye to Perse and Lucy and then to Asher, Mikkel and Liam. All three men offered to walk us home but we declined and said we were fine. I hoped Liam would insist, but he didn't. None of them did. It seemed if you told these three guys, no, they accepted it without question.

The annoying thing was, I saw Lucy and Perse join the men as soon as Diana and I reached the exit.

Sixteen

I hadn't got a lot of sleep and rather than lay awake for hours, I got up and went for a walk. The air was already humid despite it only being around 5 a.m. and the gulls soared overhead, their wings spread wide in the thermals as they twisted and turned this way and that. No one was about and the silence was almost eerie. As if someone had muted the volume of life.

I walked down to the church and past Liam's pottery, still locked up at this time in the morning. And as it was Sunday, it might remain so. I strolled down the hill towards Sea Walk and was surprised to hear a door shut to my right. I glanced over and to my astonishment, there was Liam. He was coming out of one of the cottages on Church Hill and was just opening the garden gate to step onto the pavement.

He looked incredibly handsome. His shirt was open all the way down to his navel and only partly tucked into his trousers; his jacket was slung carelessly over his shoulder and hooked over one finger. He looked tired as if he hadn't got much sleep and the shadow on his unshaven jaw made him even more sexy. His chocolate-brown hair was dishevelled in a way that you only got from rolling around in bed all night, and a sudden pain hit me in my gut like cramp. I wanted to run but as I tried to step back, he raised his head and spotted me. Our eyes met and held for a second or two and neither of us spoke.

'Hi,' I said, eventually. 'Good night?' I cursed myself for saying that and forced a smile.

'Hi.' He looked startled like a deer coming face-to-face with a hunter. He glanced back at the cottage door and then at me. 'Er. It's not what it looks like.'

'Oh? You mean you're not really coming out of someone else's house at some ungodly hour of the morning wearing the same, and if I may say so, rather crumpled, clothes that you wore last night, with a serious case of bed head?'

I didn't know whose cottage it was but I prayed to God it wasn't Lucy's.

'Bed head?'

I nodded my head towards him at pointed at my hair. 'Bed head.'

He slung his jacket over one arm and ran his other hand through his hair, which only served to make it more tousled, as he walked towards me.

'I didn't get much sleep.'

'I don't doubt it.'

'No. I meant I tossed and turned all night.'

I raised my brows and forced a grin. 'Whatever takes your fancy.'

'I slept on the sofa.'

'Yeah right. Do you actually expect me to believe that? Why would you sleep on someone's sofa when your own bed is just a few doors away?'

'Because Lucy asked me to.'

And there it was. He was coming out of Lucy's cottage after spending the night … on her sofa. A likely story. He stood beside me now and we began walking towards the beach together even though his house was in the opposite direction.

'Uh-huh,' I said. 'I see.'

'No really. She did. I walked her home and when we got there it was obvious there had been a break in. We called the police and I waited for them to arrive. Then she asked if I'd stay because she didn't want to be alone. Orla was spending the night at Becca's, so I spent the night on Lucy's sofa.'

'The sofa?' I teased him with my raised brows.

'Yes. And it's a small sofa. A two-seater at most. So as I said, I didn't get much sleep.'

'Ah. Was anything taken?'

'From the break in? Yeah. Some jewellery, her laptop, a few ornaments and her spare keys are missing.'

Perhaps he was telling the truth, after all.

'Bloody hell. That's not good. Is she okay?'

'She will be but she's shaken up, obviously. I'm asking Jonno to come and change the locks and mend the window.'

'Jonno? He drives a mini cab.'

Liam nodded and grinned. 'He's a locksmith and an odd-job man too.'

'Oh I see. That's kind of you.'

He shrugged. 'Not really. It's what any one of us would do.' He glanced across at me. 'Er. What are you doing out this early? Did you spend the night somewhere too?'

There was a definite edge to his tone but he could see I was wearing jeans and a T-shirt, not the dress I'd worn last night.

'Nope. Just wanted to see the sunrise.'

'On your own?'

I laughed. 'Yes. Why not?'

He shook his head. 'Just nicer to watch it with someone, I would've thought.'

'I'm used to doing stuff like that on my own. I like it.'

'Ah yes. Josie Parnell doesn't need to share her life with anyone. I almost forgot that for a moment.'

'And what's wrong with that? Surely it's better to be able to stand on my own two feet and do things by myself than to not do things because I don't have a 'special someone' to do them with?'

'I suppose that's true. But isn't there a danger of doing so much on your own that you forget how nice it is to do things with someone special?'

'No. I don't think so. And you could wait all your life and that someone special might never come along. Or they could already be with someone else.'

'Or you could miss the someone special because you're so busy doing things on your own.'

I shrugged. 'If it's meant to be it'll be. Fate will do her stuff.'

'Do you believe that?'

'Yes. I think I do. It may not be what we want though. That's the problem. Sometimes what we think we want isn't what we need. And it isn't meant to be no matter how much we might want it.'

'Er. Run that by me again, please.'

I tutted.

'I'm serious. Are you actually saying that if we want something – or someone – and it looks like Fate isn't going to let us have that thing or person, we should just forget it because it wasn't meant to be?'

I nodded my head from side to side as if I was processing his comment.

'Yes and no. I do think that some things are worth fighting for. What I don't believe in though, is banging your head against a brick wall. You can't force someone to love you, or stay with you. You can't stop them from loving someone else and not you. You can't fight that.'

He tensed visibly and a very unhappy snort of laughter escaped him.

'No, you're right. I agree with you on that. You definitely can't force someone to love you, or stay with you if they love someone else. But if that's the case, they weren't worth fighting for in any case. Let's change the subject. Did you enjoy last night?'

It sounded almost as if he were speaking from experience, as I was, and I wanted to ask him about it. But then I ran the risk that he might ask me. I couldn't deal with that.

'Yes,' I said. 'Very much. Especially the dancing.'

'Yes. I enjoyed that part too. Especially watching you. You're a very good dancer. Wait. Isn't that Elsie's cottage?'

He pointed to Seaside Cottage and the ambulance and police car parked outside. Without another word we both ran to the cottage as the paramedics were coming out.

'What's happened?' I yelled. 'This is my aunt's cottage. Is she all right?'

'Honeybee?' I heard Elsie's voice and I breathed a sigh of relief. 'I'm fine.'

'Is she?' Liam asked one of the paramedics.

He nodded. 'Just a few bruises. But someone should keep an eye on her because she had a nasty fall and she lay there for some time we think. She may have concussion but it doesn't look like it at the moment. And she may suffer with delayed shock. It was a rather upsetting experience.'

'What happened?' I asked, wanting to know before I saw Elsie.

'She disturbed a burglar and he pushed her over.'

'A burglar?' Liam and I stared at one another.

'Thanks,' I said and ran inside.

Liam followed behind me and I saw a police woman sitting beside Elsie, holding her hand. Another was taking a statement. Elsie looked so frail I almost burst into tears. I went and sat on the sofa on the other side of Elsie and gave her a gentle hug.

'Why didn't you stay at Diana's as she suggested?' I said. 'What happened? Are you hurt?'

Elsie tapped my hand. 'Don't fuss, honeybee. I'm fine. Really I am.'

'We've just taken some details,' the police officer beside her said. 'There was another break in not far from here last night and we think it's probably the same person.'

I was tempted to say, 'You think?' but I

held my tongue. Of course, it was the same person. The likelihood of two different burglars in such a small village on the same night was pretty remote.

'We know the other person who was burgled,' Liam said.

'It was Lucy,' I told Elsie.

'Is she hurt?' Elsie asked, worried as always about others before herself.

'No,' Liam said. 'She's fine. Just shocked. They'd been and gone by the time we got there.'

'*We* got there?' Elsie asked, raising a questioning brow.

She didn't miss a thing. And I couldn't help but smile.

'Liam walked Lucy home last night. I wish I'd walked you home.'

'Gray walked me home,' Elsie said. 'But he was tired so he didn't come in. We said goodnight, I opened my door, put my keys in the bowl by the coat stand and went to the kitchen to make myself a bedtime drink. I thought I heard a noise but I listened and all was quiet. I went up to bed and fell asleep and then I woke with a start. I definitely heard a noise. I came downstairs and there he was. Standing in the kitchen doorway. I thought Gray had come back and let himself in but suddenly I saw him move towards me and realised it wasn't Gray. I saw him raise a hand and I thought he was going to punch me in my face but instead, I felt a thud against my shoulder and I was flat on the floor before I knew it. I'm not sure how long I lay there but when I came to, it was light and the birds were singing. I thought I was dreaming until I realised I was lying on something hard. It took me another little while to get myself together and then I wondered if I'd had a fall and it was all a dream. Until I saw the drawers were open in the sideboard in the sitting room and that there was some money missing from the kitchen counter. So I called the police and these nice ladies called the ambulance. Would you like a cup of tea, honeybee?'

'I'll make it,' Liam said. 'You stay there. Anyone else?' He looked at the police officers but they shook their heads.

'We'll be off,' one said. 'We've got all we need for now. No point in seeing if there're fingerprints. You said he was wearing gloves?'

Elsie nodded. 'Yes. Definitely. I saw them when he pushed me. Black gloves with a large spider shape on the front.

'Oh Elsie,' I said. 'You're coming back to Diana's with me.'

'And leave this place empty for the young thug to come back and finish taking what he wants. No, I am not!'

'Then I'll come here and stay with you.'

'I'm not sure that's a good idea,' Liam said, from the kitchen, returning to the sitting room so that he didn't have to shout. 'I think, perhaps, we should get Jonno to change the locks and see if he can find out where the guy got in and sort that out. Then fit an alarm. That way you can go and stay at Diana's knowing that your property is as safe as it can be. I'd offer to stay here but I can't leave Orla.'

'That's good advice,' one of the officers said. 'And we'll have a car drive around every so often for the next day or two, especially as two properties in the area have been burgled.'

'I can't believe it's happened,' Elsie said. 'Nothing bad ever happens in Seahorse Harbour.'

'That's exactly what Diana said last night,' I said, feeling anxious and concerned for Diana and the kids, living in a prime property when there was a burglar running around.

I wondered if there was an alarm at Sea View Cottage. I'd have to ask Diana. If not, poor Jonno was going to have a very busy day.

Seventeen

No matter how much we tried, neither Liam nor I could persuade Elsie to stay at Diana's. At first, I thought she'd agreed but after we'd had a couple of cups of tea, Elsie got her fighting spirit back.

She repeated almost the same thing she'd said earlier: 'No young thug is going to drive me from my home. Besides, if he got in again and I wasn't here, he could wreck the place. I'm not having that. I'm staying.'

'Then I'll ask Jonno to put a lock on your bedroom door,' Liam said. 'That way if you're in bed and hear someone in the house, at least you'll be safe while you wait for the police to arrive. Make sure you have your mobile beside your bed. The burglar might cut the landline.'

A little after that, Liam said he'd better go. He wasn't sure what time Orla would be getting home from her sleepover with Becca and he didn't want to call and worry her.

'Call me if you need me, Elsie,' he instructed before he went. 'At any time, night or day. Even if you're just feeling anxious and need someone to chat to. And I can be here in a matter of seconds if you want me to come round.' He looked me in the eye. 'That goes for you too.'

'Thanks. I don't have your number though.'

'We can remedy that right now.'

We exchanged numbers and he did the same with Elsie. I then walked him to the front door.

'I'll stay and make sure she's okay and I'll call Diana and tell her what's happened. I'll tell her not to mention it to Orla. I assume you want to do that yourself.'

'Yes, please. Call if you need me. I mean it, Josie.'

'I know you do, and I will.'

He hesitated for a moment.

'I'm sorry w- ... you, didn't get to watch the sunrise.'

He almost said, 'we'.

'There's always tomorrow. I can meet you outside Lucy's if you're planning another night ... on the sofa.'

He threw me a look of reprimand and then smiled. 'I'm not. But I did sleep on the sofa, I promise you. Ask Lucy if you don't believe me.'

'I just might do that.'

The smile grew wider and he leant against the frame of the front door, his jacket once again slung over his shoulder and his other hand shoved into his trouser pocket.

'Surely you're not jealous? I can't believe that Josie Parnell would seriously want to know where I spent my night.'

There was a look in his eyes that made me nervous.

I laughed but it sounded a bit maniacal, so I gave him a playful shove.

'In your dreams, Liam Fulbright. I'm just being nosy. Now get lost because I need to make Elsie and me some breakfast.'

I closed the front door before he had a chance to respond and waited a few seconds until I heard him walk away. But my heart did a little flutter in my chest as I recognised the song he was singing to himself. It was 'If I Fall In Love' by Ali Gatie. He was one of my favourite singers. And that was my favourite song at the moment.

Did Liam know that? Or was it pure coincidence? Did Liam like Ali's music too?

I don't know why that excited me, but for some peculiar reason it did.

I felt more relaxed a little later when Elsie called Gray at what she considered a respectable hour on a Sunday, namely 9 a.m. and told him what had happened. He was at the door in a matter of minutes, although he looked a little flushed and out of breath. He didn't look quite so debonair as he had on the previous occasions when I'd seen him.

'I hadn't long been out of bed,' he said. 'Are you all right? Are you hurt?'

Both Elsie and I assured him she seemed fine.

'I've been trying to persuade her to come and stay at Diana's,' I said. 'But she flatly refuses to leave here.'

'Well then, I'll come here and stay,' he said.

I'm not sure what surprised me the most. The way he said it without asking if it was okay. Or the fact that Elsie smiled, nodded and said that was a wonderful idea.

'But what if your house gets burgled while you're here?' I asked.

'It's not my house. It's my son's. I've been staying with him for a few weeks now.' He gave me a wink and a smile. 'He'll probably be glad to be rid of me. I think I might've been cramping his style.'

'Oh,' I said. 'Well, that's that then, Elsie. It seems I won't have to drag you up the hill to Diana's, kicking and screaming.'

'Oh honeybee!' She laughed. 'As if you really could.'

'I'll stay, if you want to be getting off,' Gray said.

'Yes,' Elsie agreed. 'You run along. I'm fine and Gray will take care of me, so there's no need for you to worry.'

I got the feeling I was being dismissed. But

in a nice way. I wasn't sure if Elsie and Gray were just friends or if there was something more between them but he was lovely and Elsie seemed to be back to her usual bubbly self, so I said goodbye and left them to it.

A few metres up Church Hill, I saw Perse, the Reverend, walking from the church so I did a quick U-turn and dashed down to Sea Walk and nipped into Seahorse Bites Café on the promenade.

'With you in a sec,' a female voice called out.

I wasn't sure what to do. I'd eaten breakfast about an hour ago so I wasn't hungry, and I'd drunk enough tea and coffee to sink a ship, but I couldn't walk out now. Besides, I didn't want to talk to the Reverend this morning. It was Sunday so she'd probably try to drag me into church.

'No rush,' I replied, and sat at a table by the window, looking out into the bay.

This village really was beautiful. And so peaceful too. Putting to one side the fact that there was a thuggish and possibly dangerous burglar on the loose, Seahorse Harbour was the idyll. The perfect, picture-postcard, seaside village.

It was so different from New York. I loved the hustle and bustle of the City that never sleeps, but I also loved the tranquillity and beauty of Seahorse Harbour. I wondered how it would feel, returning to New York after spending the summer here. Would I miss this place? Would I miss Diana and the kids? I wouldn't miss Henry. I would miss Elsie. What about Liam? Would I miss him? And Mikkel and Asher and ... Now I was just being ridiculous.

'What can I get you, love? I've got some delicious, homemade croissants and I make my own raspberry jam.'

'Er. That sounds perfect.' I could always forego lunch. 'And a coffee, please.'

'Large?'

'Why not? It's Sunday.'

'Back in a jiffy.'

She hurried away and as I watched her I spotted a poster giving details of the annual summer fayre. It was called The Save the Seahorse Fayre. I got up and walked over to it, but just then my mobile rang. I half expected to see the mad Medusa getting her arse bitten by her snakes but instead it was the buxom blonde astride the plane. I must find an image to go with Liam's number now that I had it.

'Bloody hell, you old tart. This is a bit early for you,' I said, laughing into my phone.

'Hi, you old slapper. Is it early or is it late? That's the question.'

'Are you drunk? You sound drunk.'

'I bloody hope so. I necked almost half a bottle of Voddie and four Cosmopolitans. I'm in a cab on my way home from Rachel's party and I thought I'd give my best friend a call. But she wasn't home so I called you.'

'Haha. The old ones are always the best.'

'Is that what the last guy you slept with said? You are almost thirty-five.'

'Funny. At least I can remember the last guy I slept with. I'd forgotten Rachel was having a party. Damn. Was it good?'

'Brilliant. As Rachel's parties always are. Any hotties over there? Or are they all shuffling around on those Zimmer frame things?'

'Oh my God, Rhoda, you have no idea. There're at least three gorgeous guys here. I've been flirting with them all, naturally.'

I heard a bell tinkle and wondered if that meant my order was ready but I glanced sideways towards the kitchen area and saw the woman was still busy. I returned my attention back to the poster, although as I was talking to my friend, I wasn't really reading it.

'Three? I thought you said the place was tiny.'

'It is. But it must attract hot guys, obviously.'

'I need proof. Send me photos. Preferably with them not wearing very much. Better yet, wearing nothing at all.'

'Ah. I don't have any photos. Yet. I'll take some and send them.'

'Are you planning to bestow all three with

your charms? Or is there one in particular?'

'Haven't decided yet. I'm keeping my options open. There's one I fancy a bit more than the other two, but he's got a kid so that's an issue.'

'Why? You're not planning to marry the guy, are you?'

'Of course I'm not planning to marry the guy. I'm never getting married. You know that. But a kid means responsibility, doesn't it? And it cramps your style. You can't just get naked anytime you want.'

The woman poked her head round the kitchen door and smiled. But not at me. Someone must've come in. That tinkling must've been the bell above the door. I half-turned to see who it was.

'Morning, Liam,' the woman boomed out. 'Be with you in a jiffy.'

My heart leapt to my mouth. Liam had been standing in the café for the last few seconds or so and he must've heard every word I'd said. As I completed the turn and saw his face, I realised he had definitely heard. He looked at me as if I'd just thrown a bucket of iced water over him ... containing sharks ... jelly fish ... and a nuclear missile from a submarine while I was at it.

'Liam!' I yelped.

'Don't let me interrupt your conversation,' he said, his mouth a straight hard line. 'It was very ... enlightening.' He looked away and smiled at the woman but it wasn't a happy smile. 'I just popped in to tell you there's been a couple of burglaries, Lyn. I'm telling everyone I can and if you could also spread the word, that would be good. Jonno's going to be changing some locks so if you want him to look at any of yours, let either me or Jonno know.'

'Burglaries? In Seahorse Harbour? Never.'

He nodded. 'Sadly so. Lucy had a window smashed and some items stolen and Elsie was knocked to the ground. But thankfully she's okay.'

'Good gracious. Whatever next. I'll pop round and see Elsie later. Thanks for letting me know, Liam. You're a saint.'

'Hardly. Bye for now.'

He walked to the door and I dashed to his side, forgetting Rhoda was on my phone.

'Liam! I was joking. I didn't mean any of that.'

His eyes bore into me like ice picks.

'You always are, Josie. And you never do. That's the problem. See you around.'

And he was gone. Just like that.

I knew if I went after him it wouldn't do any good. He needed time to cool down. And yet. He didn't sound angry. He sounded disappointed. And hurt. As if I'd let him down or something.

I heard a voice coming from my hand and

put my phone up to my ear.

'Who was that?' Rhoda asked. 'What happened?'

'I think I've just blown my chances with one of those three hot guys. He heard every word I said to you.'

'Holy crap. Oh well. At least you've still got two.'

'Yeah. The problem is, he was the one I think I wanted.'

'Ah. That is a bit of a bugger. But perhaps it's redeemable. Turn on the Josie charm. It still might work.'

Somehow, I didn't think it would.

I chatted to Rhoda for a few more minutes but I didn't have the enthusiasm to say very much, and I slumped into the chair I'd vacated earlier, and then the woman – Lyn, brought my croissants and my coffee and I said goodbye to my best friend.

'It's none of my business, love,' Lyn said, giving me a sympathetic smile, and a tiny pot of raspberry jam that she pulled from the pocket of her bright yellow apron, 'but I couldn't help but notice there was a little bit of tension in the air just now.'

I gave a snort of derisive laughter.

'I think that's an understatement.'

'Yes. Well. In my experience, the best thing to do is tell the truth. Honesty heals more wounds than any plaster.'

I looked at her and blinked. 'I did tell the truth. Just now.'

She pursed her lips, pulled a face and tapped my hand with her fingers.

'If you say so, love. But I think we both know that what you said to Liam was anything but the truth. He won't know how you really feel unless you tell him. Let me know if you'd like more jam. There's plenty where that came from. I'll leave you in peace to have a good think about what you really want.'

I got the distinct impression she wasn't talking about more jam.

Eighteen

'Alex had a top of the range security system installed when we bought the place,' Diana said when I returned to Sea View Cottage. 'Bernice suggested it. She said that Seahorse Harbour Holiday Park sometimes had some shady visitors, and they might be tempted to see if the house was easy pickings.

'That's a bit rich as she and Alex spent every summer there for years,' I said.

'I know. But there's no point in arguing with Bernice. Or of reminding her of that. It is a bit worrying though, isn't it? And two burglaries in one night. Perhaps there're two of them. Perhaps there's an entire gang.'

'Let's not get carried away, Di. At least we've got Henry. But I expect he'd probably lick the burglars to death.'

'He might give them a scare. The sheer size of him intimidates many people.'

'Yes. I'm one of them. What's up? You're looking thoughtful.'

She was cutting boiled Jersey Royals in

half and tossing them into her homemade mayonnaise, I assumed for her delicious potato salad.

'Toby's having some friends here today for a barbecue.'

'Yes. You said last night. Do you want a hand?'

'Thanks. That would be lovely. But that's not what I was thinking. The 'friends' are boys he and Becca met at the Lido the other day. The day you took them.'

A memory of me and Liam laughing and teasing one another popped into my head and I quickly dismissed it.

'And? Oh I see. You're jumping to the conclusion that one of them may be the burglar, aren't you?'

'It's possible. Didn't you say that Elsie said it was a teenager who attacked her?'

'I said she thought it was. Mainly because he was tall and 'spritely' and had a large spider image on his gloves. She said it was the sort of thing teenagers would wear. But the burglar could've borrowed his son's gloves. Or just bought them because he needed gloves. I don't think we should start assuming the worst.'

'No. You're right. I'm being paranoid.'

'Have you called Alex and told him?' I didn't want to ask but I felt I had to.

She lowered her gaze and chopped some spring onions. 'No. I didn't want to trouble him. He'd only worry and he's got enough on his mind right now. I'll tell him if it happens to anyone else.'

For someone who had just been a bit paranoid, that seemed a little odd. Surely her husband should be the first person she would call? Or maybe she was right. Perhaps there was no point in worrying him unless she had to.

We'd already agreed not to tell Mum. Elsie and Mum weren't on speaking terms so we knew Elsie wouldn't call her, but we decided it was best if we didn't mention it either. Elsie wouldn't want us to.

I peeled the boiled eggs and chopped them into pieces, tossing them into the large bowl of potato salad and adding several dollops of Diana's mayonnaise.

'I think I may've upset Liam.'

Diana stopped chopping parsley and looked me in the eye. 'Oh? How?'

I shrugged and told her about my phone conversation with Rhoda and the fact that Liam had heard my end of it.

'Oh dear. I'm assuming one of the three hot men is Liam then?'

'Of course. To quote Becca. Duh-uh. Liam's the one with the kid.'

'And ... he's the one you like the most?'

I nodded.

'Hmm. I thought you liked him but I wasn't sure. Is it ... is it serious?'

'Me liking Liam? No. I'll be going back to New York in a matter of weeks. It couldn't get serious even if I wanted it to. And besides, there's Orla.'

'Orla's sixteen, Josie. She's hardly a kid. Although Liam does dote on her and I can see why you'd be worried. You're not really the maternal or responsible type, are you?'

'I kill all the plants you buy me. What do you think?'

'Yes. Liam would never forgive you if anything happened to Orla.'

'I'm aware of that. He even lectured me for making what he thought were inappropriate comments in front of her. Although he was wrong about that and he did apologise.'

'Oh? What sort of comments.'

'It doesn't matter. I'll tell you another time.'

Becca had just appeared at the door but that wasn't really why I stopped. I didn't want to think about that day. For some reason, it was making me feel a little miserable. The thought that if Liam remained upset with me, we wouldn't get to spend any more days like that, together.

'Need any help?' Becca said, half skipping, half dancing towards us. 'Orla's just nipped home but she'll be back later. I'm really looking forward to this. More so than last night's party. That dreamy young guy is coming, Josie. You know? The double trouble, gorgeous dark-haired guy.' She made a swoony face and leant her elbows on the counter.

'The one who splash-bombed into the pool?'

'That's the one. His name's Noah. Isn't that a lovely name?'

Diana frowned at her. 'This is the first I'm hearing of this. Who's this Noah? How old is he? Is he here on holiday?'

'Oh Mum. Don't start. He's seventeen and yes, he's here on holiday. For the summer. Just like me. He's staying with his aunt, in her caravan. She works at Seahorse Harbour Holiday Park.'

'She lives in a caravan?' Diana shot me a look of concern.

'Oh don't be a snob, Di. Lots of decent, hard-working people live in caravans.'

'I suppose that's true.'

'Don't tell Dad though.' Now it was Becca who looked concerned. 'He'd have a fit. And Gran would insist you lock me in my room or something.'

Diana nodded. 'Bernice would say that.' She gave a small smile.

'He's really nice, Mum. You'll like him.'

'You said he was double trouble. I don't like the sound of that. What did that mean?'

'Oh. That was just because when we first saw him, Orla and I scored him in double figures but Josie said he looked like trouble. He isn't. Honestly. He's really sweet and he doesn't talk about himself hardly at all. He listens. And he asks lots of questions about me, about when we come down here. About you and Dad. Oh, and he asks Orla stuff too, of course.'

Becca flushed and I had a feeling she wasn't being completely honest. I also had a feeling that there might be trouble between Becca and Orla over this Noah.

And then another thought occurred to me. Becca had just said the boy asked her lots of questions. About the house and basically when it was occupied. Was he, by any chance, the burglar? Did he befriend local kids and get info about people's homes? Becca and Toby would've told him about the cocktail party, so he would've known several of the homes were empty for a time that night.

Or was I now the one being paranoid?

I decided to keep a very close eye on Noah at the barbecue.

Which I did.

But other than the boy being very confident for a kid his age, I couldn't actually find anything to make me think he was a criminal. He was polite to Diana and to me. He even brought Diana a bunch of flowers to say thank you for inviting him into her home. I suspect that was his aunt's idea. I didn't know any seventeen-year-old boys who would do something like that off their own bat.

He even got Henry on his side. Although that wasn't difficult. Anyone could win over Henry. But when he offered to help with the dishes and roped everyone else into helping so that Diana and I could 'relax and enjoy the afternoon' to use his words, I almost fell in love with him myself.

'He's too good to be true,' I said, sipping a large glass of wine on a sunbed on the deck, while all the teenagers, including Toby, cleared up.

'Becca was right,' Diana said, with a hint of a swoon, herself. 'He is a lovely boy.'

I watched Becca and Orla vying for his attention and had to admire the way he gave equal time to both. But he did look at Becca just a little more frequently than he did Orla. Which was surprising too. Orla is the spitting image of Una, so basically, a beauty. Becca is lovely, don't get me wrong, and she's stunning in her own way, but Orla would win hands down in any beauty pageant.

'Mum?' Toby yelled. 'Can we go to the beach?'

'Oh. Don't you want to spend the afternoon by the pool? Josie and I will give you some space if that's what you want.'

'We want to go to the beach,' Toby repeated. 'We're going to paddle board.'

'In that case, we'll come with you.'

'M-um.' Toby frowned. 'We'll be careful.'

'I'll keep an eye on them,' Noah said, smiling sweetly.

'Okay then.' Diana was easily persuaded.

'Can we leave Henry with you?' Toby asked and without waiting for a reply, he and everyone else dashed off.

But not before Noah came over and thanked Diana for having him, and me for being so welcoming too.

'Was he being sarcastic?' I asked, once he was out of earshot. 'I'm not sure I was particularly welcoming.'

'You were nice after you'd finished grilling him about his life story,' Diana said, grinning. 'I think that should've been my job.'

'As Becca reminded me. I'm her godmother. I have a responsibility.'

'What you mean is you were being nosy.'

'Yeah well, I didn't get much out of him. Only that his dad drives a London bus and his mum's a school teacher. He said he's come to stay with his aunt while he decides which university he wants to go to. As if all the ones he's applied to will offer him a place.'

'Perhaps they will. He does seem very bright.'

'He does, doesn't he? But I do think Becca and Orla may come to blows over him. You might want to keep an eye on that.'

'Yes, Mum.' Diana laughed. 'Speaking of

Mum. Have you heard from ours?'

'Nope. Either she's taken the hint, or Dad's finally strangled her and maybe even moved in with the Trollope at number 25.' I laughed – but Diana only smiled wanly. Almost as if my joke had upset her in some way.

We talked about other things. Like Elsie and Gray.

'Mikkel doesn't look very much like him, I don't think,' Diana said.

'Why would Mikkel look like Gray?' And then the penny dropped. 'No way! Are you telling me that Gray is Mikkel's dad?'

Diana nodded. 'Didn't you know? I thought Elsie would've mentioned it.'

'So would I. I wonder why she didn't?'

'Perhaps she assumed you knew. He's been staying with Mikkel since ... just after Easter. That's how Elsie met Gray. Mikkel introduced them.'

I couldn't quite get my head around that. Or the fact that Elsie hadn't told me. But perhaps Diana was right. Maybe Elsie just assumed Diana – or Mikkel – had already told me.

'What do you think I should do about Liam?' I asked, already on my fourth glass of wine and feeling a little light-headed – and emotional. Not a good combination.

Diana fiddled with the strap of her white, blue and purple, floral top.

'In what way?'

Her voice was little more than a whisper and she took several swigs of her coffee. She'd gone back to being teetotal after that one glass of wine the other day. Although I'm pretty sure she had a cocktail or three at the party, but she had only drunk water at Neptune's.

'In getting him to talk to me again.'

'Isn't he talking to you then?'

I tutted. 'Diana! I told you what happened in Seahorse Bites and how he marched off, all huffy.'

'Yes. But you haven't seen him since this morning so you don't know whether he'll talk to you or not when you see him next. Why not wait and see?'

'Oh I know. Believe me. I could see it in his eyes. He looked at me like I was a bit of flotsam. Or is it jetsam? Anyway, like some bit of old rubbish floating in the sea.'

'Flotsam and jetsam aren't necessarily rubbish. Harry Boatman had several pieces in his house that were really rather lovely. In their own way that is. And I'm sure Liam doesn't think you're either. He was probably a bit peeved, and rightly so from what you told me you'd said. I'm sure he'll get over it. Liam's not the sort to ... to hold past indiscretions against someone.'

'Past indiscretions? It was hardly that. I just said a few things he might not have liked.

But the thing is...' I grabbed the wine bottle from the ice bucket beside me and topped up my glass. '...the thing is, I sent him a text message to say I was sorry. One of those GIFs with big sad weepy eyes and a big 'I'm sorry' flashing across it, and he didn't reply.'

'Perhaps he hasn't seen it yet. Perhaps he's busy.'

'Er. I sent him another one. About an hour ago. He hasn't replied to that one either. It was a photo of a polar bear sitting by a phone waiting for a call.'

She gave me an odd look. 'You do realise Liam's a thirty-eight-year old man and not a teenage girl, don't you? Why on earth are you sending him text messages like that?'

'They're cute.'

'They don't exactly scream sincerity though. Why didn't you just send a text saying 'sorry'?'

She had a point.

'You're right. I'll send him one now.'

She tutted and shook her head. 'I'm going to make some more coffee. Would you like a cup?'

'No thanks. I've got wine.'

She got up and went into the kitchen and I sent Liam a text saying simply, 'I'm sorry, Liam. Please give me a call and let me know we're still friends.' I added several emojis, pressed send, closed my eyes and waited.

The heat – and possibly the wine – and of course the sleepless night and early start, and worrying about Elsie, must've made me drift off to sleep because the next thing I knew, there was a huge commotion and I opened my eyes to see Liam standing in the kitchen.

He'd come to reply to my text messages in person! I was elated.

Until I noticed he had Orla with him and that she was in floods of tears.

But there was no sign of Becca or of Toby.

And Noah was nowhere to be seen.

Nineteen

I jumped up from the sunbed and almost fell into the pool. My head felt woozy and my eyes were blurred. I shook my head, trying to get myself together and hurried to the kitchen.

'What's happened? What's going on? Where're Toby and Becca? Where's Noah?'

Diana was crying and dashing about; Orla was sobbing uncontrollably.

Liam looked me in the eye. 'There's been an accident.' His voice was calm and firm.

'An accident?' I shrieked. 'What kind of accident? Involving Toby and Becca? Are they hurt? Are they okay? Where are they?'

He gently took my hands in his and sat me down on one of the high stools at the breakfast bar.

'Stay calm. Becca's fine. Absolutely fine. Toby's hurt. We're not sure how badly but he was conscious when the ambulance arrived.

'Ambulance?'

I stared at Orla who nodded as if her head was on a spring.

'It's ... my ... fault,' she sobbed.

'Why? What did you do?'

'She didn't do anything,' Liam said, his voice tinged with ice. 'She's blaming herself for not keeping an eye on Toby, that's all. Toby went off with some of the boys and went tombstoning. It's unclear what happened after that. All I can get out of her is that they should've been watching Toby and now he's on his way to hospital and that some boy called Noah has taken Becca there on the back of his moped. He told Orla to come and get Diana, but she came to me, of course and I came straight here. Diana's getting a few things together for Toby and I'm taking her to the hospital.'

'I'm coming too.'

'Fine.'

I dashed outside, grabbed my sundress from the back of the sunbed and threw it on over my bikini. Diana reappeared and with a terrified look on her face, she grasped my hand.

'Tell me he'll be okay, Josie.'

'He'll be fine. He's fit and strong. He'll be okay, I'm sure of it.'

We raced outside, leaving Henry barking in the hall as if he knew something had happened to his master. Diana and I sat in the back of the car and hugged all the way to the hospital while Orla sat in the front and cried. Liam didn't say a word, just looked ahead, his jaw clenched, his knuckles turning white as he clasped the steering wheel tightly.

I couldn't understand what had happened. What had Orla meant when she'd said it was her fault they weren't watching Toby? Who? Her and Becca? Where was Noah? Was he the one who'd egged Toby on to do it.? To tombstone off Seahorse Point. Something Toby knew he should never do.

'Orla?' I said in a soft voice. 'Orla, sweetie. Can you tell us what happened?'

Liam turned and glared at me for an instant but he didn't speak. Gradually, Orla's sobs subsided and she swiped at the tears streaming from her eyes. Her shoulders shook as she spoke and I could hardly hear her.

'Sorry, sweetie. I didn't hear you.'

'She said it was the other boys,' Liam snapped.

I shot him an angry look but then realised he was as anxious as the rest of us, so I mellowed.

'Thank you. Um. What other boys, Orla? The ones who were at the barbecue?'

Orla nodded.

'They persuaded Toby to tombstone?'

Diana let out a strangled sob and gripped my hand tight. Orla nodded again.

'Was Noah with them?'

'N-no. H-he was w-with us.'

'You and Becca?'

She nodded.

'What happened then? Toby obviously jumped but what happened after that?'

'Take your time, sweetheart,' Liam said gently. 'This isn't your fault. No one's cross with you.'

He glanced at me in the rear-view mirror and his expression told me to take it easy with his daughter. I thought I was. Frankly, I just wanted to shake her and get her to tell me what happened, but I knew that was wrong and wouldn't solve anything.

'Th-they dared him to j-jump. Th-they called him a s-sissy because he said he wouldn't. Th-then they took his ph-phone and refused to g-give it back unless he did. N-Noah was on the w-water with Becca and I d-didn't think Toby w-would do it. I swam out to B-Becca and Noah and t-told Noah wh-what was happening. Th-then we saw Toby on top of the P-Point. And he j-jumped.' She let out a kind of half yelp, half scream, as if she were picturing him leaping off Seahorse Point.

'It's okay, sweetheart.' Liam reached out and hugged her with one arm before returning his hand to the wheel.

'Did he hit the rocks?' Diana asked in a strangely cool tone, but her grip on my hand was getting even tighter.

'N-no. He hit the water h-hard and got swept onto th-them.'

Diana shrieked and pain shot through my hand.

'Jesus,' Liam said. 'Perhaps we should leave this until we find out how he is. We're almost there.'

'I need to know,' Diana said. 'Did he ... did he ... Did anyone get to him ... in time?'

Orla nodded.

'Yes,' I said. 'Liam said Orla told him Toby was conscious when the ambulance arrived.'

'Oh. Of course. Yes. I forgot. Thank God. I ... I ... oh God. My poor baby. I'm going to kill those boys when I get my hands on them.'

'The rip c-current caught him,' Orla continued, clearly now needing to tell the whole story.

And it seemed I was completely wrong about Noah.

Far from being in any way involved in the tombstoning, Noah was livid. He saw Toby jump and, telling Becca and Orla to swim back to shore, he paddled his hired board as fast as he could over to the rocks at the foot of Seahorse Point, dived in, and after getting thrown against the rocks himself once or twice, he rescued Toby. He somehow managed to drag Toby onto the board that had also been bashed against the rocks a couple of times by the current. Then he paddled away from the inlet, gave Toby the kiss of life while on the board and then, standing astride Toby so that

Toby couldn't slip off, Noah paddled to the shore. Becca had had the good sense to phone for an ambulance and Noah performed more CPR on Toby, who thanks to Noah, came round before the ambulance arrived.

Noah dashed off to get his moped while the paramedics did their thing, although they told Orla and Becca that Noah had already done most of their job for them. They put Toby on a stretcher and just as they were about to drive off, Noah returned. He told Orla to come and get Diana and he took Becca to the hospital because she was screaming and crying that she had to be with Toby.

'Whoever this Noah is,' Liam said, once Orla had told us everything, 'he's a pretty smart kid. And I think Toby probably owes him his life. It sounds to me as if Toby's definitely going to be okay. Noah acted quickly and that makes all the difference in a situation like this.'

'Noah was brilliant,' Orla said, having finally stopped sobbing. 'Everyone on the beach was clapping him as he rode off behind the ambulance with Becca.'

Diana was still a little frantic with worry but hearing that Noah got to Toby so fast had clearly helped ease her fears. It had definitely helped ease mine. The next time I saw Noah, I'd make sure he knew how grateful to him we all were.

It seemed I'd been completely wrong about

Noah. He wasn't trouble at all. He was anything but trouble. He was Toby's guardian angel.

A few minutes later, when we arrived at Easterhill Hospital, Diana's phone rang as she got out of the car. I assumed it must be Alex and I heard her say, 'I realise you're worried. I'm terrified. I'll call you as soon as I know.' She rang off and we all hurried into the hospital. Becca and Noah were sitting in the waiting room and a doctor was talking to them.

'I'm Toby's mother,' Diana yelled, dashing towards them.

'Mum!' Becca shrieked. 'Toby's going to be fine. He's going to be fine. The doctor just told us so.'

The doctor waited until Becca and Diana had hugged.

'As I was telling your daughter, Toby's going to be fine. Just very badly bruised, and he'll need a few days in bed to recover. But he's a very lucky boy. We're keeping him in for observation for a day or two, and we'll see how he is after that. I'm confident you'll be able to take him home by the middle of the week. We'll send him for x-rays just to be sure there're no breaks or fractures we're not aware of and as he had a nasty fall and lost consciousness for a minute or two, we simply want to keep him with us for a short time.'

'But you're sure he's okay?'

The doctor nodded sagely. 'As sure as we

can be. Yes.'

'Thank you so much, doctor. May I see him?'

'Of course. But don't stay too long. He needs to get some rest. We've given him some painkillers so don't worry if he starts to get sleepy. I'll get a nurse to take you to him, if you'll just wait here for a few minutes.'

'Yes, yes. Of course.'

The doctor smiled and walked away and Diana hugged Becca again.

'Was Dad really angry?' Becca asked, her voice as shaky as her hands still were, despite hearing Toby was going to be fine.

Diana shot a look at me and gave a small cough as she stroked Becca's hair.

'I haven't told your father yet, sweetheart. You're right, he will be angry and that won't help Toby right now, will it? Unless the x-rays show any breaks or fractures, let's keep this to ourselves for now, at least until Toby's feeling better. Your father's so busy at the moment and there's no point in him rushing down here and giving Toby a lecture, is there?'

'No. I agree. It would upset Toby even more.'

Diana glanced at all of us. 'I know that may seem strange, but the doctor did say Toby will be fine. And Alex will be so cross because he's told Toby never to tombstone off Seahorse Point. It's asking a lot, I realise, but if we could keep this ... incident to ourselves for now, it would mean so much to me. And to Toby and to Becca.'

'I won't be telling anyone,' I said.

Liam looked uncertain but he shook his head and placed his arm around Orla's shoulder.

'Neither will we. We'll keep this to ourselves, won't we, sweetheart?'

Orla smiled. 'Of course. I'd never do anything to hurt my friends.'

That seemed an odd comment, but I didn't think any more of it.

Diana hugged all of us in turn, including Noah, but when she pulled him into her arms, she hugged him really tight.

'I don't know how to thank you enough,' she said, tears rolling down her face.

Noah blushed and looked embarrassed. He also looked as if he couldn't breathe and he didn't seem to know what to do with his hands. Finally, he placed them on Diana's shoulders and eased her away.

'No need to thank me. I didn't do much.'

'Only saved my brother's life,' Becca said, wide-eyed and tearful.

Noah shrugged and looked extremely uncomfortable when Diana nodded and hugged him again.

'Er. Thanks. But I only did what anyone would.'

Liam smiled at him. 'You're a hero in all our eyes, Noah. You're going to have to get used to that.'

Noah shrugged again – as much as he could with Diana holding him so tight. She let him go when the nurse appeared, but as she followed the nurse she turned back to Noah and beamed at him.

'If there's anything I can do to repay you for what you did, please tell me, Noah. Anything. I mean it. If there's anything you need, or want, just say the word and it's yours.'

He gave her an awkward smile and glanced at Becca from beneath his long dark lashes.

'Thanks,' he said. 'But I don't need anything. And I've got everything I want, I think.'

From the look Becca was giving him, I think he was probably right. If what he wanted was Becca, that is.

And then I saw Orla from the corner of my eye, and it was clear from her expression that she wasn't very happy.

Twenty

Someone had to look after Henry while Toby was in hospital, and also, once he was home. Until Toby was able to get out of bed and take the mad mutt for the numerous walks Henry seemed to require, someone else had to do it. Somehow, and please don't ask me how because I honestly have no idea, that someone turned out to be me.

I suppose I was the obvious choice – the only choice really. Diana was to-ing and fro-ing from the hospital for the first two days. And Becca was ... I'm not really sure what Becca was doing other than going to visit Toby at least twice a day. I know she spent some time with Orla because I saw them giggling together on the Tuesday, but the giggling didn't seem quite as, well, giggly as it had been and I heard Orla snap at Becca once or twice.

'You're only fifteen, Becca,' Orla said, 'What do you know about anything?'

And on the Wednesday, when I told Becca that Noah was pulling up outside the house, just as Orla was going home for lunch, Orla turned to Becca and said in an accusatory manner, 'I thought you said you were going to the hospital with your mum to collect Toby? There was no need to lie to me.'

Becca looked stunned. 'I am going to the hospital with Mum. I didn't lie.'

'Oh? Then what's Noah doing here?'

'I don't know,' Becca said, clearly feeling defensive and a little hurt. 'Why don't you ask him?'

'I will,' she said.

And she did.

She opened the front door before he had a chance to ring the bell.

'Oh hello, Noah. This is a surprise. Is Becca expecting you?'

I could see from where I was standing, trying to clip the lead onto Henry's collar even though he thought it was a chew toy and kept trying to catch it in his large and slobbery mouth, that Noah was surprised to see Orla.

'Oh. Hi Orla. Er. No. She's not. Is she in? And how are you?'

'I'm fine. Better than fine, in fact. Of course she's in. You know she is.'

'Er. I didn't. I just came by on the off chance.'

I'd had enough of Orla.

'Come in, Noah,' I said. 'Becca's just there, in the kitchen.'

Orla glared at me and Noah squeezed past her without her moving out of his path. He gave her an odd look and then a pleasant smile and Orla sort of curled her lip.

'Hi Becca,' he said. 'How are you? I hope it's okay for me to drop round.'

'Of course it is. But Mum and I are going to get Toby from the hospital so I don't have long. Sorry. We're picking him up at 3 and Mum wants to buy him a present on the way.'

'That's okay. I just wanted to give you this.'

He held something out to Becca and both Orla and I strained to see what it was. It looked like a mobile phone.

Becca's face was a picture. She beamed at him, but it was more than that. She looked as if she wanted to throw herself into his arms, but she didn't. Perhaps because she knew Orla and I were watching.

'Toby's phone!' she exclaimed. 'You got back Toby's phone. Look Orla. Look Josie. Noah's got back Toby's phone.'

I glanced at Orla and she glanced at me. We were both impressed and I could see Orla's bad mood drift away.

'But how?' Becca continued. 'Mum wanted to report it to the police, but Toby wouldn't let her and said the boys had given it back to him and he must've lost it in the water when he jumped.'

'Yeah. I don't think Toby wanted to cause

any trouble. He probably thought the kids were just messing with him. I had a pretty good idea who'd taken it. They're staying at the holiday park. I went and had a word on Sunday, but they denied having it. I said I'd give them time to think, and when I went and had another chat with them last night, they gave it back to me. Sorry I couldn't get here sooner, but my aunt's got me a part-time, summer job as a lifeguard at the Lido, and this is my lunch break. Tell Toby the kids said they're sorry and it won't happen again. He doesn't have anything to worry about. Okay?'

'Okay. Will do. Oh, Noah. This is so great. Toby loves this phone. Mum said she'd get him a new one but he'll be so happy to have this one back. Wait. Did you say you're working at the Lido? As a lifeguard? That's brilliant. Well done.'

'Congratulations,' Orla said. 'That's fantastic.'

'Yes it is,' I agreed.

Noah shrugged. 'Yeah. Thanks. I've got all my first aid training and stuff. And it seems word's got out about me helping Toby, so they offered me the job. It's a bit of extra money and another thing I can put on my C.V. Not rocket science, but better than 'dossed around all summer'. Mum and Dad are happy, so it's all good. But it does mean I won't have as much time to hang out with you ... and Orla.'

I had definitely misjudged him. Not only was he humble ("helping Toby", not "saving Toby") he was sensible and had a good work ethos. He was also diplomatic enough to have included Orla, when what he was obviously saying was that he couldn't hang out with Becca as much. I liked him more each time I saw him.

'Never mind,' Orla said. 'I'm sure Becca and I will be spending quite a lot of time at the Lido.'

'Definitely,' Becca said, blushing.

Diana came downstairs. 'I thought I heard your voice, Noah. It's lovely to see you again. We're just off to get Toby. How are you?'

'I'm good thanks, Mrs Dunn.'

'Please, Noah. Call me Diana.'

'Look, Mum.' Becca held up Toby's phone. 'Noah got Toby's phone back. Toby didn't drop it in the sea. Those kids–'

'Found it,' Noah said. 'Some kids who're staying at the holiday park found it.'

'Oh, that's wonderful news. Toby will be so pleased. Thank you, Noah. It was so good of you to bring it to us. I think that deserves a reward. Where did I put my handbag?'

'No! I mean, no thank you, Mrs ... Diana. I don't want a reward. I didn't do anything.'

'Oh. Er. Well, what about the boys then? Perhaps something for them for handing it in?'

'No, Diana.' His voice wasn't quite so sharp this time but it was firm. 'The last thing they'd expect is a reward. If you want to thank someone, thank the Universe, and put a couple of quid in a charity box, for animals, or kids, or something.'

'I'll do that, Noah. That's a lovely thought. Your parents and your aunt must be very proud of you. But we must be off. Mustn't keep Toby waiting. He's chomping at the bit to get home and see Henry.'

'And I'd better get back to work,' Noah said. 'See you soon, I hope.' He smiled at Becca.

'Would you drop me at my place, Noah?' Orla asked, smiling sweetly. 'It's so hot again today and I'm not sure I can make it down the hill without collapsing from the heat.'

'Er...'

He glanced at Becca but before he could answer I said, 'Diana and Becca can drop you off, Orla. There's air conditioning in Diana's car so you won't be as hot as you would be on the back of a moped.'

'Of course we'll drop you,' Diana said. 'Come along.' She smiled at me, at Henry and the lead he was chewing. 'You'll be fine until we get back?'

It was a question and I laughed. 'I'm sure we'll survive. I've almost got this dog walking lark cracked.'

'Yes. I can see that.' She raised one perfect brow. 'There're several other leads in the utility room if Henry eats through that one.'

Twenty-One

It was a beautiful afternoon but very hot and humid and it felt as if there was a storm brewing. In more ways than one.

I intended to take Henry for a very long walk. I needed to tire him out. Diana said the last thing she wanted was an excited dog jumping all over Toby on his first day home from hospital. We'd agreed that I wouldn't bring Henry home until after 6 that evening so that Toby could get bathed and tucked up in bed before being reunited with his beloved dog.

I walked through Little Wood, which due to the canopy of trees, was slightly cooler, and quite eerie in one or two places. The paths were mainly earth but a couple were manmade and easier to walk on without tripping over a half-hidden tree root, or having your foot tip into a hole dug by a squirrel, a fox, a badger, or some other wild creature.

Trees of Oak, Ash, Elm, Copper Beech and Silver Birch sung a mellow tune as they swayed gently in the growing breeze and leaves of various shapes, sizes and colours rustled like millions of maracas.

We stayed there for some time; me throwing sticks for Henry and him bounding off in every direction but the one the stick had gone in. He really wasn't a very smart dog. But he seemed to be having fun, even if I was getting arm ache. You really needed to be fit to own a dog like him.

Although he didn't bring back any of the sticks I'd thrown, he did bring me some other very interesting finds. A single wellington boot; a sun hat; a broken and twisted umbrella, the spokes of which nearly had my eye out, let alone Henry's; and an unopened tin of baked beans. I'm not sure how an unopened tin of beans had got into Little Wood, but the other things seemed reasonable finds. But how someone could lose one boot and not notice was a bit of a mystery.

We left the woods via one of the many footpaths and came out almost opposite the church. I sat on the bench beneath the ancient Oak and Henry flopped across my feet, covering my pale blue pumps in dusty, dried earth, accumulated on his long coat, no doubt from the woods. I hitched up the navy-blue skirt of my dress just an inch or two so that my legs could catch the sun. It was just gone 5 and as puffy pale grey clouds were beginning to appear in the distance, it seemed the sun might not be out for that much longer, even though it would be at least 8.45 until it officially set.

I closed my eyes and leant against the bench, my arms stretched out along the top of it, my head hanging back as far as it would go, remembering the last time I'd sat there. Henry barked softly and then louder, as if greeting someone and when I opened my eyes and righted my head, I spotted Liam striding into The Olde Forge. I got the strangest feeling he'd been watching me for a moment or two.

But he hadn't come to say hello.

He hadn't even acknowledged me.

My phone rang and I saw Medusa and the snakes. I wasn't in the mood to talk to Mum, so I let it go to voicemail. But an idea suddenly sprang into my head and with a smile on my face, and a spring in my step, I made my way to Fulbright Ceramics.

I didn't want to risk taking Henry inside, so when I spotted an old iron hook embedded in the side wall of the building, it seemed the perfect place to leave him. Being on the northern side, it was in the shade and I noticed there was a large bowl of water nearby. I tied his lead to the hook, moved the bowl over towards him and he was happily slopping water everywhere when I walked around the front and went inside the old stone building.

Liam was about to sit at his potter's wheel but he glanced up when he heard me walk in.

Our eyes met and for a second or two neither of us spoke. He was the first to look away. He gave a little cough, ran a hand through his hair and promptly turned his back on me.

'Is that how it's going to be then, Liam? You refusing to speak to me unless you absolutely have to.'

He turned to face me and there was a lump of wet clay in his hand. I wondered if he planned to throw it at me but instead, he slapped it onto the flat wheel.

'I haven't refused to speak to you.'

'You didn't though. No, "Hello, Josie." You just turned your back on me.'

'I didn't hear a hello from you either. And I wasn't turning my back on you. I was getting a piece of clay so that I could get back to work.'

He had a point. I hadn't said hello.

'Let's start again. Hello, Liam. How are you?'

He looked me in the eye and then looked away, glancing along rows of shelves all containing various pots which in turn held a number of different tools. He took out a long, thin wooden one that looked a bit like a crochet hook. I remember seeing one of Mum's.

'Hello, Josie. I'm fine thanks. How's Toby?' His voice was devoid of emotion.

'Toby's good. He's coming home today. In fact, he's probably there right now. And I'm fine too thanks. Not that you asked.'

'Where's Henry?'

'Henry?' I tapped my chin. 'I know that name. Hmm. Let me think.'

'You had him with you just now.'

'Aha! I knew it.'

He gave me the oddest look as I pointed my finger at him. He had been watching me, or at least he'd seen me, but perhaps playing Miss Marple wasn't the way to go.

'What?' He frowned at me.

I waved my hand in the air. 'Nothing. Henry's tied up outside throwing water around and no doubt getting it everywhere apart from in his mouth.'

A twitch appeared at the side of Liam's mouth but it vanished almost immediately.

'Do you want something? Or have you just come in for ... a browse around?'

'I want something. I want something very much indeed.'

He gave me another odd look. 'What, exactly?'

'I want...' I walked slowly towards him, running my fingers along the edge of the central, display tables, glancing from side to side until I got within about two feet of him. 'A bowl.'

He cleared his throat. 'A bowl? What type of bowl? As you can see, I have several.'

'And they're all gorgeous. But I want a particular bowl. Wait.' I rummaged in my shoulder bag and pulled out my phone and my purse, placing them on the table to my side. I took out a packet of white tissues, another packet of tissues, this time with a Christmassy image. They'd obviously been in there a while, and I yanked out my make-up bag and added those to the table, moving one of Liam's beautiful bowls just a fraction to make room. I piled my notepad and a pen, a fold-up shopping bag and a scarf on top of those. 'It's here. I know it is. Give me just a second.' I tugged out several chocolate bar wrappers and smiled sheepishly at him. 'Toby must've put those in here. Hold on. I'll find it soon.'

'Would you like me to clear another table?' he asked.

'Funny.' I took out a second make-up bag, a mini sewing kit and a bottle of bright red nail varnish. 'Oh. I've been looking for that.'

He burst out laughing. 'How can you find anything in that bag?'

'There's a method.'

'So I see. It seems to involve emptying the entire contents onto my display table.'

'Ta dah!' I waved a somewhat worse-for-wear photo in front of his face. 'You see. I told you I'd find it. Hold onto it will you while I shove this lot back.'

'I think there's a heavy loader at the DIY store. Want me to get that for you?'

'Ha ha. You're so droll.' I opened my bag

wide and slid everything back in off the table. Then, grinning up at him, I pretended to slide one of the gorgeous, massive bowls into my bag as well.

'Nice try,' he said, laughing. 'May I?' He held the photo up.

'Yes. That's what I want.'

He studied it. 'Er. A kitchen table and four chairs? I'm a potter, not a cabinet-maker.'

I tutted loudly. 'Not the table and chairs. That.' I moved closer and pointed to the centre of the photo.

He squinted at it. 'The bowl?'

'Yep.'

'The one that's barely visible.'

'You can see it clearly.'

'If I had X-ray vision, perhaps. It's half hidden behind ... what is that? A pile of rubbish? Wait. Don't tell me. You'd been clearing out your handbag.' He laughed at his own joke.

'You're such a wheeze. That, I'll have you know, is Mount Vesuvius.'

He looked across at me and back at the photo, laughing a bit more.

'It's not. It's nothing like Mount Vesuvius.'

'It is. And it's exactly like Mount Vesuvius. It's so much like Mount Vesuvius that Mount Vesuvius thinks it's got a twin.'

'I take it from your strong defence that you made this Mount Vesuvius.'

'I did. And it would've won first prize in the 'Famous Mountains of the World' Art project ... if I hadn't dropped it on my way to school. Dad said it was the best Mount Vesuvius he had ever seen.'

'Your dad didn't get out much then? Sorry. I'm teasing. It's a fabulous Mount Vesuvius. I can see that now.'

'Thank you. I'll make you one for Christmas. So can you do it?'

'Can I do what?'

'Make the bowl.'

'This bowl?'

I tutted. 'Now you're just being silly. Yes. That. Bowl. And it has to be exact. It was porcelain. Can you make porcelain stuff?'

'I can.'

'Excellent. It had blue scrolls all around this large rim. See. This rim here.' I moved closer and stood half in front of him, half beside him, leaning in as far as I could so that we could both see the photo. 'And right there. See those little red flowers?'

He gave a small cough. 'I do.'

'They're geraniums. Or pelargoniums. Or something ending in 'niums'. Anyway. Those things there are olives. And that's an olive tree. The colours have to be just like these. Only not as faded.'

'Brighter, you mean?'

'Precisely. And I think there was

something else...'

I edged closer and my left breast brushed against the back of his hand, the only obstacle between us being the thin cotton of my blouse and my lace bra. An odd sensation shot through me and I raised my gaze to his. His gaze was smouldering and I felt my lips part.

'Hey Mr Fulbright,' a young voice said. 'Sorry to interrupt, but d'you know where Orla is?'

I quickly moved away from Liam and he cleared his throat again, ran a hand through his hair and smiled at the teenage boy standing in the doorway.

'Hi Darren. Er. No I don't. She told me earlier that she was going to the beach. Everything okay?'

Darren gave us a strange look and then smiled. 'Yeah. I just went by your house and thought I'd see if she was around, but she wasn't. I'll head down to the beach and see if she's down there.'

'Okay. If you see her, Darren, please remind her not to be late home for tea.'

'Will do. Carry on.' Darren grinned and closed the door.

Cheeky bugger. I don't know what he thought we were doing but I did know that I needed a drink of water. No. I needed a drink. A proper drink.

Liam grinned. 'I think you were saying

there was something else.'

'Yes. But I can't remember what it is right now. It'll come back to me. Or Diana might remember. So can you do it?'

'Yes. I think so. I'm sure I can. What about size?'

'It was about twelve inches across, I think. And about four inches deep.'

'And it was a fruit bowl?'

'Yes. It was Mum's favourite bowl.'

'What happened to it?'

'I broke it one Halloween, trying to fly off that kitchen table on my broomstick.'

'As one does,' Liam said, grinning at me again.

'Liam?'

'Yes.'

'I probably shouldn't say anything, but I think there's something you should know.'

'Oh?' he seemed nervous again. 'What's that?'

'It's about Orla.'

He stiffened. 'What about her?'

'I think she's a little in love with Noah.'

He laughed. 'I know. I think she's got a crush on him.'

'I think it's more than a crush, Liam. And I don't think it's going to end well for her.'

'What does that mean?'

'Don't get cross.'

'I'm not. What do you mean, it's not going

to end well for her?'

'Don't be defensive. I just mean that Noah doesn't feel the same way about her.'

'Really? And you know this how?'

'Because I've seen the way he looks at Becca and the way he looks at Orla, and believe me, he sees Orla as a friend but he sees Becca as a whole lot more.'

'Becca? Well, I suppose you would take her side as she's your niece.'

'Side? This isn't about taking sides, Liam. It's obvious that Noah wants to be with Becca. And Orla doesn't like that. She doesn't like that one bit.'

'What, exactly, are you saying?'

'I'm saying that Orla's getting jealous, and today, when Noah came to the house to see Becca just as Orla was leaving, Orla had a bit of a ... strop.'

'A strop? My daughter had a strop? Seriously?'

'Yes. She accused Becca of lying to her. And she questioned Noah on the doorstep as to what he was doing there. She's jealous, Liam, and it's going to get worse unless—'

'Unless what?'

'Unless someone has a word with her.'

'Thanks. So now you're saying I don't know my own daughter.'

'No. I'm not saying that.'

'You just told me that she was bitchy

towards Becca. That's not the Orla I know. But then I've only known her for sixteen years whereas you've known her for ... how long? Ah yes. About a week.'

'Hey. There's no need to be like that about it. I told you because I ... because when you're a sixteen-year-old girl in love and the guy you love chooses someone else, it cuts you in two. It breaks your heart so badly that you think it'll never heal. Just seeing him or hearing his name is like falling off a cliff onto jagged rocks, over and over again. And you go a little bit mad doing anything and everything you can to try to force yourself to get over him. But nothing works. Nothing. Do you want Orla to be like that? Do you? I'm not saying she will but personally, I wouldn't take that chance. I'd talk to her about it now. Try to make her see right now that it's not meant to be. Before she gets in any deeper.'

'That ... that sounds as if you're talking from experience. But you've never been in love, Josie, and you never wanted to be. You always made that very clear to everyone. But Orla's not like that girl you've just described. Orla's sensible.'

'Is she, Liam? She's a lovely girl and I'm sure she's very bright and clever and sensible, usually. But is anyone sensible when it comes to love? I can guarantee where Orla is right now. Right this minute. And it isn't on the beach.'

'Really? So what you're now saying is that my daughter is lying to me?'

'I didn't mean it like that. But if she told you she was going to the beach, then yes, she is. Because she's not at the beach. She's at the Lido. And she's been there since early this afternoon. Where Noah just happens to be working as a lifeguard. And when Orla knows that Becca is at the hospital collecting Toby. Orla's heading for a fall, Liam. I'm telling you this for everyone's good. How far she falls depends on what happens now. If you don't believe me, go to the Lido and see for yourself. I bet you anything you like, she'll be all over Noah like a rash.'

'For someone who doesn't have kids and hardly ever sees her niece and nephew, you suddenly think you're an expert? You're wrong about Orla. And I think it's probably best if you leave the parenting to those of us who are parents.'

'I may not know anything about parenting, but I know a whole lot about being a sixteen-year-old girl who's madly in love.'

I slung my bag on my shoulder, snatched the faded photo from his fingers and stormed out of Fulbright Ceramics.

His harsh words had hurt me.

But on reflection, he was probably right.

Even if he was wrong about his daughter.

Twenty-Two

I'd been calling in to see Elsie every day, especially since the break in. Gray was staying with her so I wasn't overly concerned, but I still wanted to see for myself that she was okay and hadn't suffered any lasting consequences. I needn't have worried. Elsie was back to her usual self by the very next day.

I'd called in to see her on Monday morning to tell her I'd spotted a police car driving around, so they were clearly doing their job. I popped in again in the evening to tell her about Toby's accident before she heard it from anyone else and I'd regaled her with Noah's heroic rescue and admitted how wrong I'd been about him.

I also told her that Diana said she hadn't told Alex, which we both agreed was strange, especially as I was sure I'd heard Diana on the phone to him when we'd arrived at the hospital.

I'd had coffee with Elsie on Tuesday morning, and she said the police had been round to say there had been no more incidents but they were still patrolling the area and had asked people to report anything suspicious. They were clearly no closer to solving the cases but at least they were keeping them open.

When I visited her after leaving Fulbright Ceramics, I wasn't in the best of moods.

Gray opened the door and let me in, with his usual cheery greeting.

'Hello, Josie. You're looking lovely. Elsie's in the garden, catching the last of the sun.'

'Thanks,' I replied, as he stepped aside to let me pass.

'I was just about to pop out,' he said, following me towards the garden where I could see Elsie sitting beneath the grape vine. 'I hope you don't think I'm being rude, but I promised Mikkel I'd call in to say hello.'

'Of course not.' I stepped onto the patio. 'You couldn't be rude if you tried. Unlike someone else I could mention.'

'Ah. Then I think this is probably perfect timing. Shall I make you a pot of tea before I go? Or there's Elsie's elderflower cordial in that jug on the garden table.'

'Thanks, Gray. I'll have the cordial.'

He turned to a cupboard and handed me a glass. 'Bye for now then. Bye, Elsie.' He gave her a wave and blew her a kiss which she pretended to catch in her hand and then held it to her heart.

I walked across the grass, put my glass on

the table and gave her a kiss on the cheek.

'I see you and Gray are getting along rather well.' I poured myself some cordial and smiled as I sat opposite her.

'He's such a dear man.' She glanced towards the kitchen even though he'd already left. 'Did I hear you say someone was being rude to you?'

I took a swig of cordial and my eyes shot open in surprise.

'I thought this was elderflower cordial!'

'It is,' Elsie said, grinning. '*My* elderflower cordial, which as you should know by now, contains an equal measure of gin. It's rather refreshing at the end of a hot summer day.'

I puffed out a breath and laughed. 'It certainly is.'

'So, honeybee. Tell me who's been rude to you.'

I sighed and shook my head. 'Liam. But I suppose he wasn't really being rude. He was defending Orla. And that's completely understandable because he adores her and he is her dad, after all. But he makes me so mad. And he never takes me seriously.'

Elsie leant forward and tapped me on my knee. 'Let's start from the beginning, shall we?'

I told her about Noah getting Toby's phone back and bringing it to the house.

'He's such a nice boy, isn't he?'

'Yeah. I was completely wrong about him.'

I told her about Orla's reaction and about the comments and that I thought there might be trouble.

'It certainly sounds as if there might.'

'I know, right? But when I told Liam and mentioned that he might like to have a word with her about her behaviour and about Noah, he nearly bit my head off and he told me I know nothing about being a parent and I should mind my own business and leave his daughter alone. Or something along those lines.'

'Ah. He's bound to feel protective of her.'

'I understand that. Especially as Una's no longer around.'

'Yes, well, that may be part of the problem. I wouldn't take what he said to heart, honeybee. It'll be forgotten in a couple of days.'

I took another swig of my drink. 'I wouldn't count on that. After the café incident, when he overheard what I said to Rhoda, he's clearly been avoiding me.' I'd told Elsie all about Sunday's embarrassing episode, when I'd visited her on Monday. 'Then today, we were getting on again really well until I mentioned Orla.'

'How did you leave things?'

'I told him I may not know much about parenting but I knew a lot about being a sixteen-year-old girl in love.'

'Oh my. And what did he say to that?'

'Nothing. I stormed out. Which I know

wasn't very mature, but I was cross. I'll show him one day. You mark my words. I can be grown up and responsible. I'll ... Holy crap!' I leapt to my feet, slopping the cordial all over my hand.

'What's wrong, honeybee?'

'I've forgotten Henry! I left him tied to a hook at the side of The Olde Forge.' I raced towards the kitchen and the front door. 'I'll see you later, Elsie. Bloody Liam was damn well right about me, after all.'

Twenty-Three

I was panting by the time I reached The Olde Forge. The air was heavy and sticky and the sun popping in and out between the clouds was making sweat trickle down my neck and back. The clock on the church chimed 6 as I ran to the side of the building. But to my horror, Henry wasn't there. Just half of his lead, swinging to and fro in the hot and humid breeze, like a pendulum.

I frantically looked from left to right, up the hill and down. I checked the lead. It had snapped, it hadn't been cut, so it looked as if Henry had tugged against it and made it break, probably trying to follow me earlier as I'd marched down the hill without him.

Oh God. Liam had definitely been right.

I was a terrible daughter, sister and aunt. I knew nothing about being a parent. I couldn't even take care of a dog!

'Henry!' I shrieked at the top of my voice. 'Henry. Where are you, boy?'

I ran round the front just as Liam was

coming out.

'What's...? Josie? What's going on? Was that you–?'

'I've lost Henry! Don't say I told you so. You were right. I get that. I'm hopeless. But save the rebukes for later. Just help me find him, please! Please!'

'Of course I'll help you. And I wasn't going to say ... but that doesn't matter. How did you lose him? Where was he when you last saw him?'

I grabbed Liam's arm and dragged him to the side of the building, pointing to the hook and the lead swinging from it.

'You left him tied up here? But ... you left here twenty minutes ago.'

'I know. All right! I forgot about him. I was so cross with you that I stormed off and completely forgot about Henry. I'm a terrible person. Oh God. What if he's been run over? What if someone's taken him?'

'Let's not think about that. He's probably made his way home.'

'I don't think he's that bright.'

'Let's call Diana and see if he's there?'

'She's at the hospital collecting Toby.'

'That was ages ago. She'll be back by now. Call her.'

I did as he said.

'Di? Is ... is Henry there?'

'Hi Josie. What? Henry? No. He's with you.

Oh. He's clearly not with you, is he?'

'No. I'm so, so sorry, but he's not. I ... I've lost him.'

'How can you have lost him? Wasn't he on his lead?'

'Yes. But I'd left him tied up while I went to see Liam and when I came out ... well, when I remembered I'd left him and came to get him, he was gone.'

'Remembered? What does that mean?'

'It means I forgot I had him with me. You can give me the third degree and shout at me later. But for now the important thing is we need to find him.'

'Of course we do. But he won't have gone far. He may seem like a wild beast at times but he's just a little softie. He'll find his way home.'

'Will he? Are you sure? He ... he doesn't seem that clever to me.'

'That's because you don't know him. He's got a good sense of smell and he's part blood hound, so he'll definitely find his way home.'

'Which part? If it's his tail, that won't help him much.'

Why was I making jokes at a time like this?

'He'll be fine, Josie. How long is it since you saw him? Five minutes?'

'Er. More like twenty-five.'

'Twenty-five? Oh goodness. Then he should've been home by now. Becca, sweetheart, go and look outside will you and see if you can see Henry. Don't look at me like that. Just do it will you, please? Josie? Becca's looking out the front. I'm going to look out in the garden. Where are you?'

'I'm outside Liam's pottery. I'll ... I'll go back to Elsie's. He may, by some miracle, have gone there if you genuinely think he can follow scents. Call me if he comes home. I'm really sorry.' I could hear Toby asking what was going on and why they were looking for Henry. I didn't want to see his face if I had to tell him that ... that ... 'And please tell Toby not to worry. I'll find Henry if it takes all night.'

'Call me if you find him. He's not in the garden. I'll call around and see if anyone's seen him. They all know him in the village.'

Diana rang off and I stared up at Liam.

'I've got to find him, Liam. I'll never forgive myself if—'

'We'll find him, Josie. You go to Elsie's and I'll head to the beach and see if he's gone down there. Toby often takes him there so he might've gone there to look for Toby. Ask anyone you meet on the way if they've seen him.'

'I will. Diana said everyone knows him.'

'They do. And they'll all help look for him so don't worry, okay? He'll be home safe and sound before you know it.'

But he wasn't.

Henry was nowhere to be seen and despite

almost everyone in the village, searching everywhere for him, after two hours, we still hadn't found him. Asher checked missing animal websites, phoned local animal charities and rescue centres, and searched anywhere else he could think of, but all to no avail.

Liam went as far as Seahorse Harbour Holiday Park but there was no sign of Henry. Or of Noah, he told me later, but he had found his daughter there.

The sun hadn't yet set, but it had been obscured by rain clouds long ago. Distant rumbles of thunder warned a storm was on the way. I didn't know much about Henry but I knew he hated storms. He was scared half to death by them. He'd go and hide under Toby's bed unless Toby held onto him and hugged him tight. Only then did Henry feel safe, but even then, he'd hide his giant head in the crook of Toby's arm or under Toby's jumper. I'd seen all the photos on Toby's Instagram and Facebook pages.

Without Toby nearby, Henry would be terrified. He was out there, somewhere, probably shaking with fear. Or worse. Something far worse could've happened to him.

And all because I hadn't looked after him as a responsible adult would have.

Twenty-Four

All I could think about was finding Henry. He was missing because of me. I was the one who had left him tied to a hook. Did he think he'd been abandoned? That's what some despicable people did to their pets when they no longer wanted them. Is that what Henry had thought I'd done? Dumped him tied to a hook. He could be going through all sorts of hell right now. And all because of me. All because I'd been arguing with Liam.

Heavy dark clouds rolled in across the sea and the thunder rumbled closer, deep and threatening. I spotted someone I hadn't seen before and I ran to her and asked her if she'd seen Henry, showing her the photo that Diana had messaged me. A photo of Henry sitting tall and proud giving a sideways look of adoration to Toby, who stood beside him, their eyes at the same level.

'Aww. What a gorgeous photo,' she said. 'They clearly adore each other.'

'They do. But have you seen him?'

'The boy or the dog?'

'The dog. Have you seen the dog?'

'Yes. Such a funny thing. All flapping ears, lolling tongue and a tail that was whipping from side to side.'

'That's him! When? When did you see him? And where?'

'Oh goodness me. I'm really not sure.'

'But today? You've seen him today? This evening? Sometime between 6 and now?'

'Yes. It must've been about, oh goodness, yes, about two hours ago. I was on my way home from Beach Bakers. I'd spent the day in Easterhill, having lunch with my cousin and I'd caught the last bus back. I'd just managed to get a baguette before they closed.'

'That's wonderful but where did you see Henry?'

'Who's Henry?'

If she'd still had that baguette with her, I'd have hit her over the head with it.

'The dog. This dog. The one I'm going out of my mind searching for.'

'Oh yes. Well, I was right here.' She beamed at me.

'And Henry? The dog!'

'The dog? Oh. He was going that way.' She pointed over her shoulder. 'He spotted a squirrel in the Oak tree and the squirrel ran down the tree and bounded off towards Little Wood and the dog bounded after him. Nearly knocked me over. That's why I forgot to post my letter. Which is what I'm doing now.'

'Henry ran off into Little Wood?'

'Yes. On that path right there.'

She indicated the path near the church; the one Henry and I had walked down just a few hours earlier.

'Thank you so much,' I said, as I ran towards Little Wood.

I'd seen Henry chase squirrels in Little Wood several times since I'd been here. He never caught them and I'm not sure what he'd do if he did, not that there was any chance of that, but if he'd chased one in there today, perhaps he'd got disoriented and couldn't find his way out.

The air seemed far more humid beneath the canopy of trees than it had when we were there that afternoon. Now the Oaks, Ash, Elm, Copper Beech and Silver Birch swayed and creaked and cracked and their leaves rustled angrily as the wind picked up.

Rain pitter-pattered down, playing a slow drum beat as I got further in amongst the trees and then it fell like bullets between the branches, pelting the leaves and pummelling my skin. But the rain felt warm. It was like standing under an eco-power shower, fully clothed.

Ordinarily, I loved the rain. Especially rain like this. But at that moment all I could think about was Henry and his fear of storms.

I ran deeper into the woods, calling Henry's name and dodging tree stumps. Within minutes my dress was saturated, clinging to me like a second skin, my hair stuck to my face and neck and I could hardly walk now, let alone run as my pumps squelched in the mud beneath my feet.

I stepped onto a manmade path and yelled Henry's name, over and over again until my throat was hoarse and the rain mingled with tears of anger and frustration running freely down my face.

I wasn't sure where I was and the storm clouds had brought darkness. Little Wood might not be large, but in this weather, I go could round and round in circles and never find my way out.

The battery on my phone was dying and the torch flickered dimly until it finally went out. I slipped my phone into the pocket of my cotton dress and did the button up so it wouldn't fall out if I ran, or more than likely, fell.

I'm not sure how long I was in Little Wood, calling for Henry over and over as the wind tugged at my dress and the rain fell all about.

I thought I heard my name. Faintly at first, drowned out by the roars and crashes of the thunder and the beat of the torrential rain. A flash of lightning lit up the trees for a second and they seemed to glisten for a moment before I was plunged into darkness once again.

'Josie! Are you here?' I heard it this time. And even with the competing thunder, I knew that voice. 'Josie? Henry's safe. He's found. Josie? Where are you?'

Another flash of lightning lit up the path and I recognised Liam's silhouette against the bright white light.

'Liam? Liam, I'm here!'

I ran towards him, slipping and sliding on the muddy path, the rain almost blinding me as I wiped it from my eyes. I could see that he was also making his way to me and as we closed the distance, I saw the relief on his face.

'They've got him, Josie. He's fine. He's absolutely fine. Sonya told me you came in here to find him and I've been looking for you for almost twenty minutes.'

I didn't know who Sonya was and I really didn't care. I assumed she was the baguette lady.

'Thank God!'

I threw myself at him and he caught me, hesitating for a nano-second before wrapping his arms tightly around me and pulling me closer. We clung to one another for a moment and then I lifted my face from his chest and looked up into his eyes, crying with happiness and blinking as the rain poured down my face.

I think I kissed him first. In fact, I'm sure I

did. I grabbed the collar of his shirt and pulled his face towards me. But he immediately responded, locking his mouth on mine and kissing me back with an urgency and intensity I'd never experienced before. I felt that need too. It was more than need, it was desperation, and we stumbled, wrapped in one another's arms until we fell against a tree – a noble Copper Beech, the branches heavy with red-green and red-purple leaves, catching the torrential rain with a splish-splash-thwack. The thunder growled and roared and the lightning lit up the trees and intermittent patches of sky all around us.

Liam twisted us around so that my back leant against the smooth, wet, silver-grey tree trunk as I savoured the feel of his tongue in my mouth, his fingers in my hair, his kiss urgent and possessive as he held my face in his palms and deepened his kiss.

I tugged at his shirt, pulling it free of his jeans, and tore at the buttons almost ripping it in my need to feel my hands on his bare flesh.

Thunder crashed above us and the branches overhead swayed and creaked and groaned, even louder, but I didn't care. The storm surging around us was nothing compared to the one raging inside me. Lightning flashed and crackled closer but it was a mere flicker in comparison to the electricity coursing through my body. I finally reached his skin and my hands ran over it as the rain pierced the umbrella of leaves and a cascade of water drenched us, cooling our bodies but not our desire. We laughed between our kisses and then there was nothing but us.

He groaned as I slid one hand beneath the waistband of his jeans. His hands moved from my face to my neck and tugged at the buttons on my dress. After what felt like an agonising wait, he cupped my breasts and caressed each one in turn, and then one hand fumbled for the button on his jeans as I undid the zipper, stroking him through the denim and longing for him as much as he clearly longed for me.

His mouth was on my breasts, his hands searching, exploring, stroking and teasing as I arched into him and moaned his name.

My entire body quivered at his touch and I gasped as he lifted the skirt of my dress and slid his hand inside my lace knickers. My mouth opened wide and filled with droplets of rain and I bit my lower lip as he found that spot, making me press my nails into his back as each second sent me soaring higher.

I clutched at his hair and pulled him up to kiss me again. Passionate, intense kisses as I shoved his saturated jeans over his hips and pulled him even closer, and I twisted and wriggled slightly until my knickers slid to the ground.

He lifted me in his arms and I wrapped my

legs around him; the rain beating out some primal tempo as thunder reverberated around us, lightning flashed, and rivulets of water ran down our bodies from the leaves.

'Josie,' he moaned as he plunged into me and I could no longer hear the storm or see the lightning or feel the rain. I was only aware of the rasping of our breath and the thumping of our hearts, beating in seemingly perfect rhythm as we slaked our mutual thirst for one another.

I had never felt pleasure as great as this. I had never wanted or needed any man as much. I didn't want this to end and yet the ecstasy was almost unbearable. My head swam, my heart was fit to explode and I couldn't seem to get enough of him or his body or his touch.

We kissed frantically, ignoring the deluge of water now teeming through the branches as the storm peaked overhead. We moaned one another's names, and looked into each other's eyes as I crossed my ankles pulling him in even deeper and when we both reached that moment of euphoria almost exactly at the same time, it was like glimpsing paradise and we shuddered against each other as we came back down to earth.

'Josie,' he whispered, breathless, his mouth against my ear. 'Oh God, Josie.'

'I know,' I said, gasping for air, still clinging to him, almost afraid to let go.

'Oh God,' he said a few moments later, and something in his tone made me tense.

'Liam? Are you okay?'

He shook his head slowly against mine and gently eased himself away from me, letting my feet drop to the ground and sink into the mud. His hands slid from my body and he didn't look at me as he pulled up his jeans and hastily zipped them, not bothering with the top button. He ran his hands through his hair and finally, he looked into my eyes and shook his head again.

'I'm so, so sorry, Josie. This should never have happened. I ... I ... don't know how it did.' He glanced upwards, blinking against the rain as if he'd only just noticed the weather.

'What the f–?'

I stared at him in disbelief, not wanting to say that word because that is what his words had turned that incredible experience into. I had thought we were making love. We weren't. Not in his mind at least.

Was that all this was to him? A shag in the woods in a storm?

Seriously?

'It's my fault,' he said, unable to look at me now. Or not wanting to. 'We should get out of this rain.' He hugged his arms around himself, pulling his shirt together.

I took a deep, calming breath and slapped a smile on my face. I fumbled to do up my buttons but my fingers wouldn't work properly.

'Hey. Don't worry about it, Liam. It's no big deal. It's just sex, after all. And it takes two to tango. This was as much my fault as yours. But don't get all worked up about it. It was fun. It was fantastic. But it's over. No harm done. As for the rain. I don't think we can get much wetter.'

I was shaking and so was my voice. I pushed myself away from the tree, unsure if I could stand without its support.

He was glaring at me.

'Just sex? Is that really all it was to you? Seriously? Of course it was. I'm the fool. Shit, Josie. You are unbelievable.'

He laughed but it wasn't a happy sound.

Had I missed something? Wasn't he the one who had said it was a mistake?

'Er. You're the one who seems to be regretting it. Not me.'

I wiped rain from my face but it was a waste of time and effort; more pelted us relentlessly.

'I'm not regretting it. How could I? I've wanted you since that day I saw you sitting on that bench. I wanted you even before that. Years ago when ... And I've never had ... But that doesn't matter. It shouldn't have happened because this can't go anywhere. It's not just me, Josie. I have Orla to think about.'

'Orla? I realise that. But what does she

have to ... Oh, I see. What you're saying is that you wanted to have sex with me, but I'm not the sort of woman you take home to the family. Is that it?'

'Not exactly. No. But you're not the sort of woman who wants a long-term relationship, are you? You don't want to settle down, do you? I heard you say that yourself in the café. You're never getting married. For you, life is all about fun and laughs and sex with no strings attached. I don't have that luxury. I have a daughter to think of. An impressionable sixteen-year-old who doesn't need to see her dad having casual sex with her best friend's aunt.'

'I would hope she wouldn't see us.'

He glowered at me.

'That's it. Make a joke of it. Like you always do. I'm serious, Josie. I can't do this.'

'I'm sorry. But it doesn't have to be casual, Liam.' Hope sprang up in my heart.

'Yeah right. Because you'd be happy to stay in Seahorse Harbour, would you?'

'I ... I might.'

He hesitated. 'For how long? Until you saw someone else you liked? Or until you got the craving to travel?' He shook his head. 'I can't take that risk, Josie. I can't do that to Orla. I can't do that to myself. If it wasn't for Orla, I might take that chance. But I can't. I simply can't. The pain and heartache of finding out ...

of losing someone I love. It ... it almost broke me last time. I can't go through all that again. I'm sorry.'

'Forget it. You're right. It wouldn't work. I'm no Una. And I'm no Diana either.'

I stepped forward but my shoe got stuck in the mud and I had to bend down and take it off. So much for a dramatic exit, so to speak.

'What does that mean?'

'What?'

'About Una. And Diana?'

I took both shoes off and held them in front of my chest.

'Well, Una was the most beautiful woman in the world and a pretty tough act to follow. And Diana is the perfect wife and mother. Things I could never hope to emulate.'

'You ... you know about me and Diana?' He looked stunned. Shell-shocked.

'You and...? Yes. Yes, of course. But I'd like to hear your side of the story.'

I had no clue what he was talking about. But now I had to know even though both he and I stood a very good chance of catching pneumonia.

'We should go somewhere and get dry.'

'Just tell me, Liam.'

He looked as if he wanted to run but he glanced up at the tree and found a spot where the branches gave more shelter. He reached out for me but I moved away and covered the two feet or so to get out of the worst of the rain. I didn't want him to touch me again. I thought it might break my heart. He shoved back his sodden hair, shook his head and sighed deeply.

'What did Diana tell you?'

'I want to hear your words. Not hers.'

He let out a breath and harrumphed.

'She said she didn't want you to know. She asked me not to say a word. I wonder why she told you? Guilt, perhaps?'

He was questioning himself, not me and I waited in silence for what I now knew was to come.

'It was a spur of the moment thing. I suppose it was a bit like this. Except I didn't have feelings for Diana. Other than friendship. We were sitting on the sofa in my house, comforting one another in our misery. Una had ... been gone for a month or so and I wasn't coping with what ... with everything. Diana was a shoulder to lean on. We had too much to drink and ... one thing led to another and ... well. You know the rest. It was a mistake and it never happened again. Ever.'

I couldn't believe it.

Diana and Liam. Liam and Diana.

They'd had sex. And then they'd decided it was a mistake. Just like Liam had decided tonight was a mistake.

I looked at my toes, sinking deeper into the mud and I wanted to be sucked down, to disappear from here. I smoothed down my dress because I had to do something or I think I might've lashed out at him.

'Well,' I said, as calmly as I could after taking several deep breaths. 'You need to be more careful. It seems you make a lot of mistakes when it comes to sex. First, my sister. Now me. It's getting to be a habit. I wonder who your next mistake will be.'

'Josie! That's not fair.'

'Not fair? Don't give me that. You have the nerve to tell me that I'm some tart who likes to sleep around and isn't fit to cross your threshold, yet you seem to be the one who's doing that.'

'I didn't call you a tart. I'd never call you that. That's not what I was saying. That isn't what I meant.'

'How dare you? How dare you try to pretend that we couldn't have a relationship because of me. You're the screw-up, Liam. At least I don't try to make excuses.'

'Josie!'

He reached out for me but I slapped his hand away.

'Don't touch me. Don't you ever touch me again. Don't look at me. Don't speak to me. Don't ... don't come anywhere near me. You're a bastard, Liam Fulbright! A total and utter bastard.'

I traipsed through the mud, aware of the

ridiculousness of the situation as I clutched my sodden pumps, my dress sticking to my legs. I couldn't run; I'd just slip and slide. I could feel his eyes watching me. I heard him call my name once more but then there was just the torrential rain, the rumbling thunder, the dazzling lightning – and my tears.

Twenty-Five

Diana was waiting for me in the kitchen, looking out through the torrential rain towards the woods, her mobile phone pressed against her chest.

Had she been calling me?

Or had Liam called her? Perhaps to tell her he'd told me his version of events.

Had he also told her we'd just had sex? The most incredible sex ever. At least for me. Clearly not for him.

The kitchen looked warm and welcoming, the bright lights like a beacon in a stormy sea; Diana, a shark, between me and the comfort of a cosy bed. I was feeling a trifle melodramatic.

Despite the humidity, unbroken by the storm, I now felt cold and couldn't seem to stop shivering. Diana tossed her phone on the counter when she spotted me, grabbed a towel she'd obviously had waiting and opened a section of the folding doors.

'You're drenched!' She wrapped the towel around me and began to rub me dry. 'I was so worried about you. Henry's safe and he's already fast asleep on Toby's bed. He–'

'Stop it, Diana.' I pushed her and the towel away. 'I know about you and Liam.'

She swallowed hard and nodded.

'I know you do.'

'He called you, didn't he? Just now.'

She nodded again.

'What did he say?'

She shook her head and held out the towel to me, a crestfallen expression on her face, her eyes filled with unshed tears.

'Diana. What. Did. He. Say?'

She bit her lower lip and half-turned away, draping the towel over the chair nearest to me.

'Diana!'

She spun round to face me.

'He said he'd told you about us because he thought I'd already told you. You seemed to know. But he realised you didn't and it was just a guess.'

'A guess I didn't expect to be true. My sister. My perfect sister. The perfect wife and mother, having sex with the dad of her daughter's best friend. To say I'm gobsmacked is an understatement.'

'You don't understand, Josie. You have no idea what my life's been like.'

My mouth fell open. A second later, I laughed. I grabbed the towel because I was shivering still and needed to get dry.

261

'No. It must've been hell. Being married to a gorgeous, talented heart surgeon. Not to mention, rich. Did I forget to mention gorgeous? Oh and the nannies, the gardeners, the cleaners. Yes. Being the beautiful, perfect wife, running a successful business of her own, having two wonderful kids, two fabulous homes. No, three. I forgot the ski chalet in Courchevel. Absolute hell. Oh, and I'm forgetting. Also being the favourite daughter. My heart bleeds for you. I can see how you needed to screw Liam to relieve the awfulness of all that.'

'It wasn't like that. It isn't like that. You don't know anything.'

'Then tell me. Tell me what's it's like. Because I just don't get it, Diana. I would've given anything to have...' I stopped myself from saying it. 'Just tell me why. Why Liam? Do you ... do you love him? Is that what that heated discussion on Wednesday was about?'

No! Of course not.'

She flopped onto a chair and hung her head. I stripped off my saturated dress, only then realising that I no longer had any knickers and they must be in the mud somewhere at the foot of that Copper Beech tree. I quickly wrapped the large, soft bath towel around me and sat on a chair opposite her.

'For God's sake, Diana. Bloody well talk to me. I deserve that much at least.'

She raised her eyes to mine and a strange smile lifted one side of her mouth.

'You think I've got the perfect life? You couldn't be more wrong. Oh yes, I've got the homes, the cars, the staff, the money. Well, I don't have that. Bernice does. But we're by no means poor, I accept. And I have the money from my own business. That's hardly enough to live on though. Not like this.' She waved one arm limply in the air and let it drop into her lap as she shook her head. 'You think it's easy trying to be the perfect daughter, wife and mother. Running a business that wasn't meant to be a business, just a little hobby. From something I loved that made me happy to something that has almost taken over my life. And running a book club for some friends, to chat and laugh and unwind, which turned into a social event with bitches, and gossip and books I'd never want to read. Hosting dinners and parties for people I don't like. Having beautiful women in my home and wondering which one of them my gorgeous, rich and successful husband would be screwing next. And all the while, knowing that my husband, the man I adored, would rather have been with my sister.'

'Wh-what?'

She laughed. Well, not laughed exactly. It was more of a cackle.

'You think I didn't know that Alex dated

you long before he turned to me? Oh I knew, Josie. I've always known. Everything.'

'Everything?'

She nodded slowly. 'Everything. I wanted Alex from the first time I saw him. Not in a sexual way.' She laughed again. 'I mean, we were only ten and he was twelve. But I knew then that I wanted him to be mine. I wanted to marry him when we grew up. And Mum had always told me I could have anything I wanted. But as we grew older, I began to realise that wasn't true. Because Alex didn't want me. He wanted you.'

I almost fell off the chair. She knew. How? I'd been so careful. Hadn't I?

'Yes, Josie. You. And you thought I didn't know. I watched you playing with Liam and laughing with Liam over the years as we grew up. I prayed that the two of you would fall in love. But I was watching Alex, and Alex wanted you. And what Alex wanted, Alex got. Usually. I saw you gradually move away from Liam. I watched as you fell for Alex. My Alex. Except he wasn't mine. And he never would be all the while he was with you. I watched the two of you kiss and I seethed with jealousy. I watched as you used to creep away to be together. I saw you make love and at first I couldn't look away. And then I hatched a plan and I put it into action.'

'You did what? You watched us?

Eeeuwww, Diana. That's disgusting. But you knew? All these years, you knew?'

'That he was in love with you and that you were besotted with him? Yes. I knew. I'm not proud of myself, Josie. Sometimes I hate myself for what I did. But as I told you the other day, I loved Alex beyond all reason. I still do. I would've killed to make him mine, I think. But I didn't need to do that. All I needed to do was make sure Bernice found out the two of you were lovers.'

'Bernice?'

I had a sick feeling right then. But it couldn't have been Diana. It couldn't. My sister wouldn't do that to me.

'One night, I followed you to the beach and I waited. When the time was right, I crept up and saw you. You were behind the rocks. He was on his back and you were astride him, his hands were on your breasts, his head tipped back either in agony or sheer pleasure, I wasn't sure. I hadn't ever had sex, so I had no idea what it was like. Your head was back and your nails were digging into his chest. I took a photo and I printed it out. I put it in an envelope and typed a note to Bernice saying, 'Look what that tart Josie Parnell is doing to your son.' I knew how she would react. I'd heard her say, so many times, that girls who had sex outside of marriage were nothing but tarts. I made sure I just happened to pop in to see her at their caravan in the holiday park shortly after I'd dropped the note and the photo into the mail box for their caravan. I pretended I was looking for you and had come to ask if she or Alex knew where you were, because I couldn't find you. I said Mum was cross because as usual, we were late for something. I can't recall what else I said, but I knew that you were with Alex. And I knew what Bernice would do.'

It took a moment or two for her words to sink in. At first I couldn't believe it, but then it all made sense. Perfect. Awful. Sense.

'Diana! Shit.' I leapt up from the chair and paced the kitchen, the tiles cool beneath my bare feet. 'You were the one? You ... you did that? To me? To Alex? How could you?'

'I don't know. I honestly don't. But I told you. I loved him beyond all reason.'

'So did I, Diana! Didn't you care about that?'

She shook her head. 'No. Because I truly believed you'd fall in love with someone else. For me, there would never be anyone other than Alex. I was sure of that. But you could have anyone. You were always the popular one with boys. You were always the life and soul of the party. And you were all about having fun. I honestly thought you'd get over Alex and find someone else. Whereas I thought I'd die if I didn't have him.'

'Christ, Diana. I still loved him. I didn't get

over him. Why do you think I never came back here to spend the summer? It was far too painful. Why do you think I never come to your home? Or spend Christmas at your chalet?'

'I know. Over the years I realised that. I realised you still loved him. And that hurt me deeply. But it also meant I couldn't have you around. Just in case. Why do you think I never pushed you to come and stay? I never pleaded with you. I was relieved you didn't want to come. I was glad I could keep the two of you apart. I was always scared that one day ... Well. What I hadn't realised was that Alex would never love me the way he'd once loved you.'

'But ... but how? I don't understand. I thought Alex started dating you because Bernice convinced him that he should. That Dad would help him if he did. And that if he continued to see me, he would lose any chance he had of becoming a respected doctor. I thought you had no idea about me and him.'

'I know. I knew Bernice wanted Dad to help Alex, and I threw her a few breadcrumbs and dropped a few hints to Dad. More than a few. After Alex ended things with you, Bernice persuaded him to ask me out, and then she suggested that he should propose. And the weird thing about Alex is that he always did what Bernice wanted. He still does. Just like I always did what Mum wanted. He and I have that in common if nothing else. Bernice only has to click her fingers and Alex does what she says. Even now. I told him I wouldn't sleep with him until we were married. That seemed to make him keener.'

I was stunned. How could my sister have done that?

I flopped back onto the chair and glowered at her.

'So when Bernice saw that photo and forbade Alex to see me again and he complied, you knew that's what would happen? And you knew she would persuade him to be with you? Jesus Christ, Diana. Do you know how painful it was for me? We sat in The Seahorse Inn and he told me he loved me but that his mum said I wasn't the type of girl a decent man would marry. I'll never forget those words. And he said that she'd told him you were the type of woman he needed by his side. Obedient, devoted, sensible, practical, intelligent ... and decent. He said he didn't want to dump me, but he was going to be an eminent surgeon one day and he needed a wife who could be an asset. Not a wife who was a party girl. I can still remember almost every word.'

Diana nodded. 'I know. And it's all so ironic. Because here's another thing you don't know. Mum is always telling you that you should be more like me. Well, Alex started telling me that he wished I were more like you. Not at first. At first, we were fairly happy. Becca came along quickly and then Toby was born and we were the perfect family. Then Bernice won all that money. I think she might've suggested Alex trade me in for a better model if it hadn't been for Becca and Toby.' Diana gave a little laugh. 'She decided I could stay. But Alex was becoming a successful doctor and now he was rich. He no longer needed Dad. Or the perfect wife to get him where he wanted to be. He decided it was time he had some fun. Only not with me.'

I couldn't believe this. Any of it. All this time I'd thought Diana had the perfect life. She hadn't. All this time I thought my love for Alex and his for me had been a secret. It hadn't.

We'd kept it secret because it was obvious from the day we met, that Bernice didn't like me one bit. And her dislike only grew over the years. When Alex and I fell in love we thought it was best if no one knew. I was sixteen, he was eighteen and keeping our relationship secret was exciting for us both. Having sex was legal, but we knew how Bernice would react if she found out. And my mum wouldn't have been thrilled.

And then, after several months, Bernice did find out. Someone had sent her a photo.

Alex had told me that was why his mum insisted it had to end between us. She said I had no morals and that if I was willing to have sex with him, he wouldn't be the only one. Which wasn't true. I loved Alex deeply. But Bernice didn't care. She said that if we stayed together, someone might've made the photo public, and there was no way her son was going to be humiliated over a sex photo. We never knew where that photo had come from. Alex and I were both so embarrassed I'm not sure either of us wanted to find out. At least Bernice didn't tell my mum, so she spared me several lectures. That was something, I suppose.

The only person I ever told about all of it was Elsie, because I was heartbroken and I had to talk to someone, and that was never going to be my mum. Or, for some reason, Diana. We'd always been close and yet I hadn't turned to Diana. I thought it was because I didn't want her to look down on me, or something.

When she and Alex dated, I wanted to scream at her not to see him, but she was so happy and I couldn't do that to her. I felt one of us should have some happiness in our lives. So instead, I avoided them and I stayed away from Seahorse Harbour, getting a job as crew on a luxury yacht, through a friend of Elsie's. It meant I didn't have to stay in constant touch with anyone back home.

Diana and Alex were engaged after only a few months together. "A whirlwind romance", Mum called it. I couldn't quite believe it. But I'd never seen Diana so full of life and excitement. She positively oozed happiness.

And yet, all that time, Diana had been the reason for my heartache.

'And Liam? Where does he fit into all this?'

She sucked in a breath.

'Because a few years before she died, Una and Alex started having an affair.'

I gasped at that.

'Una and Alex! No way. I don't believe it.'

'It's true. And it got pretty serious. Alex even considered leaving me for her. So I made sure Bernice found out about it and, after a while, a long while, Alex ended it. I thought he was going to finally rebel against Bernice, but he didn't. Then Una got cancer and Alex literally backed away.'

'Does Liam know?'

She nodded. 'Una told him when she was dying.' She snorted derisively. 'Wanted to get it off her chest, apparently. Anyway, I was at Liam's one night. We were both miserable. Me, because Alex was already sleeping with someone else. A nurse from his hospital. Liam, because Una's cancer had torn him to shreds but her deathbed confession had almost broken him. And because Orla knew too. She heard her mum confess to him. She was standing at the door and heard every word.'

'Orla knows her mum and Alex had an affair! Oh my God. This just gets worse. Does ... does Becca know?'

'No. When I told Liam I knew about it, he

told me that he'd explained to Orla that it was something they must try to keep to themselves. He told her he didn't want anyone to think badly of Una and said it would break my heart and Becca's if we found out the truth about Alex. He didn't know then that I already knew the truth, long before he did. Orla's so grown up for her age, and such a lovely, considerate girl. She wouldn't do anything to hurt her best friend, or her best friend's mum. And she still loved Una in spite of it. But she became withdrawn and Liam said he was riddled with guilt at asking her to keep the secret. He couldn't handle any of it. At first he threw himself into work and then, over the weeks as Orla became more sullen, he came to his senses, pulled himself together and left the bank.'

'And ... and you and him? Was that some sort of pay back for Una and Alex?'

'For me, perhaps. Not for him. That night, when he and I were sitting on his sofa, it was just two miserable people consoling one another as friends. I'm ashamed to say, I was the one who started it. I'd found out about the nurse and I was hurt and angry. I wanted to play Alex at his own game, I think. I'm not really sure. I'd been drinking. As for Liam, I think he simply wanted to feel something other than pain and sadness and depression for just one brief moment. But he stopped almost immediately and pulled away. I tried to get him to continue, but he wouldn't. But we had … well, you know. Strictly speaking, we had had sex. Even if the actual deed only lasted for a matter of seconds before he backed off.'

'A matter of seconds? Seriously?'

She nodded. 'Yes. Because he wouldn't let it go on for any longer. I told you, he pulled away. And he literally leapt off the sofa. He said it would ruin our friendship. That he didn't have those sorts of feelings for me. That he didn't want to have an affair. We agreed to put it behind us and never mention it again. Then you came to stay, and I was terrified you might find out about it. I begged Liam not to tell you. I could see you liked him and I needed to know how he felt about you. Because one thing I know about Liam is that he's honest and decent and if you two grew close and started a relationship, I thought there was a chance he'd feel he had to tell you what happened between us. Because we did have sex, even if it was only for a few seconds. I couldn't risk him telling you. But it's all come out now anyway. And a lot more besides. So now you know. I expect you hate me for what I did to you and Alex. But I want you to know that I love you Josie. I really do. I was a stupid, selfish girl, but I honestly, truly believed that you'd get over Alex pretty fast and it wouldn't affect your life at all.'

We sat in silence for a while. Both trying to

take in all that had been said.

Eventually, I reached out and took her hand in mine and looked her in the eye.

'I was furious and hurt and I felt betrayed when you first spoke. But I didn't hate you, Di. I could never hate you. The odd thing is, I actually feel as if some sort of burden has been lifted off me. I think I've been in love with the idea of me and Alex all these years. The memory of us. Not with the actual man. The first thing I thought when Mum told me she was sure there was something wrong in your world was that Alex was having an affair. So my instinct has always been not to trust him. Ever since he broke my heart, I suppose. I think I've always known what he was like. That he's a fantastic surgeon, and he may be gorgeous, but he's a weak man in many ways.'

'He is. That's one thing I don't like about him. He's not far from forty and he still does whatever his mum tells him to. And he can't keep his hands off other women.'

'Is he … is he seeing someone now?'

'Oh yes. Marina. From my book club. That's why me and the kids are here without him. After Una, he promised me he wouldn't cheat again. Then I found out about the nurse. That ended pretty quickly and I thought we were going to be okay. He said we needed to work on our marriage. And we did. But a few months ago, I discovered he was seeing

Marina. I thought it might just be a fling, but I think it's getting pretty serious. We've been rowing about it for a few weeks now. He ... he suggested we need to spend some time apart. To see how we really feel about each other.'

'I'm so sorry, Di. I honestly had no idea. Why didn't you tell me any of this?'

'I suppose for the same reason you didn't tell me about you and Alex all those years ago. I wanted to keep it secret. Other than that, I don't really know. Perhaps I thought that if I told you, or Mum, it would make it real. Sometimes I try to pretend it isn't happening. That it doesn't matter and everything will be fine. As Mum would say, I've made my own bed and I have to lie-in it. While my husband lies in everyone else's.'

'Oh, Diana. I don't know what to say. Except, don't think for one minute that if he and I had stayed together he'd have been any different with me. He'd still be having affairs, I'm pretty certain of that. And probably telling me that he wished I were more like you. The strange thing is, I think I'm more upset about you and Liam than I am about what you did to break up me and Alex. And I have to say, for a sixteen-year-old going on seventeen as you were at the time, that was some plan. But then you always were the clever and practical twin.'

'And devious. And bitchy. And jealous. And selfish. And spoilt.'

'Yeah. And those things too. But I love you. Nothing's going to change that. Unless you now make a play for Liam. Then, I'm sorry to say, you and I might fall out.' I tried to make light of it.

'No. I can promise you with all my heart, that was a one-off. That'll never happen again. Neither of us want that. And even if I did, Liam isn't interested. He wasn't then. He certainly isn't now. No. Liam and I are just friends.'

'Well, it doesn't matter anyway. Because nothing else is going to happen between me and Liam.'

'Why not?'

'Because just like Alex, Liam thinks I'm not the type of woman a decent man should marry.'

'That's utter crap. He doesn't think anything of the sort.'

'Oh yes he does. He just told me so. We'd just had the best sex I've ever had in my life and he suddenly tells me it was a mistake because he can't let Orla see him having casual sex with me. Or words to that effect. And that I'm not the settling down type. And, well, yadda, yadda, yadda.'

'You ... you just had sex with Liam? Just now?' She was clearly astonished.

'Yep. In the woods. Up against a Copper Beech tree.'

'In a thunder storm and torrential rain?' Diana gasped.

I laughed at that.

'Yep. Didn't he tell you when he called?'

'No. He didn't. He just said that he'd upset you and that he'd told you what happened between him and me because you'd sounded as if you knew, but it was obviously just a guess.' A slow grin spread across her face. 'You honestly had sex up against a tree, in a storm?'

'Not the sort of thing you'd do, I'm guessing.'

Diana shook her head. 'No. Although I think I'd like to. But I don't believe what you say Liam said. He wouldn't say such a thing. And not to you. You must've misunderstood.'

'I didn't. I assure you. He made it pretty clear. And he kept apologising and saying it shouldn't have happened. But I suppose he said that to you.'

'Actually, no. He didn't. He just said it was wrong and that it would never happen again. Which it hasn't and it won't. But it does still feel a little awkward between us sometimes even after almost three years. That's the trouble with sex, I think. You can't quite go back to the way things were before it.' She let out a long, sad sigh. 'Would you like a glass of wine? I think we could both do with a drink.'

'Actually, I'd rather have a cup of tea. I'm bloody freezing.'

'Oh my goodness, Josie. Why didn't you say so? Go upstairs, have a hot shower and get into bed. I'll make some tea and bring it up. And leave your dress and shoes. I'll deal with those.'

'Thanks, Diana. That would be great.' I went to go upstairs but stopped. 'Is Henry okay? Liam told me he'd been found and was safe and you said he's asleep on Toby's bed, but where was he for all that time, and was he hurt in any way?'

Diana grinned and shook her head. 'We're not quite sure how he got there, but he was found in the back of a delivery truck. He was last seen chasing a squirrel into Little Wood but he must've come out again, perhaps chasing the same squirrel. The delivery driver who found him said it's possible Henry jumped into the truck when the doors were open and as the driver was wearing ear buds, he didn't hear Henry's barks. His next delivery was fifteen miles away and he didn't see Henry until his final delivery. You know how Henry is with storms. He'd curled up in the corner behind the final large parcel, and that's where the driver found him. Thankfully, the lovely man called us as soon as he read the name and number on Henry's tag. Noah stayed here with Toby, while Becca came with me to get Henry. The driver met us half way, which was really good of him. Liam said he'd look for you.' She grinned. 'And obviously, he found you.'

I didn't want to be reminded of that.

I was so relieved Henry had been safe all that time, although sad that he'd been scared. I'd have to make it up to him.

I dashed upstairs and got in the shower, going over and over everything Diana had said.

All these years I'd been wondering what my life might've been like if Alex had chosen me. Or if I hadn't made the decision to sleep with him. Or that photo had never existed. Or if Bernice had thought I was good enough for her beloved son.

All this time I'd thought I still had feelings for Alex and was worried that, if we were too long in one another's company, something might happen between us. I could never do that to Diana. But Alex was hard to refuse. I'd seen the way he'd looked at me more than once after they were married.

So I'd tried never to be alone with him; I'd avoided him whenever I could. Staying away from my sister and her kids so that I wouldn't have to spend too much time with Alex. And yet, when she'd told me just now what she'd done all those years ago, I felt sorrier for her than I did for myself.

Diana didn't break my heart; Alex did that by not standing up for us. For what we had. For bowing to his mum's ideas and believing that the only way to get ahead was with help from my dad. And he seriously believed – or Bernice did – that the best way to get that was to marry

Diana.

How ridiculous it all seemed now. He could've made it on his own. It might've been more difficult; Dad definitely opened doors for him, got him his first job and introduced him to all the right people. But Dad would've done that anyway.

And what if I'd told Dad about me and Alex? That would've scuppered his plans. And Bernice's. But I suppose they knew I wouldn't. Alex knew I wouldn't do anything to ruin his chances of becoming the doctor he longed to be.

As for Liam. Well. I mustn't think about him. He'd made his feelings clear. I would never be quite good enough. That hurt far more than anything Alex had said all those years ago.

And I think that was the most surprising thing of all.

I couldn't care less about Alex Dunn.

I was falling in love with Liam Fulbright.

For all the good that would do me.

Twenty-Six

'I've decided I'm going to tell Mum,' Diana said the following morning.

'Tell Mum what?' I eyed her anxiously over the rim of my third cup of coffee.

After my shower last night, Diana had brought up a pot of tea, a chocolate fudge cake and a tub of salted caramel ice cream just in case I fancied it, and we'd sat in my bed, chatting into the early hours.

She'd told me more about Alex's affairs and how upset she'd been when she'd found out about what she thought was the first one, only to discover years later when she confronted him about his affair with Una, that it had been his third. Una had been his eighth, and there'd been two more after Una that she knew about. The nurse and now Marina. Her love for him was her Achilles' heel.

She'd told me about how her baby clothing business had become a chain around her neck, and the book club now the bane of her life.

'All I ever wanted was to be a wife and a

mother. I was never interested in having a business. I made baby clothes because it kept my mind off who Alex might be sleeping with. Then a friend of Alex's decided the baby clothes were 'fab', told him I should set up a business, became a silent partner and the whole thing spiralled out of control. I started the book club to lose myself in someone else's happy ending, even if it was only fiction, and to have a laugh and a chat with my friends. Then the wife of another of Alex's friends heard about it and brought some of her friends along. Before I knew it my friends stopped coming and we no longer discussed books at the book club, just networked and gossiped and put on a show.'

'Why didn't you just say no and put a stop to it?'

'Come on, Josie. You know me. When have I ever said no? All my life I've tried to 'people please' and look where that's got me.'

'You said you want to make some changes. Was that true or were you just saying that?'

'No. I do want to make some changes. I want to sell my business. I want to end the book club. I want ... I want to stop loving Alex. But I don't think I'll ever do that. I honestly can't imagine my life without him in it.'

I'd nudged her arm. 'You might, Diana. Take it from someone who knows. It is possible to get over Alex Dunn. The important thing is to want to.'

We'd fallen asleep not long after, but this morning she seemed different. More determined. More ... alive.

'I'm going to tell Mum the truth.'

'About Alex?'

'About everything.'

'Everything! Are you sure that's wise? Something as important as all that should be done face-to-face. That's why I came over here. I knew whatever was upsetting you had to be discussed in person.'

She burst out laughing and it was a happy laugh, not forced or strained.

'Well, we've certainly done that. I suppose you're right. But the thing is, if I don't tell her now, I think I might chicken out. And I really don't want to do that. Last night was an epiphany for me.'

I raised my brows. 'It was a bit of an epiphany for me too. Especially up against that tree.'

She smiled at me. 'Yes. And I've decided I want to do things like that. I want to have fun. I want to let my hair down. I want to make love in the rain. I want to see ... do other things.'

She coughed lightly and poured herself more coffee, holding up the pot to me. I shook my head.

'Threes enough for me, thanks. Are the kids up yet?'

'No. I think all the excitement of yesterday,

283

not to mention the last few days, has caught up with them. Even Henry didn't seem to want to go out for his morning pee. But I managed to persuade him with a couple of doggy treats. He did what he had to and trotted back up to Toby's bed.'

We sat in silence for a while, both staring out into the garden, deep in our own thoughts.

'Er. Diana?'

'Yes.'

'Is there something going on between you and Mikkel?'

'M-me and Mikkel?' She darted a look at me and then around the room as if following the flight of a trapped fly. 'Wh-why did you ask that?'

'Because you and he seem to be walking on eggshells when you see one another. And at your party, you both came out of Alex's study looking a little ... flushed. And when Toby had his accident, I heard you on the phone to someone who clearly cared about Toby. And I know it wasn't Alex because you said you hadn't told him.'

She looked me in the eye and sighed heavily.

'Oh God, Josie. I don't know what's happened to me. I still love Alex. I really do. But ... well, when I found out about Marina, I think I lost my mind for a while. Oh hell. I think I lost my mind the day that I met Alex. But over the last few years I've turned into someone I don't recognise. I suppose I may as well just say it. Something did happen between us. Again, because I'd had a few too many drinks. You asked why I really gave up alcohol. Well, that's why. I wasn't an alcoholic by any means but every so often, when I got very depressed, I'd drown my sorrows with wine. Rather a lot of wine.'

'How didn't I know this? How didn't I see? Why didn't you talk to me about it and tell me how unhappy you were?'

She smiled wanly and shook her head. 'I knew you and Mum and everyone thought I had the perfect life. I wanted you all to keep thinking that. And after I tried to seduce Liam – which let's face it, is what I did, I stopped drinking for a while. It began again at Easter when I discovered Alex was sleeping with Marina.'

'Oh Di. It must've been awful.'

She shrugged. 'Alex took the kids to our chalet in Courchevel for Easter. I wasn't feeling well so I didn't go but I came down here to get some sea air and to think. I spent a lot of time in the pub. Elsie was away on a cruise and I was feeling pretty lonely. One night, after I'd had a lot to drink, Mikkel brought me home and put me to bed and I literally threw myself at him. I begged him to have sex with me but he wouldn't. I was so embarrassed the following day.'

'Oh my God. But I can't imagine Mikkel rubbing that in your face.'

'He didn't. He came to see how I was feeling and told me to forget about it. He made me coffee and asked if I wanted to talk and I poured my heart out to him. He sat and listened and then he took me out for the day. Just as friends. I think it was one of the happiest days of my life. He took me for a picnic the next day, and the day after that, to an open-air concert at Easterhill Hotel. The next time I asked him to stay, I was perfectly sober and we spent the best part of two days and nights in bed. Neither of us wanted to get dressed. I've never felt like that before. And then I went back to Blackheath and to Alex and the kids and I realised I could lose everything. I hadn't seen Mikkel since, until that day on the beach. He'd called and texted me several times but I told him it was over and then I stopped taking his calls and finally, I blocked his number.'

'Diana! And that day in the study?'

She flushed crimson. 'He ... he told me we needed to talk. He wanted to know why I wouldn't speak to him. He said he thought we had had something special. I told him we hadn't. That it had just been a fling. And I said, 'You've moved on anyway, because you're already flirting with my sister.' I was jealous, of course, but I didn't tell him that. He told me he had no idea you were my sister until that day on the beach, but that he liked you. And that if there wasn't going to be anything between me and him, he needed to get on with his life.'

'Wow. I suppose I should be flattered in a way. What did you tell him?'

She shrugged. 'I ... I told him I still loved Alex. And that he should get on with his life.'

'Oh, Diana. But hold on. How did he call you at the hospital if you'd blocked his number?'

'I unblocked it after I saw him ... and you on the beach that day. Because that's the problem. I ... I actually think I might have feelings for Mikkel. I like him. I like him a lot. But I do love Alex. And there're the kids to think about and...' Her voice trailed off and she shook her head.

'Are you saying what I think you're saying? Are you saying that you'd like to continue seeing Mikkel?'

She looked me in the eye. 'I don't know what I'm saying, Josie. I'm not even sure how I feel anymore. This is why I need to tell Mum. All of this, everything I told you last night and this morning is why I've been upset. That's why I keep crying. That's why I'm driving myself insane with guilt and longing and fear and ... a host of other things I don't even understand. I loved Alex beyond reason. I still do. I can't imagine my life without him, as I keep saying.

And yet after Easter, and especially as the summer grew closer, I started to imagine a life with Mikkel. And it terrified me to death. Not the thought of a life with him. The fact that I was starting to wonder what a life with him might be like. Does that make any sense at all?'

I nodded. 'It does, Diana. It absolutely does. Perhaps you're right. Perhaps you need to talk to someone else about all this. Apart from me. But I don't think it should be Mum. Not yet. I think it should be Elsie. She was the only one I told about me and Alex all those years ago. I think you have some serious thinking to do, and Elsie may be able to help you. She listens without judging, and she's wise, and kind and caring. She'll help you to see things you might not have thought of. And if you do chicken out of telling Mum, you can always ask Elsie to do it for you. That'll get them speaking again and it'll get you out of the line of fire for a while.'

Diana laughed. 'That doesn't sound like a bad idea. And what about you? You and Liam? What are you going to do?'

'There is no me and Liam. He made it very clear that there's no way we could have a relationship. I'll stay here until you sort yourself out and then I'm heading back to New York. Life was so much simpler there.'

Twenty-Seven

It rained all that day.

Toby stayed in bed and Henry stayed beside him. I ventured into Toby's room, half expecting Toby to tell me to get out, and for Henry to growl at me for abandoning him. Instead, Henry bounded over and licked my face and Toby invited me in. I had taken Henry a bone, and Toby a large glass of Coke and four chocolate biscuits, so that might've had something to do with my warm welcome.

I was so thankful they were both okay and I think Toby felt the same. When I cuddled him, he didn't try to push me away. I even cuddled Henry.

Becca and Orla spent the morning together in Becca's room, doing whatever girls do these days when it's pouring with rain. I spent most of the morning staring out into Little Wood, watching the rain and remembering the night before. Liam's arms tight around me, his kisses, his touch, his voice, his ... everything. I remembered every second. And I told myself I had to forget.

Diana went to see Elsie and she didn't get back until lunchtime. She couldn't tell me what was said because Becca and Orla came downstairs for lunch. I'd made a lasagne and was going to take some upstairs for Toby, but he decided to come down too.

'Are you sure you should be up?' I asked.

'I'm fine. I don't want to spend all day in bed. I've been in bed for days.'

'You're not going out in this weather,' Diana said. 'I'm not having you catching pneumonia on top of everything else.'

We watched the rain as we ate lunch, all feeling a little down in the dumps and all for differing reasons.

'Why don't we have a party?' I said, in an attempt to lighten our moods.

'Today?' Becca looked doubtful.

'No. For mine and your mum's birthday. It's in three weeks. And it's a special one because we're going to be thirty-five.'

'A birthday party?' Diana looked even more doubtful.

'I can't imagine being thirty-five,' Becca said. 'It seems so old.'

'Don't worry, kiddo. With remarks like that you won't be. You'll be dead.'

'Funny,' she said.

'Oh God, Orla!' I'd just realised what I'd said. 'I'm so sorry.'

She shrugged. 'It's fine. Don't worry about it. And Mum was thirty-six when she died.'

Oh, so that's okay then. I didn't say that. Sarcasm wasn't the way to go. But sometimes Orla surprised me. One minute, she was just a kid; the next she was so grown up and mature. I suppose that's what being sixteen is about. Crossing over from one to the other. Sometimes you slipped back.

'I think a party's a great idea,' Toby said, and then his enthusiasm dwindled. 'Will Dad be coming?'

Diana shot a look at me. 'If we're having a party for my ... for our, birthday, Alex will expect to be here.'

'Of course he will,' Becca said. 'I know he's so busy at work but he'll make sure he comes to Mum's birthday.'

'He wasn't at Mum's last birthday,' Toby said.

'No. But he was working.' Becca glanced at Diana. 'And Mum didn't have a party for that one. This one is special, as Josie said. Dad will definitely come. I know he will. Oh, let's have a party, Mum. It'll be such fun.'

Orla, I noticed, didn't say a word.

Diana smiled at Becca and Toby and then looked me in the eye.

'Well, Josie. It looks as if we've got a party to arrange.'

Suddenly, it didn't seem such a good idea,

after all.

Twenty-Eight

We'd spent Thursday afternoon and most of the evening making lists for our party – and that included Orla, who seemed to perk up as soon as Noah arrived and joined in. He had the afternoon off; there not being much call for a pool lifeguard in the pouring rain.

Once again, everyone in Seahorse Harbour would be invited, which meant, like it or not, I'd have to spend an evening watching Liam enjoying himself with everyone but me.

Why had I suggested a stupid, birthday party? I really was a glutton for punishment – my own worst enemy.

And Alex would be there too.

Elsie laughed when I told her about it on Friday morning.

'Oh honeybee,' she said, 'you don't need enemies when you've got yourself to stick the knife in your own wounds.'

'It isn't funny, Elsie, and I'm surprised you think it is. I may be over Alex, but I'm still not sure I want to spend my birthday in his company. And now I've got to sit there like a lemon while Liam, no doubt, flaunts Lucy or someone in front of me.'

'If you stopped being so glum for a moment, you'd see the funny side too. And why would Liam flaunt anyone in front of you? He's not the type of man who plays games. That's the sort of thing Alex would do, not Liam.'

That was probably true. All those years ago, after Alex said it had broken his heart to stop seeing me, he held hands with Diana in front of me, or sat with an arm around her during family occasions. He even suggested we could still meet up in secret now and then – for sex, he meant, although he didn't actually say it – but I told him I couldn't do that now he was with my sister. And after he'd proposed to Diana, when I returned from the yacht, he asked if we could "have one final time together", to which I'd thankfully been strong enough to say no, even though there was nothing I wanted more at the time. I'd quickly got a job as a holiday rep in Hawaii. Again, via someone Elsie knew. I needed to be as far away as possible.

'Yes. You're probably right. All these years, I've been in love with a memory. An idea of what could've been. But the reality of a life with Alex wouldn't have matched up to the fantasy.'

Elsie nodded. 'As poor, dear Diana soon found out. I can tell you this, now Diana has told you and I everything. The reason your mum and I fell out was because I told her Alex was having an affair with Una. Tibby wouldn't hear of it, of course. No one would cheat on her wonderful daughter. She said I was making it up. I was seeing things that weren't there. I was being cruel because I didn't have children of my own and I was jealous.'

'Mum said that to you? That you were jealous?'

Elsie grinned. 'Tibby's always had a flair for the dramatic. You know how she is. She watches all those soaps on TV and believes she's starring in one. God forbid we should lead normal, sometimes boring, sometimes wonderful, everyday lives. Tibby needs to have at least one small drama every day. She said that until I apologised for the comment about Alex having an affair with Una, she wouldn't speak to me. I told her that in that case, we wouldn't be speaking to one another until it all came out and that I didn't think Una was the first. She slammed the phone down on me and we haven't spoken since.'

I shook my head. I could almost hear Mum saying that.

'It amazes me how different you and Mum are. But then again, Diana and I are twins and we're like chalk and cheese.'

'Just because we're sisters, it doesn't mean we have to be alike. Although we are in many ways. We both adore dancing. We both love gin. We both love the sunshine and the sea.'

I grinned. 'Almost everyone loves those things.'

Elsie laughed. 'Not everyone loves gin, honeybee. And you and Diana aren't so different. You're very alike in many ways.'

I raised my brows and pulled a face. 'Really? How?'

'You both fell in love with the same man. You both love your mum even though she drives the pair of you insane sometimes. And you've just proved you love one another no matter what. Like me and Tibby, you both love dancing. You both love the rain. And snow. You both love yellow. Oh, the list is endless. I could go on for some time. But I'll say one final thing that you both have in common. You both want to love one man, and for him to love only you. To settle down with him and to have a happy family. Neither of you cares about money, or fame, or travel, or constantly having fun. Even though you, Josie, put on a fairly good show of pretending you do, and saying silly things like you'll never get married. When what you really want ... what you've always wanted ... is to love that special someone and for him to love you back.'

I lowered my gaze. 'Everyone wants that. Deep down.'

'Not everyone, honeybee. Alex doesn't.

Bernice doesn't. I don't. I only got married to shut my mother up. If Eric hadn't died, we'd have got divorced.'

I shot a look at her. 'Really? What about Gray?'

She laughed. 'What about him? We're just having fun. He'll go back to Hell in a few weeks and I'll carry on as I was.'

I tutted. 'Elsie! Gray's lovely. He doesn't come from Hell.'

She laughed out loud. 'Oh he does. He honestly does. Both he and Mikkel. He showed me on the map. It's a village in Norway, about thirty kilometres northeast of Trondheim. I'm going to visit him there this winter. Just so that I can have a photo of me in Hell when it freezes over.'

Twenty-Nine

Saturday was the first day of August, and I couldn't believe it was only two weeks since I'd made that fateful call to Diana. So much had happened in such a short time and I knew my life was going to be completely different by the time I returned to New York.

'You are coming back, aren't you?' Rhoda asked, when she video called me from her phone.

'Of course I am. You're up early for a Saturday. I've just had lunch, so that means it must be about 7 a.m. there.' I recognised the Pulitzer Fountain in Grand Army Plaza, as she walked.

'Just gone 7, yep. But not up early. Haven't been home. Shona, Rachel and I met some guys in a bar, and you know how it is. I think I can safely say that I got the really hot one. Scorching, in fact. Gonna need several cold showers just to stop thinking about the sex last night.'

'I know the feeling.'

'Yeah? You've had sex with someone in Seahorse Harbour? Was it that hot guy you fancied, or someone else?'

'The hot guy. Against a tree. In a thunder and lightning storm. You think your sex was scorching. This was blistering hot.'

'You got blisters? That's gotta hurt.'

I roared with laughter as she grinned and pulled a face.

'Blistering in the figurative sense, not the literal.'

'Ah. Okay. And is there gonna be a repeat performance?'

'Sadly not. He doesn't feel I'm the sort of woman he can take home to his mother. Or his daughter, as it happens. He thinks I just want fun and that I couldn't handle a serious relationship. So he says it won't ever happen again.'

'That's a bit harsh. He sounds like a tosser.'

'No. He's not. He's perfect, I think. I just have to find a way to make him see I'm not as bad as he thinks I am.'

'Hey. Don't go changing who you are just for some guy. There're plenty more where he came from.'

'I'm not sure they make many like him. And it's not really a question of me changing. I think it's more a matter of me realising what I want. What I've always wanted.'

'That sounds deep. Are you okay?'

'Yeah. I'm good. Oh. But I won't be back for my birthday. My sister and I are having a birthday party here. You can come if you like. It would be fantastic to have you here.'

'Oooh, get you. "My sister and I". You sound like the Queen or something. Thanks. But no can do. You know how much I hate flying. We'll have to neck several bottles of bubbly when you get back. Right, you old slapper. I've gotta go. I'm almost home and I need to crash. Let me know what happens on the sex front.'

'Will do, you old tart. Go and get some sleep. Lots of love.'

We waved frantically at one another and blew each other several kisses before we said our final goodbye.

I was sitting on one of the high stools at the breakfast bar, and I watched Becca and Toby in the pool, pushing Henry around on a lilo. Henry was on his back with his paws in the air and his tail was wagging faster than a propeller, half in, half out of the water, sending showers over both Toby and Becca. They looked so young, so innocent. And my heart did a tiny flutter.

Did I want kids? The thought surprised me and I sat bolt upright.

Liam already had Orla. She was sixteen now. Would he want more?

Why was I wondering about him wanting

kids? He'd made it perfectly clear we wouldn't be having a relationship.

But hadn't I just told my best friend that they didn't make many guys like him and that I thought he was perfect? Hadn't I also said that I just had to find a way to make him see I'm not as bad as he thinks I am?

So what was I waiting for?

'Are you ready?' Diana called out from the hall.

'Ready? Er. Ready for what?'

She walked into the kitchen, cocked her head to one side and gave me an odd little smile. She was wearing a deep lemon sundress and matching pumps and she looked like a ray of sunshine, especially as her hair, which was usually the colour of dark honey kissed by bees and sprinkled with gold dust, was much lighter now and almost glowed as if it had a halo around it. Or perhaps I was being a little fanciful. But she did look stunning.

'Oh, Josie. How could you forget? I only told you yesterday. I'm helping out at the Save the Seahorse Fayre. I told you I do it every year and you said last night that you'd help too.'

'Ah. How many glasses of wine had I had when you told me? I'm joking. I do remember. But I hadn't twigged that it was actually this Saturday.'

'I told you it's always on the first Saturday in August.'

'Yes. I remember. Oh God, yes. That's today. Damn. Er. Give me ten minutes.' I glanced at her dress. 'No. Better make that fifteen. Or you can go ahead and I'll meet you there. Are Becca and Toby coming?'

'No. Becca's going to look after Toby while they wait for Noah to finish his shift. He's going to come down with them later. He finishes at 2, so they'll only be on their own for half an hour. I'll wait, if you're really only going to be fifteen minutes, but I'm taking over the tombola at 2 and I need to make sure I've got everything ready and that Perse has put all the raffle tickets in the drum. Last year she left them in the book and then we had to tear them all off and put them in. Unfortunately, it was a breezy day, and a few of them blew away. We don't want a repeat of that.'

'No indeed,' I said, laughing as I jumped off the stool. 'Apart from the likelihood of riots by people whose tickets didn't get a chance to be drawn, just think of the litter pollution. Hardly right to have bits of paper flying into the sea when it's all about saving the seahorse and keeping the beaches litter free. Back in just a jiffy.'

I dashed upstairs, unbuttoning my blouse as I went, hopped out of my shorts and tossed them on the bed as I ran into my room and searched for a dress as pretty as Diana's. I picked a halter neck sundress with tiny pink, lilac and purple flowers on a white background. Summery and virginal, yet sexy and suggestive at the same time, with its low neckline and strapless back. I slid my bare feet into a pair of purple-blue pumps, dabbed mascara on my lashes, swiped a natural-coloured shimmering lipstick over my lips and ran towards the stairs, remembering just in time that I needed to clean my teeth, having only just finished lunch.

'Two minutes to spare,' Diana said, glancing at her watch and laughing. 'You look lovely.'

'Bit rushed but it'll do. Why didn't you remind me when you went upstairs earlier to get ready?'

'I did. I said, "Josie. It's almost 1 o'clock so I'm going to get changed." You said, okay.'

'Ah. But it didn't register that you meant I should get changed too. Next time, any chance you could be more specific? Like, get off your arse and go and get changed because we've got to leave soon.'

'I'll say exactly that the next time. I've told the kids we're off.'

'Is that what the smell is? I did wonder.'

She laughed and shook her head as we headed towards the front door.

'Don't ever consider trying to earn a living as a comedienne, will you?'

'I won't. But I do need to consider a way to earn a living when I get back to New York, so I need to think of something.'

'Oh? Er. I know this sounds silly, but I'd almost forgotten you'd be going back. I ... I wish you weren't.'

I glanced at her as she closed the front door behind us.

'Yeah. I think I'm kind of starting to wish that too.'

Thirty

The Save the Seahorse Fayre was an annual event. They'd held something a bit like it, but on a much smaller scale when I was here all those years ago. Diana told me it seemed to grow larger every year.

Stalls lined several streets, selling cakes and other foods, dog food and collars, T-shirts, beach bags and towels, beach shoes, and lots more besides. There were street entertainers, a band, and of course, The Seahorse Riders were handing out leaflets and getting people to sign up to the Save the Seahorse Fund. The village was packed from top to bottom and all along Sea Walk in both directions.

There were also games and competitions on the sand – volleyball, a sort of mini rounders, a tug of war, a best sandcastle competition, a beach run, a kayak and a paddleboard race and a 'Who can make the best sea person?'. This entailed burying someone in the sand so that only their face and arms were showing, and then designing a mermaid or merman's body, or a fish, or crab, or seahorse from the sand around them. That sounded like fun – but not necessarily for the person buried.

In addition to the games and competitions on the beach, there was the tombola, to which local businesses and some from Easterhill donated prizes. That was positioned on Sea Walk, close to Nice Ice. Amongst the various stalls, there was a 'Guess the number of pebbles in the jar', competition and, outside of Fulbright Ceramics, a 'How much does this seahorse weigh?' – which was a beautifully crafted, ceramic seahorse, glazed in turquoise, teal, pale blue, Royal blue, lilac and cream. It was designed and made by Liam and signed by him and it was the most gorgeous ornament I'd ever seen. The eyes of the seahorse seemed to follow you as you walked by.

When Diana and I walked past, well, hurried past so that Diana wouldn't be late, Lucy was making a guess. I couldn't help but notice that she had her hand on Liam's bare forearm and I'll admit I wanted to march over and remove it. She was laughing and smiling at him and he was smiling right back, but he did glance in our direction when we shot past. And he did look a little flustered. Or perhaps that was my imagination.

Perse had forgotten that the ticket stubs needed to go in the drum, so the first thing

Diana and I did was tear them carefully and make sure none escaped to the sea. We spent the next couple of hours calling people over and persuading them to buy as many tickets as we could. And it seemed I had a knack for it.

'You're very good at this,' Asher said, when he stopped off to buy two tickets at 50p each and I got him to buy ten tickets instead.

'Excellent,' I said. 'I'm going to add first-class tombola ticket salesperson to my C.V. That's bound to open so many extra doors along my career path.' He gave me a questioning look and I added, 'I need to find a job.'

'A job? Really? It just so happens my veterinary nurse gave me notice this morning. She and her husband are moving to Scotland. You'd need to do some training, of course, but it's an idea if you're interested.'

'Aww, thanks, Asher. There're just two teensy problems with that. I'm not good with living things, remember? And the commute from New York each day would really mess with my social life.'

He laughed and nodded. 'Ah yes. Can't even keep a plant alive. I recall you saying. But I'd completely forgotten you're here from New York.

'Yeah. There's a lot of that going around. Now can I interest you in another ten tickets? Those cute little seahorses are depending on you to save their lives and a fiver's nothing really, is it? But it's ten more chances to win one of these gorgeous prizes.'

'Oh, go on then,' he said.

As I handed him his tickets, tore off the stubs and turned to put them in the drum, I saw Liam standing in a queue at the cake stall beside us, and from his position in the queue, he must've heard my entire conversation with Asher.

Asher must've known Liam was there because he turned to him and said, 'I'm glad you offered to buy the cakes, mate. Josie's just taken all my spare cash. I'll need to nip to the ATM later.'

'Ah,' I said, jutting out my jaw. 'How many tickets would you like, Liam?'

He looked me straight in the eye and said, 'You tell me. That's seems to be how it's working.'

'In that case I think you should have the same as Asher. That's twenty tickets for ten pounds please.'

He pulled a tenner from his wallet and handed it to Asher who handed it to me. I sent the tickets to him via Asher and I smiled as I put his stubs in the drum.

'Good luck to you both,' I said, and turned away to sell more tickets.

I didn't see either of them again until much later, but I did see Mikkel hovering nearby once or twice and he seemed to be deciding whether or not to come over to us. He eventually appeared with Gray and Elsie and all three, each bought twenty tickets.

'You seem to be enjoying yourself, honeybee,' Elsie said, as Mikkel was paying Diana for all of the tickets.

'I am. This is a lot of fun. And it's for a good cause so that makes it even better. It's been a hot afternoon though and I could kill for some of your cordial and several ice cubes.'

'You're welcome to pop in, but we're going to the pub first. Why don't you join us there? And speaking of ice cubes. Are the waters still icy with you know who?'

'Riddled with icebergs, sadly. But I'm working on a way to melt them.'

'That's my girl. And how's my lovely Diana?'

'Hot, but having fun.'

I opened my mouth and was going to say: 'That's what all the men tell her', but thankfully, I realised that might be inappropriate given the situation, so I closed my mouth again and smiled. Instead I said, 'We might see you at the pub then.'

'Oh!' Diana looked anxious. 'I'll need to get Toby home. He's still recovering. He's been in the pool all morning and he's on the sand this afternoon. I don't want him to overdo it. You go though, Josie.'

'We'll see,' I said.

'Come along then, Mikkel,' Gray said with a smile, tapping Mikkel's arm. 'We've got a tug of war to win.'

Two other women from the village came and relieved me and Diana, and we wandered down to the sands to watch some of the competitions. Toby, Orla, Becca and Noah were there and Henry was being unusually well-behaved. Even buried up to his neck, with just his ears and his front paws sticking out, he was unbelievably relaxed. They'd given him the sand body of a sailor, and had drawn a hat in the sand, and stripes as if on a T-shirt. He looked so cute that they actually won second prize.

It had been a lovely day but one thing spoilt it for me. Or should I say one person.

Lucy Willis.

Every time I saw Liam, Lucy wasn't far behind. She was a bit like a shadow. But Liam didn't seem to mind. Which only made it worse.

I was thinking about going to the pub later, but Diana was adamant she wouldn't, so before the Fayre wound down completely, she and I and the kids, walked back up the hill to Sea View Cottage. On the way, we passed The Olde Forge, where Liam was once again taking guesses about the seahorse's weight – and Lucy was hovering nearby.

'Let's guess, Mum,' Becca said, so we all did, except Orla. Although she said she had no idea, she felt it wasn't right for her to guess, as she was after all, Liam's daughter.

I wrote down my guess on the piece of turquoise paper Liam gave me, along with my name and phone number, as instructed, but I added, 'please call me, even if I don't win' on mine and made sure I folded it up so no one could see it. I popped it in the box and smiled as I handed him my pound coin, the cost of a bid. You were only allowed one per person. I suppose because Liam didn't want to have to go through hundreds of guesses to find out who had won.

'I hope I'll get a call,' I said.

His eyes narrowed in a question for just a second and then he said, 'Oh yes. The winning call. Good luck.'

Thirty-One

We had just finished supper when the doorbell rang and Becca jumped up to answer. Toby had taken Henry into the garden and was throwing him some sticks. As usual, Henry was returning to Toby with everything but the stick he'd thrown. Diana, Noah and I were laughing.

'It's Liam and Orla,' Becca called out, as they followed her into the kitchen.

We'd left Orla with her dad on the way up the hill, although she seemed reluctant. No doubt due to the fact that Noah was still with us and now, when she came in and saw Noah seated at the table, she glowered at him and at Becca.

'Hello, you two,' Diana said. 'This is a nice surprise. Would you like a beer, Liam? And Orla? What would you like?'

Liam looked unsure, but as I smiled at him, he seemed to relax.

'If we're not in the way,' he said. 'A beer would be great, thanks.'

'Of course you're not in the way,' Diana

assured him.

'Would you both like some ice cream, or some lemon meringue pie? There's plenty left of both.'

She went to the fridge and got Liam a beer and Becca got Orla a Coke. Orla went and sat at the table, pulling up a chair between Noah and what was obviously Becca's place.

'Not for me, thanks. I need to watch my figure.' Orla ran a hand down her side and I saw Liam give her a concerned look.

'Sit down, Liam,' Diana said, and pointed to a chair near me.

He hesitated. 'I'm fine. I'll stand. I feel as if I've been sitting for most of the day.'

For someone who supposedly didn't tell lies, that was a corker.

'Toby? Don't throw those sticks too far,' Diana called out, but it was too late, Henry bounded after the stick leaping over one hedge and crashing through another until he disappeared from view.

'Damn. He's gone into the woods,' Diana said. 'Toby. Don't go after him by yourself. Wait for me.'

'I'll go,' Liam said, placing the canvas bag he'd been carrying on the floor.

'It's okay. I'll go. You've just got here.' Noah dashed out without waiting for a response. 'Stay here, Toby. I'll get him.'

'Such a lovely boy,' Diana said, as Noah

unlocked the gate leading out to the woods.

'Yes,' said Liam. 'He is.'

Orla looked as if she might go too but she must've thought better of it.

'Er. I came to bring you this,' Liam said, reaching into the canvas bag on the floor. He pulled out the gorgeous seahorse prize and looked directly at me.

'Is that for me? Did ... did I win?'

'You did,' he said, with a look that suggested I might've won more than just the seahorse, although to be fair, the seahorse was a fantastic prize.

'Wow! I don't think I've ever won anything in my life. I can't quite believe it.'

He placed it on the table in front of me. The seahorse and Liam looked me straight in the eye.

'I couldn't believe it either,' Liam said. 'When I read your ... guess, I was really surprised.'

'Why?' Diana laughed. 'My sister's not just a pretty face you know.'

'I know,' he said, his gaze still fixed on me. 'And the guess was almost spot on.'

'It's so beautiful, Liam. It really is. Thank you.'

'Thank you for entering.'

'It was for a good cause.'

'Henry!' Noah was laughing. 'Henry, come here!'

Henry bounded through the open gate and ran to Toby. He had something in his mouth but it obviously wasn't the stick. It hung down limply on both sides and was white and brown.

Noah came in, closed the gate and locked it and tried to grab Henry who was circling Toby as if he wasn't sure whether to drop what was in his mouth at Toby's feet or to keep hold of it.

'Was is that in his mouth?' Diana laughed.

'No idea,' I said. 'Something unpleasant, I suspect. Although it looks a bit like a long white moustache with lumps of mud on it.'

Henry's nose twitched and he raced up the garden and dashed into the kitchen, with Toby and Noah close behind. He ran to me and dropped his treasure at my feet.

'Two prizes in one night,' Becca said, laughing. 'What is it?'

We all peered at it. Just as Toby was about to pick it up, I realised what it was.

'No!' I shrieked, reaching out to grab what had once been my white lace knickers. The knickers I was wearing the night of the storm when Liam and I had made love against the Copper Beech tree.

Henry thought it was a game and picked them up and ran off again.

I'm sure I turned the colour of the red wine I was drinking and I shot a look at Liam.

As if he could read my mind, his mouth

315

opened a fraction and a grin formed on his lips.

Before I could get to my feet, Liam had grabbed Henry by the collar. He retrieved my knickers, scrunched them up in his hand so that no one could see they were knickers and dropped them in his canvas bag.

'You can put it in the bin,' Diana said, giving him a rather curious look.

'It might be covered in all sorts of things. I'll dispose of it. I'll put it just outside the door for now.'

He walked to the front door, opened it and dropped the bag on the step.

As he walked back towards us, he said, 'Today was a great success. How much do you think the tombola made, Diana?'

Having changed the subject from my knickers, he came and sat down, pulling out a chair close to me, and with Diana and everyone now chatting about the day, the grin on his face grew wider and wider as he sipped his beer and threw me surreptitious looks every few seconds.

I wasn't sure if I wanted to thank him, or thump him, but to be honest what I really wanted to do, was kiss him.

Thirty-Two

Liam and Orla left around 8.30 just as it started to rain. Diana said she wanted a long bath and an early night and I said I was doing the same. The kids and Henry went upstairs to bed too. The sun and the fun had taken it out of all of us and now the rain seemed to make us all feel sleepy.

Except I didn't have a bath and I didn't go to bed. I sat by my window looking down towards the village through the teeming rain towards The Olde Forge, and I thought about Liam. He'd been giving me looks all evening. Rather sexy looks, full of meaning. And yet he hadn't phoned.

Perhaps bringing the prize to me was his way of saying that he was ready and willing to talk and now it was up to me to convince him. Perhaps that's what I needed to do. And I'd do that first thing in the morning.

'There's no time like the present,' I could almost hear Elsie say.

That was true. Why wait? Why spend the

whole night wondering? Why toss and turn and run through scenarios in my mind when all I had to do was run down the road and go to him. I knew where he lived. It was the last house in Wood Lane. Not that far from Elsie's.

The four or five glasses of wine I'd drunk might have given me a sense of bravado, or at least courage. And what was Love without courage?

I jumped off the bed, still wearing my sundress and tip-toed downstairs. I didn't want to wake the whole house although it was only 9.15 and I opened the front door as quietly as I could.

It was pouring and the rain fell in long straight lines. I grabbed an umbrella and ran down the hill, skipping over puddles and dodging splashes from the one or two cars that passed.

When I reached Liam's front door, I took a deep breath and thought about what I would say.

I'd lower the umbrella and stand before him in the rain, my hair clinging to my face and my dress soaked as he opened the door.

'I can change,' I would say. 'I can be responsible. I can be serious. I can be the woman you want. The woman you need. I know I can't replace Una as Orla's mum, and none of us would want me to, but I can try and be like a big sister to her, or a really good older friend. I just need you to give me a chance, Liam. To give us a chance.'

'Come in out of the rain,' he'd say, looking at me as if he couldn't quite believe I was standing there or that I'd just said what I had. 'Do you mean it, Josie?'

'Yes,' I'd say. 'I mean it. I love you, Liam.'

And he'd say he loved me too. And he'd pull me into his arms and we'd kiss and... I rang the doorbell and waited, a smile of hope and excitement on my face, butterflies in my stomach feverishly flapping their wings in expectation. I lowered the umbrella.

'Josie?'

It wasn't Liam who opened the door.

It wasn't even Orla, although I hadn't given that a thought.

It was Lucy. Lucy Willis. And she was wearing nothing but a dressing gown. That much was obvious from the amount of skin I could see beneath the loosely tied robe.

'L-Lucy? W-what are you doing here?'

She smiled and cast her eyes down her own body.

'I would've thought that was obvious. Did you want something? Liam's just popped out to get a bottle of wine.'

'A bottle of ... wine,' I repeated like an imbecile.

'Yes. It seems he's run out. Of wine that is.'

319

Who went out for a bottle of wine when it was pouring with rain?

But who went out to tell someone they loved them when it was pouring with rain?

'Oh. Er. Okay.'

I couldn't take this in. Liam had been grinning at me and giving me suggestive smiles just a couple of hours ago.

Or had he been grinning because he knew he'd be seeing Lucy tonight?

Had the smiles been gloating?

Lucy was gloating now.

'Do you want to leave Liam a message? I can give it to him when he gets back.'

'What? Oh no. Er. He ... he had something of mine, that's all. It doesn't matter. Don't bother to tell him I was here. It's not important.'

'Okay then. You'd better get out of this rain. Good night, Josie. Oh, and pleasant dreams.'

Pleasant dreams! I'd like to give her pleasant dreams.

No. I'd like to give her nightmares.

So that was it then. I'd got my answer. Liam was sleeping with Lucy.

Liam, like Alex, had chosen the future, 'perfect wife'. And the perfect wife was never going to be me.

Thirty-Three

To my surprise, Liam did try to call me that night. But I didn't answer.

He tried again about half an hour later, around 10.30 and again ten minutes after that, but I didn't answer those either.

Had Lucy told him I'd been there? Is that why he was calling?

Or was he going to tell me, belatedly, that he and Lucy were dating? More than dating. Sleeping together.

How long had that been going on? Was that the real reason he thought that having sex in the woods with me had been a mistake?

So much for Diana saying he was an honest and decent man. Clearly, he wasn't that much different from Alex.

Whatever it was, I didn't want to hear it, so I took a leaf out of Diana's book and I blocked the number and deleted the image of the god Apollo, riding his chariot across the sky, which had been the image I'd allocated to Liam's number.

And then I cried myself to sleep, which was something I hadn't done since Diana and Alex's wedding.

But I didn't sleep for long. I tossed and turned and cried and bashed my pillow and used it to muffle my screams.

Sunday morning came. I got up early and went for a walk.

Asher didn't work on Sundays.

But he did go for a run. He'd told me that at Diana's cocktail party when we'd chatted. He ran every morning, in fact.

My eyes were puffy, and my head felt like my brain had turned to slush but I put on a little make-up and concealer and headed down to Sea Walk, leaving a note for Diana.

I didn't have to wait too long. I saw Asher pounding the pavement towards me and I have to say, if it hadn't been for the fact that I was crazy about Liam bloody Fulbright, I could easily have fallen for Asher Bryant.

I waved at him and he waved back, making a slight detour and coming and standing in front of me, jogging on the spot.

'Good morning,' he said, beaming at me.

'Good morning.' I let my head bounce up and down in an exaggerated fashion and he stopped jogging and laughed.

'Sorry. Didn't want to break my stride.'

'Everyone deserves a break.'

'You're not into running then, I take it?'

'Only if something's chasing me. Something I don't like, I should clarify.'

'You're out early? Couldn't sleep? Or do you enjoy an early morning walk?'

'I enjoy an early morning coffee. But I wanted a walk because it felt so fresh this morning after the heat of yesterday and then that … rain.'

I didn't want to think about that rain. I didn't want to think about last night.

'Yes. I love mornings like this. Have you just started your walk or are you just finishing it?'

'Finishing. I need more coffee. I don't suppose anywhere around here's open yet, is it? I could do with some before I face that hill.'

'Not at this time on a Sunday, no. Er. I'm headed home. If you want to, you're welcome to come in and have a coffee.'

'Really? Are you sure? That would be great.' I gave him a beaming smile, clamping my teeth together in a jokey way.

He laughed again. 'Yes, I'm sure.'

'You're not going to make me run there, are you?'

'No. We'll walk.'

I fell into step beside him and we walked to his cottage. Slightly faster than I would normally walk but at least we didn't jog.

'This is it,' he said, opening the door. 'Excuse the mess.'

His cottage was a little smaller than Elsie's but it was modern, shiny and stylish, whereas hers was quaint and shabby chic. The modern kitchen was sleek and black with red tiles. The sitting room had dark green walls and black leather furniture; even the wood was black. Ebony, perhaps, or a very dark stained Oak, maybe. Apart from a shirt folded over a chair and a neat pile of magazines on one of the sofa cushions, the place was pristine. If he called this a mess, he'd call in the local council rubbish clearance if he saw my apartment.

'This is lovely,' I said.

'Take a seat. I'd suggest sitting in the garden but everything's wet from the rain. It's all wooden furniture out there so even with cushions, you'll get a damp rear.'

'And no one wants a damp rear,' I remarked.

I took a seat and waited for him to bring in the coffee. He brought a pot on a tray, two cups, a sugar bowl and a milk jug.

'I thought I'd be posh as you're a guest.'

'No need to go to any trouble on my part. You don't have to try to impress me.'

'I'd like to.' He glanced over at me. 'Impress you, that is.'

'What makes you think you don't?'

He held my gaze and smiled.

'I got the feeling you might have your eyes on someone else.'

'No.' I pursed my lips and shook my head. 'No one I can think of.'

'Really?'

'Nope. No one. What about you? Have you got your eyes on anyone?'

'Yes. They're on her now.'

I glanced around the room and then looked at him and grinned, fluttering my lashes.

'Me? You've got your eyes on me?'

'Uh-huh.'

'Well then,' I said. 'I think perhaps, we should do something about that, don't you? But I must say one thing first.'

He was giving me a look that suggested he wasn't quite sure what was happening.

'Okay,' he said. 'I'm listening.'

'In a little under three weeks, it'll be my birthday. And Diana's of course. We're having a party on Friday the 21st. That's our birthday. I'll be leaving the very next day and going home to New York.'

'So you're saying...?'

'I'm saying that I'm only here for a little under three weeks. And I'm not sure when, or if, I'll be coming back to Seahorse Harbour.'

'It would just be a summer fling then, is that what you're saying?'

'Yep. Something like that.'

'No strings. No commitments. No tearful goodbyes. No promises to try to keep in touch.'

'Exactly.

'That works for me.'

'Okay then. But there's just one more thing you should know.'

'Shoot.'

'I need to go out on a date before I even consider sleeping with you. Possibly a couple of dates.'

'Seriously? That sounds more like the start of a relationship than a fling.'

I shrugged. I was already getting cold feet.

'Fling was your word, not mine. I'm weird. What can I tell you? I don't like one- night stands.' That wasn't entirely true. I'd had a few of those in my life, but he didn't need to know that.

'It wouldn't be one night. We'd being seeing each other for just over two weeks.'

'I know. But them's the rules, gov'nor. Take it or leave it. Your choice.'

'I'll take it. Without question.'

'Great.'

'Are you doing anything tonight? Shall we have our first date?'

'Yep. That works for me.' This was going faster than I'd expected.

'Excellent. I'll pick you up around 7 then.'

'See you at 7. Thanks for the coffee.' I got to my feet but I felt a little shaky. 'And Asher?'

'Yes.'

'For Heaven's sake. Tidy this place up, will you?'

He looked around the room, concern written on his face until he saw my grin.

'It'll be spotless the next time you're here.'

He walked me to the door and for a minute, I thought he was going to try to kiss me. I pretended to be searching for something in my handbag and hurried out the minute I could.

And almost walked right into Lucy. Which was weird.

It was only about 6.30 and if she'd been heading home from Liam's, she would've been walking in the other direction. She must've been coming from her own house.

Which could only mean either she'd left Liam's really early and gone home and got changed and was going out again. Or she hadn't spent the night at Liam's.

Not that that changed anything. She'd still been naked save for a dressing gown last night. And he'd still gone out and got them some wine.

'Hi Lucy. You're out early.' I forced a smile.

'Hi Josie. So are you.' Her smile was as fake as mine.

It was only when I saw the look on her face and her eyes dart from me to Asher's front door, that I realised what she was thinking.

That I might've spent the night with Asher.

Thirty-Four

'Have you heard the news?' Diana said, as I walked back into Sea View Cottage.

'That Liam's having sex with Lucy? Yes.'

'What? Liam's not having sex with Lucy.'

'He is. I know that for a fact.'

'Gosh. I wonder when that started? But that wasn't what I meant. Obviously, as I didn't know that. I meant about the burglaries?'

'No. Have they found the crooks?'

'No. There have been three more. Yesterday. During the day. While everyone was at the Save the Seahorse Fayre. All three of them were on Seahorse Cliffs. The East Cliffs, not this side. One was in The Heights and two were in Rock Road.'

'Jonno lives in The Heights. I hope it wasn't his place. Was anyone hurt, like Elsie was?'

'No. And no one saw anything, so the police have no further clues.'

'I don't think they had any clues, let alone further. How did you hear about it?'

She lowered her gaze. 'Mikkel called me. He lives up on Seahorse Cliffs and when he went for his run this morning, one of the residents of Rock Road who was walking their dog, stopped and spoke to him.'

'And Mikkel called you because...?'

'To let me know, and to tell me to be careful.'

'That's nice. Are you going to tell Alex about them now? The burglaries, I mean.'

A thoughtful expression covered her face and she didn't answer for a while. I went and poured us both some coffee, seeing that her mug was empty.

'I don't know,' she finally said. 'I should. I know I should. He's my husband, this is our house and his children are here. It's the sort of thing a wife would normally tell her husband. But the odd thing is, I really don't want to. If I do, he may come down, and I ... I'm not sure I want that. And what can he do that we aren't doing? We lock up. We set the alarm. We close all the windows when we go out. And we've got Henry.'

'Well, I'd rather he wasn't here, if I'm being honest.'

'Henry?'

I tutted. 'Alex. I'd rather Alex didn't come down. I'm over all that, especially now I'm ... that doesn't matter. I just think it might be a bit awkward for all of us if Alex were here.'

'I agree. So we won't tell him.'

'Okay. But what if one of his cronies from the golf club or the air club happens to speak to him and mentions there've been burglaries? Won't he be furious with you for not telling him?'

'Probably. But he'll be furious anyway because I didn't tell him right away, so when he finds out is sort of irrelevant now.'

'Are you ... are you telling him about our party? Because I'm not sure you can keep that from him really. Although, as we did discuss, you could tell him we just had a few drinks with some friends and it turned into a party. But if he calls the kids and speaks to them, they might say something.'

'He never calls the kids. He calls me and then speaks to them. Although he rarely calls me either. I think I'm going to tell him on the day, and pretend I told him when we first decided. He's always so busy and he never listens to me so he won't be absolutely sure.'

'Diana! You really are making some changes, aren't you? And what about Bernice?'

'I'll tell her you didn't want her here.' She laughed suddenly. 'Oh, wouldn't that be great? I can see her face right now.'

'That works for me. I don't want her here.'

'We can't say that. Can we?'

'Absolutely. I'll call her and tell her myself if you like. That woman changed my life.'

Diana lowered her eyes and her voice. 'No, Josie. I did that. Bernice just reacted as I knew she would.'

'Yeah. But if Bernice hadn't made Alex into some super-obedient son, he would've told her to get stuffed when she forbade him to see me. It's her fault. I've decided. Let's change the subject. I'm going on a date with Asher tonight. You don't mind, do you?'

'With Asher? No of course I don't mind. But why with Asher?'

'Because he likes me and Liam's now with Lucy.'

'I still don't believe that. They're friends, yes. But lovers? I just can't see it.'

'That's because you didn't see her, naked, save for a dressing gown at Liam's house last night. And Liam had gone to get wine. In the pouring rain. That's serious.'

'Who told you this?'

'I saw it with my own eyes. Er. I nipped out last night.'

'Why? To see Liam?' The surprise was in her eyes and her tone.

'Yes. I ... I was going to tell him how I felt about him and that I could change and be the woman he wants me to be. Sort of. I had a whole speech planned. And then Lucy opened the door in a damn dressing gown.'

'Oh, Josie. I'm so sorry. I had no idea he was seeing her. And he ... he can't have been seeing her long. He would never have had sex with you in the woods if he was seeing Lucy.'

'He did say it was a mistake. Perhaps that's what he meant. It was a mistake not just because he thinks I'm a party girl but also because he was seeing someone else.'

'No. I know him well enough to know that he would've said that. And I don't think he would've ... continued. He would've stopped himself immediately. Like he did with me.'

My phone rang and, from the Medusa and the snakes, I saw it was Mum.

'Mum's clearly getting worried. It's only just gone 7 and I can't hold her at bay much longer. I've been sending her the odd text saying I'm still working on it and I'd let her know as soon as I found out what was worrying you.'

Diana sighed and then smiled. 'Perhaps it's time we told her what's been going on. Having discussed it all with Elsie and of course with you, I feel better about it, I think. Now's as good a time as any.'

'Okay. Let's do this. Hi Mum. Hope you're well. Listen. Before you say anything, Diana wants a word with you. We both do. With you and with Dad. Will you go and get him from the study and we'll video call you both in ten minutes. Okay? Bye.'

I rang off and took a deep breath.

'Okay,' Diana said. 'We need coffee and we

need chocolate cake. And then I'm going to tell Mum that, sadly, I'm not as perfect as she thinks. This should be fun.'

Thirty-Five

'I'm gobsmacked, Diana. Utterly gobsmacked,' Mum said, when Diana had finished.

Dad rubbed his chin and said, 'Well, well, well. There's a turn-up for the books. I often thought there was something about Alex that I didn't quite like, but I could never put my finger on it. I assume you're going to divorce him.'

'Divorce him?' Mum shrieked and Dad shot back, sticking a finger in his ear as though she'd deafened him. 'Why would she divorce him? So the man wandered once. They can get over that.'

'It wasn't once, Mum,' Diana said. 'It was several times. And he's still doing it. You've met Marina?'

'Marina? Oh yes. Didn't like her at all.'

'Well Alex does. He's sleeping with her right now.'

'Good gracious. Well, that's a different matter. Perhaps you should divorce him. But you'll need to get good lawyers. Bernice can be a nasty piece of work. Always said that about her. You make sure you get your fair share of the money.'

'I don't want the money. But I would rather like this house. I ... I haven't quite decided yet though. What I want to do about me and Alex, I mean. I'll let you and Dad know once I've decided. But ... Alex isn't the only one who ... has been seeing other people. I've met someone and I think ... I think I want to see him again.'

'You ... you've what?' Mum yelled. 'Diana! How could you?'

I'd had enough.

'Very easily, Mum,' I said. 'Di's been unhappy for years. Alex has behaved like a shit. She's met a man who makes her happy. We all deserve a bit of that. Don't make a big deal out of it. People fall in and out of love all the time. It's not the end of the world. The kids know him and they like him. I've met him, and he's great. Elsie is seeing his dad. Not that that's relevant but I thought I'd mention it. Oh, and I've fallen in love but he loves someone else. Right. I think that gets us all up to date. Dad, you go back to your telescope. We'll talk again soon. Mum, have a good think about what's important here. Your daughter's happiness, if you need a clue. We'll give you a call in a few days. Bye for now. Love you both.' I disconnected the call and grinned at Diana. 'Do you mind that I stepped in?'

Diana laughed. 'No. I'm glad you did. What do you think she'll do?'

'I think she'll call Elsie and Elsie will tell her something similar. After that, it's up to Mum. She'll either accept it and support your choices. Or she won't.'

Thirty-Six

My first date with Asher didn't go well. And neither did my second. It's always the way. The minute you fall in love with someone, you can't seem to flirt or pretend to like someone else. Everything they say or do, you compare to the person you love. Every touch. Every look. Every word. Asher was a lovely guy. A really lovely guy. He just wasn't Liam.

I hadn't seen Liam since the Saturday when he brought me the seahorse, and it was Wednesday now. By 6 a.m. it was obvious it was going to be a scorcher. All I wanted to do was collapse by the pool, preferably with a vat of chilled white wine. But the kids wanted to go to the Lido. Becca to see Noah, and Toby to show the boys who picked on him that he wasn't scared of them. So they asked me to go with them.

Diana had made one firm decision. She was going to sell her baby clothing business, so she stayed at home with Henry to try to broker a deal to do that. The silent partner, a friend of

Alex's was keen to take it over. They just had to agree a price.

And Mikkel had offered to help. With several business ventures of his own, he knew a thing or two about negotiation and he was talking Diana through the entire process. Just as a friend. Nothing else. But even a fool could see that things were moving along with him and Diana. Albeit slowly.

Naturally, Orla joined us at the Lido. Part of me hoped Liam might too, but in a way I was glad he didn't.

We sat and watched Toby, who had Noah to give him support as he approached the boys who had bullied him and basically told them not to even think about bothering him again. I had no idea if it would work but bullies are really just cowards, trying to pretend they're better than they are. And Noah was sure it would work on these particular boys. As they left the Lido shortly after, it seemed that Noah was right.

'How's your dad?' I asked Orla. 'I haven't seen him since Saturday.'

'He's okay. Working most of the time.'

'And Lucy?'

'Lucy? Yeah. She's okay too.'

I wasn't going to get much out of her. But as she was watching Noah's every move, I suppose she wasn't really listening to me.

I noticed the ginger-haired man with the

sombrero. The one I'd given a four. He was as loud today as he was before, but this time I saw that he had two sons. They were almost the spitting image of him, even down to the hat.

'Hey look,' I said to Becca and Orla. 'Sombrero man must have a wife. He's got two kids. They're about your age.'

'I don't fancy yours much,' Orla said.

'You can have them both,' Becca replied.

'I don't want them! I've set my sights higher than that.'

'Me too,' said Becca. 'And I don't like tattoos. Especially not spiders.'

I looked over at sombrero boys and I saw what Becca meant. Both boys had a spider tattoo on their wrists. A large spider. I bet that put off a lot of girls. Imagine that hand with that spider working its way over your body. It made me shake just thinking about it. I'd never hurt a spider if I could help it but I had a bit of a phobia about them and I certainly wouldn't want that spider near me. Even if it was attached to Liam, I wouldn't. Okay. Maybe I could tolerate it if it was on Liam's wrist.

I closed my eyes to avoid looking at it, but the image kept popping into my head.

And then suddenly I remembered that it wasn't the first time I'd seen it. Elsie had described the spider she'd seen on the glove of the person who had pushed her. The image that had been drawn was almost identical to the tattoos on those boys' wrists. It might be a bit of a long shot and there might be hundreds of boys with that tattoo, but what if the tattoo was what Elsie saw, and not on a glove, but on a wrist above a glove? Perhaps the light from the moon, or the intruder's torch made it more prominent. Or perhaps it was some sort of glow in the dark affair. Did tattoos glow in the dark? Was that even possible?

I pretended to take photos of Toby and Noah but I took lots of photos of the boys' tattoos. Gray had got the contact and crime number at the police station so I'd get that from him and give them a call.

I wasn't sure if I expected anything to come of it, but two days later, a police officer called round to Elsie's and said they had arrested three suspects after receiving information. Officers had gone to the static, mobile home where sombrero man and his family were staying. The sliding doors had been wide open, allowing the officers to see inside. They spotted some of the stolen items listed and, as soon as sombrero man realised the police were there, he and his sons confessed.

'Wait till I tell Dad,' Orla said when she came to the house and we told her. 'You said sombrero man had potential.' She laughed.

'He did have potential,' I said. 'Potential to be a thief. Just not a very good one. He clearly wasn't very bright. Who leaves stolen goods in plain sight? And who leaves the doors to their mobile home wide open for everyone to see those goods? But at least now we can all sleep soundly in our beds.'

Thirty-Seven

I was waiting for Asher, about to go out on our third date when it happened.

It was Saturday night and Diana and Toby were watching a film on Netflix and Henry was curled up beside Toby, fast asleep.

The front door burst open and Becca raced in, charging to Diana and standing in front of the TV screen. Tears were rolling down her cheeks.

I instantly thought either she'd had a row with Orla over Noah. Or Noah had dumped her.

'Is it true?' she screamed, and Henry's ears shot up as he stumbled to his feet. 'Is it? How did Orla know and not us?'

I realised it was worse than I thought. Orla had told Becca about Una and Alex's affair.

'Is what true, sweetheart? Whatever is the matter?'

Diana shot me a look and tried to wrap her arms around Becca but Becca flung her off.

Henry barked, Becca screamed, Toby yelled, 'What's going on?'

'Dad! Dad and Una. Did they have an affair? Were they in love? Was he really going to leave us all for her?'

'What? Who told you this?'

'Orla!' Becca's voice was loud enough to pierce ear drums, and getting louder by the minute. As was Henry's bark.

Asher appeared at the open front door and stepped inside.

'Hel-lo. Er. Is this a bad time?'

Talk about stating the obvious. I jumped up and went to him.

'Yes. Sorry, Asher, but it is. Can we leave tonight, please? I think I'll be needed here.'

Becca was still screaming and crying and almost incoherent now.

'Of course. Is there anything I can do?'

'Yes. If you see Liam, tell him I was right.'

'About what?'

'Sorry. Nothing. Forget it. I was being silly. I'll call you tomorrow. Or in a day or two when this settles down.'

I ushered him out with an apologetic smile and closed the door behind him.

It was going to be a long night.

And not in the way I'd expected.

Thirty-Eight

It had taken some time to get Becca to calm down. And not just her. Because once Toby realised what Becca was saying, he started getting upset too. Even Henry was whining.

Eventually, Diana and I managed to calm all three of them, Henry being the easiest to placate with a chewy treat. Although in the end, treats had worked equally well to settle Toby and Becca – chocolate fudge cake for Toby, chocolate fudge ice cream for Becca. Wine helped soothe mine and Diana's frayed nerves.

Diana had explained that sometimes, two adults can love one another but still fall in love with other people, which is what had happened with Alex and Una. She said that she didn't know whether Alex would have left them or not, but that even if he had, he would never have stopped loving them, and that, no matter what, Alex would always be their dad and would never cause them hurt intentionally. She was so convincing, she had me believing her.

But she also said that if she and Alex did

decide to live apart, it would be because they thought it was the best thing to do for all of them. That surprised me. It was the first time I'd actually heard her say that was an option. Until then she had said she couldn't imagine her life without him in it. Now she obviously could. Although he would still be in her life in one way or another. He *was* the father of her children.

Becca and Toby went to bed, a lot later than usual, but reassured that the world hadn't ended and that even though life may be different from hereon in, it would still go on and many things would stay the same. Only one or two things would change.

'I may be wrong,' I said, when Diana and I sat in the sitting room, drinking brandy, around midnight, 'but I get the distinct impression you came to a decision tonight.'

Diana was still shaking a little and her face was damp from all the tears she'd shed, but as I wrapped my arm around her I felt her body relax as she expelled a long and sorrowful sigh.

'Yes,' she said, her voice calm, cool and determined. 'I think perhaps I have.'

Thirty-Nine

We decided to have a pyjama day on Sunday, and in keeping with the general mood, it was raining. Toby seemed a little more subdued than normal but on the whole, no different than he had been the day before the 'Orla incident' as Diana and I had come to call it.

Becca was the worst affected. Not only had she discovered the truth about her dad – well, part of the truth at least, she only knew about the one affair with Una, not the other eight or ten or twelve affairs he'd also had of which Diana had lost count – Becca had also lost her best friend. And because of that, it was going to take her longer to accept.

Through her tears and sobs and prolonged silences, we'd ascertained that, late on Saturday afternoon, around 6, as she and Orla were leaving the Lido, Orla had seen Noah take Becca's hand and pull her to him for a gentle kiss. And Orla had realised, from the way Noah and Becca behaved, that kiss wasn't their first. It was in fact, Becca told us, their third.

Orla went 'bat shit crazy' to use a non-medical term. She accused Becca and Noah of lying and cheating and having sex and laughing at her behind her back. Of betraying her and deceiving her and breaking her heart in two as well as breaking up their friendship. She said she never wanted to see either of them again and that as far as she was concerned, Becca may as well be dead, because she was dead to her and always would be from then on.

But that wasn't all dear, sweet Orla had said.

She'd also said that she was going to tell everyone that Becca Dunn was a tart, just like Lucy had said Becca's aunt Josie was.

Well. I was ready to give Orla a stern talking to before I heard that. Now she and I were definitely going to have to have words. And so were me and Orla's dad. Not to mention his sodding, not-so-perfect, girlfriend, Lucy.

'I'm just popping out for a while,' I said to Diana, when both Toby and Becca had fallen asleep on the sofa.

Toby was cuddled up to Henry, whose long legs were dangling over the edge, and Becca was cuddled in Diana's arms, her long legs tucked beneath her. Becca got her legs from her dad. Everything else about her, she got from Diana. Although she did have slightly bigger boobs than her mum.

Which was another thing dear Orla had

apparently commented on: that Noah only liked Becca because she had big boobs. An odd proclamation, seeing as how Orla had the better and most seductive figure of the pair of them.

'You're going to have a word with Liam and Orla, aren't you?' Diana said. 'Please don't say or do anything you might regret later.'

'Would you rather I didn't say anything? Apart from all the dreadful things Orla said to Becca, let's not forget the little treasure did call me a tart. And maybe, in Lucy bloody Willis' eyes, I am. Perhaps in Liam's too. And there might be some truth in it. But girls shouldn't go around calling other girls – or women, tarts just because they like to have sex. Orla needs to understand the difference. And Liam needs to tell her that. She also needs to learn to respect her friends. And that true friendship is far more important than squabbling over a boy. Or a man, come to that.'

Diana smiled. 'Go. And good luck. But please don't let me hear that Lucy Willis has been punched on the nose.'

'As if. You know I'm not into violence. However much it may be called for.'

I marched down the hill to Liam's, the umbrella gripped tightly in my hand, the irony of the situation not lost on me. Last time I walked to Liam's in the rain was the night I was going to tell him I loved him. Today, I was going to tell him something else entirely.

I rang the bell, half expecting Lucy to answer the door in her dressing gown again, but it was Liam who flung the door open, with a deep frown on his face and tension rippling through him if the muscles in his neck were anything to go by. They looked tighter than violin strings.

'Josie! Wh-what are you doing here?'

'I've come to have a word with you and Orla, if I may.'

'Er. This isn't really a good time. Orla's rather upset.'

'So is Becca. And Noah, I should imagine. And so am I.'

'Oh? Er. I'm not sure I follow, but you had better come in then.'

He stood aside to let me pass and I walked into the hall as he took my umbrella from me.

This was the first time I'd been in Liam's house but it was just as I'd imagined it would be. Warm and welcoming and lived in.

'We're in the kitchen,' Liam said. 'Through there.' He pointed towards an open door.

'Is Lucy here?'

'Lucy?' he sounded surprised. 'No. Why would Lucy be here?'

'I was hoping to have a word with her too.'

'With Lucy?'

'Yes.'

'Oh. Then I'll give you her address.'

'No need. I know where she lives.'

'Of course.' His voice had a gravelly edge to it and his eyes flickered strangely. 'She lives close to Asher. You would've seen her.'

'I saw you coming out of her cottage early one morning, remember?'

'Oh yeah. I'd forgotten about that. Er. I heard we all have you to thank for catching the burglars.'

'Dad!' Orla shouted. 'I don't want to see anyone. I'm too upset. I don't ... Oh! Josie. I thought ... I...'

She looked as if she'd been crying too and I wondered what she'd told Liam. He didn't seem to understand why I was there.

'Hello, Orla,' I said. 'I can see you're upset, as Becca is. Although perhaps not quite as upset as her. May I sit?' I glanced at Liam.

'Yes. Yes, of course.'

He cleared a pile of books from one of the kitchen chairs and held it out for me.

'Well, Orla. I'm not sure what you've told your dad about yesterday, but would you like me to tell him what Becca has told us?'

She darted a worried look at me and then one at her dad.

'Dad ... dad will believe me.' She jutted out her chin and swiped at a tear running down her cheek.

'Of course he will. He's your dad. But I believe the truth is better. And the truth always comes out in the end, Orla. You, of all people, should know that.'

'Josie?' Liam was giving me a look of caution. 'I'm not sure what you mean by that but I don't think I like the direction in which this conversation is heading.'

'Then you'll like it even less when I tell you that Orla here has threatened to tell everyone that Becca is a tart, just like her aunt Josie.'

'What!' Liam glared from me to Orla and back again. 'That isn't true! It can't be.'

'Which part? That Orla made the threat? Or that Becca isn't a tart, like I apparently am? Because I can assure you, Liam, and you Orla, that my niece is as far from being a tart as it is possible to be. She's sweet and kind and lovely. And right now her heart is breaking because, thanks to you, Orla, she has lost her best friend, and also her boyfriend, having told Noah she can't see him again because she doesn't want to hurt you even more than she already has.'

'What?' Liam said again.

'W-what?' Orla repeated.

'Yes, Orla. You got what you wanted. Becca is no longer dating Noah.'

'I ... I ...'

'What's going on?' Liam said. 'Will someone please tell me something? You said Becca had upset you, sweetheart, but you wouldn't tell me how. Is ... is this all about Noah? What is Josie talking about? Did you call

Becca hurtful names? Did ... did you call her ... and Josie, tarts?'

He sounded genuinely horrified.

'She was jealous and angry at the time,' I said. 'I'm sure she didn't really mean it. But the thing is, Orla, you shouldn't go around saying things like that about people. Especially people you care about. And telling Becca that her dad was going to run away with your mum wasn't the nicest thing to do, especially not to your best friend.'

'What the fu-flipping ... heck is Josie talking about, Orla!' Liam was livid. He shot upright and glared at his daughter's bowed head. 'Orla. I'm talking to you. I want an answer and I want it now. And the truth, Orla. Forget about Josie. Forget about what you told me earlier. Just tell me the truth right now and we can sort this out.'

She raised tear-filled eyes to him. 'We can't! We can't, Dad. Yes, I did tell Becca that. And yes I did say awful things to her. But she broke my heart! Okay? I wanted to hurt her the way she'd hurt me.'

'You did what!' he almost growled at her. 'You told Becca about your mum and her dad?'

I placed a hand on his arm and shook my head. He looked at me and his mouth dropped open as I spoke.

'She didn't hurt you intentionally, honey,' I said, trying to soften my voice and my body language as I reached out and squeezed Orla's hand, my other hand still on Liam's arm. 'She loves you, Orla. You're her best friend. And Noah didn't mean to hurt you either. Sometimes people fall in love and they can't help themselves. They don't do it to hurt anyone else. And because Becca loves you so much, she's thrown away her happiness to hurt you less. Do you really want to repay her by telling lies and spreading gossip? Of course, you don't. Because you love her too. And take it from someone who knows. Noah may seem like the only boy in the world you'll ever love, but believe me, he won't be. Not if you accept that, no matter how bad it feels right now, you'll get over Noah. And you'll find someone who loves you in the way you deserve to be loved. You need to forgive them both, Orla, and you need to ask them to forgive you. Okay?'

Orla looked me in the eye and ever so slowly, she nodded.

'I ... I'm sorry. I truly am. And Dad, I ... I didn't mean to tell Becca about Mum and Alex. It ... it all just tumbled out because I was hurt and angry and ... and I don't really know why. But if I could take it all back, I would. If I hadn't seen him kiss her, none of this would have happened.'

'You saw Alex kiss–'

I squeezed his arm, and shook my head when he looked at me.

'Orla saw Noah kiss Becca, yesterday,' I told him in a low voice.

'Oh. Oh! Oh I see.'

Orla coughed and said, 'And ... and I'm sorry about what I said about you, Josie.' Her head was down and she wouldn't meet my eyes at first, but as I spoke she looked up at me.

'I forgive you, Orla. Remember though, just because a woman sleeps with more than one man in her lifetime, it doesn't make her a tart or a bad person. Women are allowed to sleep with more than one man. It's just not wise, or terribly kind, to sleep with more than one man at a time. Only date one man at a time is what I'm saying. I'm not very good at this.'

'Aren't you?' Liam said. 'You seem to be doing a pretty good job to me. Josie's right, Orla. Take her advice.'

'Praise indeed,' I said, throwing him a tiny smile.

Orla smiled a little too and then she looked at her dad.

'I'm really sorry, Dad. I didn't mean to let you down. I didn't mean to make you cross. I shouldn't have lied to you. It won't happen again, I promise. I ... I really don't know why I did it. I was jealous and I just ... I just went crazy.'

He stood up and pulled her into his arms and he squeezed her tight and kissed her head, stroking her hair as he did so.

'It's okay, sweetheart. It's okay. Just know that you can tell me the truth about anything. Anything at all. I may be cross at first but I promise I'll try not to be. We'll get through this. It'll be fine. I promise.'

I was kind of hoping he'd do and say all that to me, but some things aren't meant to be.

'Right,' I said. 'I'm off. You can come with me if you like, Orla. Or you can come up later, with or without your dad. Becca would love to see you. And if ... if you can find it in your heart, it would be fantastic if you could tell her and Noah that they can date if they want to. It'll be painful for you, I know. Believe me, I know. But it'll help you grow in ways you might never imagine.'

Orla nodded. 'I ... I'll try. I'll come up later, if that's okay. I ... I need to have a shower.'

I laughed a little at that.

'That's great. May I tell Becca that you'll be coming?'

'Yes,' she said firmly. 'Yes please. And ... and tell her I said I'm so, so sorry.'

'I'll walk you to the door,' Liam said.

He handed me my umbrella but he didn't let go of it at first.

'Josie. I don't know what to say, except, thank you. And you were right. You said this would all blow up and it has. I should've listened to you.'

'That's okay, Liam. But do me a favour, will

you?'

'Anything.'

'Tell that bloody girlfriend of yours that if she has anything to say about me she can say it to my face and not to your daughter. Okay?'

'My ... my girlfriend? I don't understand. I don't have a girlfriend.'

I gasped. 'So all that stuff about you not being able to have casual sex with someone was a lie?'

'What? No. I can't. I won't. And not because I think casual sex is wrong. I don't think that at all. It's just not right for me. Not now. I'm really not sure what you're talking about? I'm not seeing anyone. Casually or otherwise. I was hoping we...' His voice trailed off and he ran a hand through his hair.

'Oh really? So Lucy wasn't here in her dressing gown the other night and you hadn't gone out to get a bottle of wine to drink before, during or after having sex with her then?'

'What? When? Lucy in her...? Oh. Oh dear God. Is that what you think?' He laughed and then his face grew serious. 'How did you see Lucy? And who told you about the wine?'

'I saw Lucy because I rang your bell last week and stood right here and she answered the door in nothing but a dressing gown and a triumphant smile. She told me you'd nipped out to get some wine.'

'You saw Lucy? Here? In her dressing

gown?'

He cursed under his breath.

'Yep. Trying to keep it a secret, were you?'

'No, Josie. I wasn't. Because there is no secret. There's nothing to tell. Lucy was here because a pipe had burst in her cottage and she had to turn her water off. Well, she called me and I turned her water off. Then I called Jonno and asked if he thought he could fix it, or if Lucy needed to call a plumber. He said he'd pop round right then and take a look. Lucy said she needed a shower, so I told her she could shower here and I said in addition to giving Jonno some money for his time and effort, I'd get him and Sandra a bottle of their favourite wine as a thank you for coming out on a Saturday night after 9 in the evening. I left Lucy here and went and met Jonno at her cottage. We were there until about 10, I think and then I told Lucy it was all fixed and I walked her home. And then, if I remember rightly, I tried to call you. Several times, in fact. But there was no reply. I suppose that was because you were spending the night with Asher.'

He suddenly looked cross and as I took in all that he'd said, I realised that Lucy wasn't a very nice person. She certainly wouldn't be on my Christmas card list.

And I also realised something else. Liam was jealous because he thought I'd slept with Asher.

Something had clearly occurred to him too.

'Unless ... unless Lucy was lying about you leaving Asher's?' The hope in his eyes faded as quickly as it arrived. 'But I know you're dating him. Because he told me you two had been out a couple of times.'

I sighed. 'Lucy didn't lie about seeing me come out of Asher's early last Sunday. But I hadn't spent the night and that's the truth. We'd met while he was running and he invited me in for coffee. That was it. But we did agree to go out on a date. And we have. Just a couple of dates. Nothing has happened. We have kissed once, but that's it. Just a kiss. Nothing else.'

'That's good to know. Are you ... are you seeing him again?'

'We were supposed to be going out last night, but it got cancelled because of all this stuff with Becca and Orla.'

'And ... are you still going to go out with him? Or is there...? He coughed. 'No. Sorry. You're going back to New York in a week. You are going back, aren't you?'

'That's the plan. Unless ... unless something happens to persuade me I should stay here.'

'Could anything persuade you to do that?'

His landline phone was ringing but he ignored it.

'I think there's one thing that might.' I moved closer to him but then I saw Orla hovering nervously in the background, as if she needed to talk to her dad. 'Sorry, Orla. I'm just leaving. I'll see you both later.'

'You can count on that,' Liam said, smiling.

'Bye Josie,' Orla said, as I opened my umbrella. And then I heard her say. 'Dad. It's Lucy on the phone.'

'Lucy? Good. I need to have a word with her.'

Forty

Orla and Liam came up to the house later that morning, but things got off to a bit of a shaky start, mainly because Noah had turned up to ask Becca to reconsider dumping him. Orla saw his moped outside and lost her nerve. Thankfully, Liam persuaded her that it would all be fine, and it was.

Becca didn't even make Orla grovel, which I might've done if I'd been in Becca's shoes. Orla had hardly finished her apology when Becca held out her arms and they'd run to one another and hugged and made a pact that nothing and no one would ever come between their friendship again.

Noah had been equally magnanimous. Especially when Orla said she wished that he and Becca hadn't broken up and that she wanted them to get back together.

I think I fell a little bit more in love with Orla at that moment. I'd liked her the moment we'd met, and not just because she was Liam's kid. I'll admit, when Becca had told us what

Orla had said, I didn't like Orla quite so much, but she'd quickly admitted she was in the wrong and that proved she was a good kid at heart. And when she told Becca and Noah they should get back together, well, I know how much guts it took to do that and I felt proud of her.

Toby and Becca were dealing with the news about their dad rather well and I was sure life in Sea View Cottage would soon return to almost how it was before the Orla incident.

With one exception.

Two, actually.

I decided I didn't want to continue dating Asher. Liam had spent the morning smiling at me and making it fairly obvious that if it hadn't been for the fact that I was returning to New York, there was a very good chance that he and I might be dating.

The second thing was that Diana had invited Mikkel round for dinner. Liam and Orla were invited too, and so was Noah, and we sat around that table like two happy families. Diana and her kids with Noah and Mikkel. Me with Liam and Orla.

Except we weren't actually two happy families.

But things soon got back into a routine.

The following day the weather was fantastic. Diana, Becca, Toby and I spent the morning by the pool. Noah was working, so he couldn't join us and Orla was at the dentist in Easterhill, with Liam.

We headed to the beach in the afternoon and on the way, I popped in to see Asher. I'd told him the day before that I felt it was best if we stopped dating and, as I'd expected, he took the news quite well. He did seem a little disappointed though.

'Hi,' I said, popping my head into the reception area of his surgery and seeing Asher standing there.

'Hi,' he replied, his smile not quite reaching his eyes.

'We're off to the beach so I thought I'd say hello as I was passing. Toby's going to teach me to paddle board. Or so he says. If you've got an hour free, you're welcome to join us.'

'I'd love to,' he said. 'But I can't. Appointments all day long, I'm afraid.'

'Ah. Er. We are okay, aren't we, Asher? I mean, we are still friends, yes?'

He nodded. 'Yes. Don't worry. No commitments. No strings. No anything. We agreed, remember? I'm fine. Just a little sad to have missed out on what I think might have been something rather great.' He winked at me. 'Go and have fun. And try not to drown.'

'I can't promise either of those. But thanks. Have a lovely afternoon.'

I came out of Asher's feeling happier. And bumped into Liam who didn't look quite so pleased.

'Oh hi,' I said. 'Fancy meeting you here. Going in for your check up, are you?'

He furrowed his brows. 'Asher's a vet.' A tiny smile hovered on his mouth. 'Oh. Very funny. If your boyfriend's not too busy, I was going to ask if he fancied a pint.'

'If you mean Asher, he's very busy, sadly. But he's not my boyfriend. We parted ways yesterday afternoon.'

'You did? You didn't mention that last night.'

'The subject didn't really come up. I know I'm a bit weird but even I wouldn't dream of blurting out, during what was effectively a dinner party, that I was no longer dating Asher.'

'I wish you had,' he said, the smile taking hold.

'Why? Would it have made a difference?'

He looked thoughtful.

'It might. I don't know. Are you still going back to New York next Saturday?'

'That's the plan. Unless something happens to change it.'

'Like what, exactly?'

'Oh I don't know.' I tried to sound nonchalant. 'Like me having a good reason to stay.'

'What sort of reason would you need?'

'Josie?' Toby yelled. 'Are you coming or

not?'

Henry barked several times as if he were equally impatient.

'Yes. I'll be with you in a moment.' I smiled at Liam. 'I think my nephew is in a hurry to try to drown me. He's teaching me to paddle board. Feel like joining us?'

Liam raised his brows. 'I just might do that. I've got an hour free. Orla got a text from Becca earlier so she'll be down there soon. I dropped her at home so she could get changed.'

'Great. I'll see you on the beach then. I'll be the one clinging to the board for dear life. Or on my way to France. I'm not sure how good I'll be at steering this thing and if I get tired, I might just drift away with the tide.'

Liam grinned. 'The tide's on the turn, so you won't drift away to France, and the sea's flat calm today, so you'll be fine. And if you're not, as I'm a member of The Seahorse Riders I can jump in one of our inflatables and race to your rescue. Just try not to drown before I get back.'

'I can't make any promises. I'm now in the hands of a thirteen-year-old ... and a crazy dog. Anything could happen, so don't be long.'

I smiled as I headed down the hill and by the time I'd stripped off to my bikini, got into the glass-like water and up onto the board, both Orla and Liam were wading towards us, their paddle boards under their arms. Becca was on her board, Toby was on his and I was on and off my hired board in about two seconds flat. Diana stood, ankle-deep at the water's edge and laughed and Henry swam around the boards trying to clamber onto each one in turn until Toby helped him onto his.

'Need a hand?' Liam asked, pushing his board out towards me and leaping onto it with ease.

'Nope. I think I've got this cracked.'

I couldn't even get back on it and he paddled over to me as Toby, Becca and Orla paddled off, all laughing.

'Yes. So I see.'

He bent down and reached out for my board holding it steady so that I could clamber onto it, in a rather ungainly fashion, and then he held my hand while I got my balance. I managed about three strokes of the paddle before I fell off again but by the end of an hour, I was doing fairly well, albeit it a little wobbly.

'I'm doing it!' I yelled, paddling frantically but almost falling off again.

'I knew you would,' he called out. 'But I think you should turn around. You're heading towards the inlet.'

No sooner had he said that than I fell off again and a wave appeared from nowhere and washed me and the board closer towards the inlet.

Liam was beside me before I had time to

panic. 'Take my hands,' he said, and when I did, he pulled me onto his board and then he grabbed the rope on my board and tied it to the back of his. 'You okay?'

I nodded. I was tired but elated. 'Yep. I've really enjoyed this.'

'Me too.' He smiled at me. 'Stand up slowly so you don't rock the board.'

I did as he said and stood face to face with him, our bodies just inches apart. Water trickled off me and I saw his gaze wander down to my breasts and then he looked directly into my eyes before gently twisting me around so that I had my back to him. He eased me closer and our bodies touched as he held me steady with one hand.

'This is a bit like that scene in Titanic,' I said, trying to remain calm. I was fighting a losing battle. My heart was beating wildly. 'Only we're much closer to the water. And in no danger of hitting an iceberg.'

'Spread your legs,' he said.

I almost had us both in the water when I glanced at him over my shoulder, a mock-shocked expression on my face.

'Liam Fulbright!' I said. 'Sex against a tree in a storm is one thing. Sex on a board on the open water in bright daylight, with my family not too far away is quite another.'

The sexiest grin I'd ever seen swept across his face.

'I meant, so that you could steady yourself as I paddled us back to shore. But that's not such a bad idea. I could paddle us both out of sight. Sadly though, I've got to get back to work. Someone is coming to my pottery this afternoon from one of the big stores in Easterhill. I think they're going to place a rather substantial order.'

'Wow. That's fantastic. Rain check, perhaps?'

'If you weren't leaving next week, I'd say definitely, yes.'

'Liam?' I inched my way in a circle so that I was facing him again. 'Why is that so important to you? I mean, why should that stop us enjoying each other's company right now?'

He stiffened. And not in a good way. He held the paddle stationary and the board rocked gently as he looked at me.

'I told you, Josie. I can't have casual sex. Not even with you. In fact, especially not with you.'

'Thanks.'

'You know what I mean. I ... I can't start something that I know will have to end. You now know about Una and Alex. Her cancer nearly killed me. Knowing you're going to lose someone you love is heart-breaking. Then she told me about her and Alex and her betrayal devasted me. I realised I'd lost her long before I knew about the cancer. I've never experienced pain like that. I never want to experience it again. If I had a relationship with you, I'd feel that pain every day.'

'I understand how you felt about Una, but this isn't really the same, is it? Why are you focussing on the ending? On the negative? You could be having a lot of fun in the meantime. We could be having a lot of fun.'

'And fun is so important to you, isn't it? But I'm not like you, Josie. I take relationships seriously. Sorry. That's not really what I meant.'

'I think that's exactly what you meant. Not everything in life has to be so dramatic, Liam. People can have a good time together without breaking each other's hearts?'

'Maybe you can. I can't. It's just not who I am. Not when ... not when I have feelings for someone.'

'You're saying you have feelings for me?'

'I ... I think I could have. And that's why I can't do this. I can't get involved with you in that way. I can't put myself through that again. And I won't let Orla see me broken, like I was after Una's confession.'

'But I won't cheat on you, Liam. I won't.'

'You say that now, Josie. But you've never had a long-term relationship, have you? And you're off to New York in a matter of days.'

I couldn't lie about either of those things. But I still didn't get it. The only glimmer of hope in what he'd said was the bit about him thinking he could have feelings for me. Not that that meant anything.

'Fine.'

'I ... I think it might be best if we keep a bit of distance between us.'

'What? God, Liam. You really know how to put a damper on things don't you?'

'I don't mean to.'

So much for him asking what might make me stay in Seahorse Harbour. It seemed he couldn't wait for me to leave.

'Yeah well. You do. I think I need a swim. Will you return the board for me, please?'

I didn't wait for his response. I dived into the water and swam as fast and as far away from him as I could.

Forty-One

'I really don't follow Liam's thought processes at all,' I told Diana and Elsie later that afternoon as the three of us sat in Elsie's garden beneath the grape vine, drinking her elderflower cordial. Henry was sprawled out on the grass in front of us, a bowl of water by his side.

Noah had come down to the beach and we'd left him in charge of Becca, Toby and Orla. Another teenager called Darren – the one who'd popped into Liam's pottery the day I was asking him about Mum's bowl, had also joined them, so we were pretty sure they were safe. And Elsie's cottage was just across from the beach and up a small incline from the road.

'Nor do I,' Diana said.

'I understand about the pain of losing Una,' I continued, 'and I completely get the shock and heartbreak of her betrayal. But what I don't understand is why he would intentionally deprive himself of something he seems to want, just because he can't bear the thought of what he might experience in the future. What's that famous Tennyson quote? '"Tis better to have loved and lost than never to have loved at all." Perhaps I should get a T-shirt printed and send it to Liam.'

'But he has asked you whether you'd consider staying, hasn't he, honeybee?' Elsie topped up our glasses.

'Sort of. But he hasn't actually said the words. I mean he hasn't asked me to stay.'

'Would you?' Diana queried. 'If he did ask.'

'I honestly don't know. I'd need to be sure that he really wanted me to. To be with him, I mean. To have a relationship. And he's never said that. All he's ever said is that I'm not the sort of person who has relationships. It's like he's only capable of seeing negatives as far as I'm concerned and never the positives.'

'So are you saying he'd need to ask you to marry him or something before you'd consider staying?' Diana sounded surprised.

'No. Of course not. But I would need to know that he does actually have feelings for me. All he said today was that he thought he could have. What the hell does that mean?'

Elsie smiled. 'It means he's a man who has been badly hurt and who isn't prepared to open himself up in case he crashes and burns again. I hate to say this, but I think, if you really care about him, you might have to be the one to tell him how you feel, before he tells you.'

'And what if he says he doesn't feel the same?'

'Then the two of you will never have a relationship. But you'll never have a relationship anyway unless one or other of you opens up about your feelings. He's terrified of being hurt again. You think you're not good enough to be truly loved by someone. You've both been hurt in the past. You both need to be prepared to take a chance on your future.'

'Yeah. But he keeps going on about me just wanting to have fun. As if there's something wrong with having fun. And the thing is, I don't really know him, do I? We do have fun together. We laugh. We tease one another. And the sex was sensational. I only have to look at him and I literally feel things in places I didn't even know existed. But I like having fun. I like my silly jokes. I like my life. I'd just like to have someone special to share it with. What I don't want though, is some misery telling me I'm enjoying myself too much. I get enough of that from Mum.'

'I think what Liam means by that is that he believes you never want to settle down with just one man. With him, for example. That you want to keep your options open. I'm sure if he believed you loved him. Truly loved him, he'd be as much fun as you could handle. What I'm saying, honeybee is this. You need to decide how you feel about him. Don't make promises you can't keep. But if you love him and feel that he's the one for you, then I'm pretty certain all you need to do is tell him that.'

'And prove you mean it,' Diana said.

'How do I prove I mean it?'

'By staying, perhaps.' Diana smiled. 'And Elsie, the kids and I would love that too.'

'I … I'm not sure I can do that. I have my apartment in New York. My friends. My life there. I can't just stay here and never go back. I'll have to give this all some serious thought. Let's change the subject and talk about our party.'

Which is exactly what we did.

I didn't see Liam again for the rest of the week. It was pretty clear he was avoiding me. And to a certain extent, I was avoiding him. I'd been completely honest with Elsie and Diana. I was definitely falling in love with Liam bloody Fulbright – but was it the real thing? Was this true love, or just another fantasy, like Alex? Was Liam 'The One'? More importantly, could I ever be 'The One' for him? Or had that been Una? Would I just be second best? In truth, perhaps I would. Was I prepared to accept that? She was the most beautiful woman in the world. That was an act I'd never be able to follow.

I discussed it with Rhoda and to my surprise she said much the same as Elsie.

'You need to decide how you feel, Josie,'

she said. 'Unless you're sure this is for real you can't say anything to Liam. You can't give the guy false hope. You can't break his heart again. And I think that's what's holding him back. Just his fear of that happening. Which tells me that the guy is actually more than a little crazy about you already. He's simply trying to put the brakes on so he doesn't crash and burn again.'

'That's almost exactly what my aunt said!'

'There you are then. Great minds think alike. But you know what? I sort of hope you decide he isn't 'The One', because if he is, that means you won't be coming back, and it's breaking my heart just to think of that.'

'That's half the problem. I've got to choose and I don't want to. If he didn't have Orla, maybe he could come to New York once a month or so and I could come back here. We could have a long-distance relationship.'

'Yeah. I'm not sure that would work. I think it's pretty simple. If you love him, and mean really love him, you'll want to stay.'

'But doesn't that work both ways? If he loves me. Truly loves me. Wouldn't he just ask me to stay? Or wouldn't he want to try to make the long-distance thing work?'

'I think we're going round in circles. The only ones who can decide are you and him. And the thing is, I think you'll know. When it's time to get on the plane on Saturday, you either will or you won't. But if you don't, you'd bette promise me right now that you'll still come back and see me. See all of us.'

'Of course I will. You're my best friend, Rhoda. And maybe, if I did decide to stay, you could overcome your fear of flying and get your arse over here. You'd love this place. You really would.'

'Okay,' she said. 'Let's not get too carried away. I'm still kinda hoping you'll get on that plane and come back.'

Forty-Two

Invitations had gone out, party decorations had been hung, food and drink spilled from every fridge. Diana had three fridges. Three! And two huge freezers. She really did have the perfect house, if maybe not the perfect life.

Once again, Diana had used her name to get us massages and mani-pedis at Easterhill Spa, only this time she had actually booked in advance. Becca and Elsie came too, but not Orla. This was a family day out. And Orla wasn't family. She didn't seem to mind one bit.

'Darren's taking her to the Lido for the day,' Becca said. 'I think she really likes him. He's been around for ages but she says he's matured this last year. He was a bit of a nerd before but he's suddenly got muscles and a tan and he's grown a couple of inches. He's also just had his hair cut and updated his style. He's cool now and we're thinking of going out on a double date. Her and Darren and me and Noah.'

It sounded a bit like history repeating

itself. Liam had been a nerd and Una the most beautiful girl in Seahorse Harbour when they met. I hoped that was the only part in this Darren and Orla relationship that would be repeated.

'I'm certainly pleased to hear that she seems to have got over Noah pretty quickly. I wish I'd done the same when I...' I let my voice trail off.

Becca didn't know about my past with her dad and she didn't need to. All of that was strictly between Diana and me and Elsie.

After our morning at the spa, we returned to Sea View Cottage where we opened the champagne. There were piles of presents and cards and to my surprise, several of them were for me. My friends in New York had clubbed together and sent me flowers, and chocolates, and a little Statue of Liberty ornament. She was wearing a banner one of them had clearly had made – no doubt Rhoda, saying, 'Don't carry a torch for someone. Just light up their life the way you light up ours. The world is yours, so take it.'

I was pretty sure what it meant and if Rhoda, Rachel and Shona hadn't called me and sung a rather raucous, Happy Birthday, I would've called them.

'So are you getting on that plane tomorrow?' Rhoda asked, just before we ended our chat.

377

'I honestly don't know,' I said.

And it was the truth. I didn't.

Although as I hadn't seen Liam for days, I was veering towards a 'Yes'.

Alex had sent Diana a present. It was a diamond bracelet and she seemed fairly certain he'd got his secretary to buy it, wrap it and send it out. She did however, call to thank him, and told him about the party we were having in a few hours' time. He wasn't exactly thrilled. They had a bit of a row and it ended with Diana slamming the phone down on him.

Most of the village came to the party. Sea View Cottage is big but it was almost bursting at the seams. Since arriving here I'd got to know quite a few of the residents and they already felt like friends. Leaving here would be harder than I thought. And not just because of Liam.

In spite of all the people, I found myself watching the door for his arrival. I'd bought another new dress and it was low cut with a plunging neckline and an equally plunging back. It meant I couldn't wear a bra. I also wore no knickers. I felt sexy and racy and actually rather horny even before the man arrived. Imagine how I felt when he walked in, kissed Diana on the cheek, scanned the room as if looking for someone and then made his way towards me.

He looked like a piece of heaven had fallen

from the sky. Even more tanned than before, his hair more lustrous, his dark blue eyes more sparkly, his smile a real winner, I wasn't sure I'd be able to speak when he finally stood in front of me.

'Happy Birthday, Josie.'

He placed his hand on my arm and sent electricity racing through me. He kissed me on the cheek and I felt my face flush with heat. But best of all, he held out two gifts.

'What are these?' I asked, shaking them – until I saw his expression.

'They're breakable,' he said, with a grin and a shake of his head.

'Not a diamond ring then?' I joked.

A thrill shot through me when I saw a look in his eyes as if he were asking, 'Would you like me to give you a diamond ring?' He didn't ask me though.

I opened the large round present, which he instructed me to open first.

I couldn't believe my eyes.

'It's not really a gift for you, I know,' he said. 'But in a way it is.'

It was the bowl I'd wanted him to make for me. The bowl I'd broken all those years ago. Mum's bowl. Mum's favourite bowl. And it was exactly as I remembered it. I placed it carefully on the table.

'Oh, Liam!' I shrieked. 'This is the perfect gift. Thank you, thank you, thank you!'

I threw my arms around his neck, almost knocking the bowl off the table in the process. It was actually a rather awkward moment as he didn't seem to know what to do with his hands so he held them out to the sides. I quickly let him go.

'But how did you remember what it looked like? I took the photo with me when I left that day?'

'I asked Diana. She had a photo of it too. A better photo than the one you showed me. That's how I managed to get all the details right.'

'I don't know what to say. The fact that you went to so much trouble really means a lot. And Mum will be thrilled. I may even get to be the favourite daughter for a day or two.' I smiled and opened the other present.

That was definitely for me. And my heart skipped a beat when I saw it. It was the most gorgeous heart-shaped vase I'd ever seen, and it was bright yellow with beautiful, sparkly red hearts and blue flowers dotted here and there.

'I love it,' I said. And I did.

'I thought you might be able to keep flowers alive if you can't keep plants. And perhaps, if I send you some, you might think of me ... of us, once or twice and ... smile.'

'And the heart shape and the hearts and flowers? Are they a tiny piece of your ... of yours and Orla's hearts for me to take back to New

York with me?'

He flushed crimson. I swear to you he did.

He coughed, ran a hand through his hair and gave me an odd sort of smile. Half happy, half sad.

'Yes,' he said. 'Exactly.'

'And you should know, Liam. I'll be leaving a lot more than a tiny piece of my heart here with you. With you and Orla.'

Other guests arrived and we didn't get another chance to talk until much, much later. It was twilight, fading into the night as clouds rolled in from the sea. He was standing by the glass folding doors leading to the garden and to Little Wood.

'It looks like there's going to be a storm,' I said.

I stared out at the woods as rain began to pitter-patter against the glass.

I could feel Liam looking at me but I couldn't look at him and we stood in silence for a moment or two with just the sound of the rain and the muffled whistle of the wind while the buzz of conversation and laughter echoed all around us.

'Fancy going for a walk in the woods?' he said, and I could hear the amusement in his voice.

But there was something else. Something akin to ... hope. And also maybe a hint of sadness.

I turned my head to look at him and I saw the curve of his lips, the longing in his eyes; I could see his chest rising and falling beneath his crisp white shirt as his breath deepened just a little.

'Wouldn't that be a mistake?' I didn't try to hide my laughter, or the hint of sarcasm, but neither could I hide my excitement.

He shook his head slowly. Oh so slowly.

'The only mistake is that I was a jerk. I have been for weeks now.'

Our eyes met; our gaze locked.

'I can't argue with that.'

'You're leaving for New York tomorrow.'

'I am.'

'So ... this is our last night together here?'

'Yes. I suppose it is. Although we're not strictly speaking, together.'

'We could be.'

'For one night? So what are you saying? That we should nip into the woods for a quickie against a tree? I didn't think you did casual sex.'

His jaw clenched and his eyes hardened.

'No. That wasn't what I was saying at all. Quite the opposite, in fact.'

'Oh?'

'I haven't been with anyone since Un died. Apart from you.'

'And technically, my sister. Sorry. I don't know why I said that.'

'Fine. But I don't have feelings for Diana.'

'Are you saying you have feelings for me?'

'Yes. I am. I ... I want you, Josie. I can't stop thinking about that night. I can't stop thinking about us. Do you have feelings for me?'

I was stunned. Of all times to say it he'd chosen now. My last night here.

'Liam, I ... I...'

'Of course not. I keep forgetting. You don't want commitment. You're not the type to settle down.' He sounded cross.

'No. That's right. You know me. I'm all about fun.' I couldn't keep the edge from my voice.

'I thought, for a minute, I'd been wrong about you. I thought you wanted the same thing I do. But that's my problem, isn't it?'

'I do want–'

The front door burst open, bringing with it a shower of rain and a swirl of wind so strong that it swept a pile of napkins to the floor and made several dresses flap and flutter. All eyes turned towards the door, including mine and Liam's.

'Alex!'

I couldn't believe my eyes.

'Sorry, I'm late to the party,' he said, banging the door closed behind him and scanning the room. 'I've been rather busy saving lives.'

A cumulative exclamation went around the

room, followed by some clapping and cheering
Diana looked as if she were glued to the spot. A
spot where she was standing, rather close to
Mikkel. There was a look of horror on her face
as Alex threw his coat on a chair, but all I could
think about as I watched that incredibly
handsome face, bask in what he saw a
adulation was ... you total and utter prat.

'Was he expected?' Liam said and there
was a cold, hard edge to his voice.

'No,' I said. 'He wasn't. I think tonight i
going to be interesting.'

'I thought that earlier,' he said, throwing
me a hurt look. 'But it seems I was wrong about
that.'

'I think we've both been wrong. Excuse m
for a moment. I must go and make sure Diana'
okay.'

I didn't wait for a reply. I marched across
the room and on the way, asked Elsie to keep
an eye out for Becca and Toby, who wer
somewhere with Henry, Noah, Orla an
Darren. Probably upstairs, knowing them
playing on computer games or something.
took Diana by the hand, smiling reassuringly a
Mikkel.

'End this right now,' I said to her. 'Tell Ale
you need to have a word. Take him into hi
study and tell him the game's up, that his kid
know the truth and that you want a divorce
Don't let him worm his way back in here, an

nto your heart. He's no Mikkel, and you know
t.'

Alex was chatting to some people he knew
and knocking back champagne. I wasn't sure
Diana could do it but I prayed to the Universe
o give her strength, and I think it must've
worked. Just fifteen long minutes after Alex
had arrived, he came out of his study, a
thunderous look on his face, quickly replaced
by a smile, and gave his apologies to those who
were standing nearby.

'I'm afraid I have to leave. No rest for the
wicked, or the wonderful. Duty calls, I'm sad to
say.' And he turned and walked out, coming
back briefly to grab his coat and to tell Diana
that he'd come and see the kids tomorrow.

'No,' she said. 'You won't. You'll see them
one day next week. We'll arrange a time and
place to suit us all.'

'Are you saying I'm not welcome in my own
house?' He glared at me. 'Josie? Why do I feel
you have had a hand in this? I was astonished
when Diana told me today you were here.'

'I hope I did have a hand in this, Alex. And
I think you'll find this is half Diana's house. She
bought it with you with the money left to her by
Grammie Yates. Goodbye, Alex. See you soon.'

He stormed out without another word. No
doubt to call Bernice and ask her what he
should do.

Diana gripped my hands in hers. 'I can't

believe I just did that. But I'm so relieved I did
I ... I still love him. Even now. But I can't go on
like this. I can't live my life with a man who
doesn't respect me and I can't keep being a
total bitch every time he has an affair. I wish
you were staying so that you'd be here when he
does see the kids. I could use some support. But
I know you can't.'

'I think Mikkel will happily provide you
with any support you might need. But as it
happens, I've been thinking. How would you
feel if I stayed? Just for the rest of the summer
After all, I did come here to spend the summer
at my sister's. And it's still only the 21st of
August.'

'Oh, Josie! I'd be thrilled. Delighted. Please
stay. Stay for as long as you like. If Alex and I
do get divorced I'm going to ask for this house
So you can stay forever. I'd love you to do that.

'Forever is a long time, Diana.' I looked
over at Liam who was standing exactly where
I'd left him, looking over at me. 'Although
sometimes, forever isn't long enough. I'll see
you later, Di. I think there's a tree out there
with my name on it.'

She threw back her head and laughed
'Don't leave your lace knickers under it this
time,' she whispered.

'You saw them?'

She nodded. 'I realised shortly after Liam
put them in that canvas bag. The expression

on both of your faces sort of gave it away.'

I laughed and hugged her and gave her a kiss.

'I'm not wearing any tonight so that won't be a problem. Don't wait up.'

'I won't,' she said, after giving a little gasp of surprise. 'There might not be a tree with my name on it, but there's definitely something that is. Or should I say, someone.'

She walked towards Mikkel and I hurried towards Liam.

I would have to return to New York at some stage, if only to hand in the keys to my rented apartment and to spend some time with my friends.

But I definitely wouldn't be going back tomorrow.

And if I had my way, Liam Fulbright and I would be spending more than just one night together.

We'd be spending a lifetime of nights.

But as I made my way back through the crowd, I couldn't see Liam anywhere.

I did see Asher again though. I'd seen him earlier and he'd wished me a happy birthday and given me a present. It was a wind-up puppy toy.

'You won't be able to kill this one,' he said, laughing.

'I wouldn't bet on that,' I replied. 'If this wind-up bit is still working by the end of the month, I'd be surprised.'

Now I asked, 'Have you seen Liam?'

'No,' he said. 'Not for a while. Has Alex just left? He didn't stay long.'

'Er. He had to get back to the hospital, I think. Emergency call or something. Excuse me. I need to find Liam.'

I searched for him for about ten minutes but being so short I couldn't see over the heads of most of the guests. I was about to climb on a chair and stand on the table when I remembered what had happened to Mum's fruit bowl all those years ago, and decided it probably wasn't the best idea.

'Happy birthday!'

I turned to face Reverend Perse.

'Thanks,' I said. 'I don't mean to be rude but you haven't by any chance seen Liam, have you?'

'Liam? Yes. He walked out the front door a couple of minutes ago.'

'He left?'

'Yes.'

'Is he coming back?'

'I have no idea. I was over here. I glanced across and saw him. That's all I can tell you.'

'Was he on his own?'

'Yes. Orla told me earlier that she's staying here the night.' Perse was giving me a rather curious look. 'Is everything all right?'

'No. Everything's wrong. Very wrong.

Sorry, Perse but I have to go. Enjoy the party.'

I knew Orla was staying with Becca. That wasn't what I meant. But I assumed if Liam had left with someone, Perse would've mentioned it.

I headed towards the front door, grabbed my coat and umbrella from the coat cupboard and stepped out into the rain.

Forty-Three

I had to smile as I dodged the puddles o
Church Hill. Every time I'd gone to Liam's i
had been raining.

I thought about one of the previous time
when I'd gone down to his house; the time I'
gone to tell him how I felt. I'd planned exactl
what I was going to say and imagined what hi
replies would be. That hadn't turned out wel
Lucy had opened the door in her dressin
gown. I didn't think there was any chance c
that tonight, but I prayed the door wouldn't b
opened by some other gorgeous woman.
prayed Liam would be alone this time.

I turned into Wood Lane and saw wate
was cascading down the banks from Littl
Wood which all the cottages in Wood lan
backed onto. It really was pouring now.

When I reached Liam's front door, I took
deep breath and thought about what I woul
say. Exactly as I had done on that previou
occasion.

I rang the doorbell and waited, a smile c

hope and excitement on my face and the butterflies in my stomach feverishly flapping their wings in expectation – just like before.

When he opened the front door, I lowered the umbrella and stood before him in the rain, my hair clinging to my face, my raincoat soaked. At least my dress was dry.

'Josie!' He was clearly surprised to see me.

I looked up into his eyes and he looked deep into mine.

'Why did you leave the party?'

'I ... I needed to make some calls and use the internet. Come in. It's pouring and you're getting soaked.'

'What would you say if I told you I won't be leaving tomorrow?'

'You won't?'

He looked as if all his Christmases had come at once.

'I won't. I think I have a very good reason to stay. At least I hope I do. I can change, Liam. I can be responsible. I can be serious. I'll never replace Una and I'm not even going to try. I just want to be a friend to Orla, or whatever she wants me to be. I just need you to give me a chance, Liam. To give us a chance.'

He blinked as if he thought he might be dreaming then he shook his head quickly and stepped forward to reach out for me.

'Come in out of the rain. We can talk about this inside.'

'If you're going to tell me you've decided you don't want me, then I need to know right now.'

'I'm not going to tell you that. Please come in.'

He reached out for me again but I backed away.

'Are you saying we have a chance? I need to know because I want that more than anything.'

'Do you mean it, Josie? Please come inside.'

'I mean it, Liam. I'll change and I'll prove it to you.'

'I don't want you to change. And you don't need to prove anything to me. I just want you to come in out of this rain.'

'What are you saying? You're going to tell me that you like me but that this won't work, aren't you? You're going to say you've got to think about Orla.'

'I do have to think about Orla. And I have. But that's not what I'm going to say.'

'Oh? What then?'

'Please come here and I'll tell you.'

'No. Tell me now. I need to know. Because I love you, Liam. I really, truly love you.'

He stared at me for a second.

'Is that really true?'

'Yes. It's true. I almost wish it weren't. But it is. I love you.'

He sighed, shook his head and stepped outside, letting the door swing shut behind him. He closed the distance between us with two long strides and stood looking down into my eyes. He brushed a lock of wet hair from my cheek and gently eased it behind my ear before cupping my face in his hands.

'You make me so mad sometimes, Josie.' He was grinning as it said it.

'I know I do. I'm sorry.'

'Don't be. What is it about you and rain?'

'I love the rain,' I said. 'And I love you.'

'I love you too. I love that you make me feel like that. I love that you make me feel so much. I love that you only have to glance in my direction and I turn into a madman overwhelmed by desire. I love your smile. The crazy things you do. Your sometimes ridiculous, crude comments and innuendoes. I love your voice. The sound of your laugh. I love that your face crinkles if you don't like something but that you try to hide it. I love that you're happy to stand here and get soaked. I love everything about you, Josie. I love you just the way you are. The only things I don't love are the thought of you returning to New York without me. The thought that you didn't want to settle down. The doubt as to whether I'd be enough for you. But if what you said is true, I don't care about any of that. You're worth the risk. I want to take that chance. Because from the moment I saw you sitting on that bench, knew I didn't want you to leave again. And yes I know things might not be easy if we're together. We'll probably both make mistakes But I also know I don't want to live my lif without you in it. I want you by my side. An Orla wants that too. She told me earlier tonigh that I was an idiot if I let you go. And she i right. I was an idiot for thinking I could. I wan to wake up with you beside me every morning That's what I want. And if I have to follow yo to New York to show you that, I'll do it. That' why I came home. I came to book a ticket fo tomorrow. A ticket to New York. Well, tw tickets to be honest. I can't leave Orla naturally. Now will you please come inside?'

For a second or two I couldn't speak. couldn't move. I was so stunned by his word that I honestly couldn't manage a reply.

Finally, I said, 'Uh-huh.'

'Uh-huh? That's it?' He threw back hi head and laughed and then he looked into m eyes as rain ran down his hair and face an soaked his shirt. 'Okay then.'

'Can you get a refund?' I asked.

'On the tickets? I don't know. I expect s but I really don't care about that.'

'Perhaps you could get the dates change(I do have to go back at some stage to clear ot my apartment and to see my friends. I'd lov

you to meet them and them to meet you and
Orla.'

'Then that's what we'll do. We can talk
about that later.'

He kissed me then, softly at first and then
deeper and more passionately as his hands slid
from my face, over my shoulders, down the
length of my arms and finally around my waist.
He pulled me tighter to him and I could feel his
need for me growing as I kissed him back with
equal need. The kiss was as good as those kisses
beneath the tree. I didn't want it to end but he
eased away from me and took my hands in his.

'Wow,' he said, staring at my mouth and
then into my eyes again. 'Now can we please get
out of the rain and go inside, get dry and talk?'

I slowly shook my head and smiled. I had
never been so happy in my life. Apart from
maybe once, beneath that tree in the woods.

'Nah-uh,' I said. 'I don't want to talk. I've
got a much, much better idea.'

His smile was full of happiness and love.

'When I said talk, what I actually meant
was something else entirely. I love you, Josie.'

Now we couldn't seem to stop telling one
another how we felt.

'I love you too, Liam. And I'm going to
show you that I can be the woman you want.
The woman you need.'

'You already are the woman I want. The
woman I need. The woman I love. Now can we

please get out of this rain? We don't have any tree branches here to shelter us. And you're shivering!'

'I'm not shivering, Liam.' I laughed. 'I'm quivering with excitement. I'm tingling with longing. I'm ... Oh what the hell. You get the picture. Take me to bed and make mad passionate love to me, please. After all, it is still my birthday, and every girl deserves a special birthday treat.'

His smile told me he thought he was also getting a special treat.

'I can definitely do that. And not just on your birthday. Plus, we do need to get out of these wet clothes without delay.'

'Excellent,' I said. 'And just so that you know, there's no chance of me leaving my knickers anywhere for someone to find because I'm not wearing any.'

He gave a tiny gasp and then his eyes sparkled with anticipation as the sexiest grin spread across his face.

'I love you, Josie, and I'm going to show you just how much.'

'I love you too, Liam. And as you were planning to fly to New York tomorrow, I think you already have.'

He swept me up in his arms and kicked the front door open with his foot, kissing me again as he kicked it shut behind us.

My thirty-fifth birthday was turning out to be the best birthday I had ever had.

And I had a feeling that every birthday from now on, was going to be equally as good.

Coming soon

Christmas at Aunt Elsie's

A distant relative. A blizzard.
A Christmas of surprises.

Charlotte (Lottie) Short isn't looking forward to Christmas. Her boyfriend, Clark has decided their relationship has run its course. Apparently, he needs to 'find himself' … on a three-week skiing holiday with his friends. Now Lottie and her beloved spaniel, Merry, are going to have to face the festive season – and a bleak future, without him.

But a Christmas card and 'round-robin' letter from a distant relative gives Lottie cause for hope. And as the first snowflakes fall, she's on her way to Seahorse Harbour. She'll spend a few days in a cosy B&B and get some bracing sea air. That might help heal her broken heart.

What Lottie doesn't plan for is a freak snowstorm, or Merry needing treatment from the local, and rather gorgeous vet, Asher Bryant, meaning Lottie will have to stay in the tiny seaside village for longer than expected. But at least there's a warm welcome at her aunt's cottage. And in the village pub … along with a roaring log fire.

And that's not all that might bring a rosy glow to Lottie's cheeks this Christmas. Asher's pretty hot. And so are one or two of the guests in Seahorse Harbour Holiday Park. This Christmas might be better than Lottie expected. And perhaps she'll find she doesn't need her ex-boyfriend, Clark, after all.

A delightfully festive, feel-good romance and the perfect Christmas treat.

This is the second book in my new series of standalone novels set in the tiny, seaside village of Seahorse Harbour.

A Note from Emily

Thank you for reading this book. If you loved it and want to be the first to find out about my new books, and also, chat with me and other fans, ask to join the exclusive <u>Emily Harvale's Readers' Club</u> Facebook group. Or go to: <u>https://www.emilyharvale.com</u> and subscribe to my newsletter via the 'Sign me up' box.

A little piece of my heart goes into all my books and when I send them on their way, I really hope they bring a smile to someone's face. If this book made you smile, or gave you a few pleasant hours of relaxation, I'd be delighted if you'd tell your friends.
I'd also love it if you have a minute or two to post a review. Just a few words will do, and a kind review makes such a difference to my day – to any author's day. Huge thanks to those of you who do so, and for your lovely comments and support on social media. Thank you.
A writer's life can be lonely at times. Sharing a virtual cup of coffee or a glass of wine, or exchanging a few friendly words on Facebook, Twitter or Instagram is so much fun.

I mentioned my newsletter just now. It's absolutely free, your email address is safe and won't be shared and I won't bombard you, I promise. You can enter competitions and enjoy some giveaways. In addition to that, there's my author page on Facebook and there's also my lovely, Facebook group. You can chat with me and with other fans and get access to my book news, snippets from my daily life, early extracts from my books and lots more besides. Details are on my website but you'll find all my contact links in the Contact section following this.

I'm working on my next book right now. Let's see where my characters take us this time. Hope to chat with you soon. In the meantime, I'm sending you love and virtual hugs. I can't wait to bring you more stories that I hope will capture your heart, mind and imagination, allowing you to escape into a world of romance in some enticingly beautiful settings.

To see details of my other books, please go to the books page on my website, or scan the QR code below to see all my books on Amazon.

Acknowledgements

My grateful thanks go to the following:

Christina Harkness for her patience and care in editing this book.

My webmaster, David Cleworth who does so much more than website stuff.

My cover design team, JR.

Luke Brabants. Luke is a talented artist and can be found at: www.lukebrabants.com

My wonderful friends for their friendship and love. You know I love you all.

All the fabulous members of my Readers' Club. You help and support me in so many ways and I am truly grateful for your ongoing friendship. I wouldn't be where I am today without you.

My Twitter and Facebook friends, and fans of my Facebook author page. It's great to chat with you. You help to keep me (relatively) sane.

Stay in touch with
Emily Harvale

f you want to be one of the first to hear Emily's news,
nd out about book releases, see covers, and enter free
competitions, then sign up to her Readers' Club by
visiting:

www.emilyharvale.com

nd subscribing to her newsletter via the 'Sign me up'
box. If you love Emily's books and want to chat with
her and other fans, ask to join the exclusive

Emily Harvale's Readers' Club Facebook group

Or come and say 'Hello' on social media:

@EmilyHarvaleWriter

@EmilyHarvale

@EmilyHarvale

Printed in Great Britain
by Amazon